Praise for the
MRS. MURPHY SERIES

"As feline collaborators go, you couldn't ask for better than Sneaky Pie Brown."

—*The New York Times Book Review*

"This engaging series remains fresh."

—*Fredericksburg Free Lance–Star*

"Rita Mae Brown provides a perfect diversion for a cold night, complete with a cat or a dog on your lap."

—*Richmond Times-Dispatch*

"Brown's signature asides—on such subjects as local and national politics, traditional art, race, God, and just about anything else that strikes her fancy—give readers plenty to think about."

—*Publishers Weekly*

"Fun and satisfying . . . an essential purchase for all mystery collections."

—*Booklist*

"Clearly the cat's meow."

—*Library Journal*

Furmidable Foes

A MRS. MURPHY MYSTERY

Furmidable Foes

RITA MAE BROWN &
SNEAKY PIE BROWN

Illustrated by Michael Gellatly

BANTAM BOOKS

NEW YORK

2021 Bantam Books Trade Paperback Edition

Copyright © 2020 by American Artists, Inc.
Illustrations copyright © 2020 by Michael Gellatly

Published in the United States by Bantam Books, an imprint of Random House, a division of Penguin Random House LLC, New York.

BANTAM BOOKS and the HOUSE colophon are registered trademarks of Penguin Random House LLC.

Originally published in hardcover in the United States by Bantam Books, an imprint of Random House, a division of Penguin Random House LLC, in 2020.

ISBN 978-0-593-13005-6
Ebook ISBN 978-0-593-13004-9

Printed in the United States of America on acid-free paper

randomhousebooks.com

4 6 8 9 7 5 3

Book design by Diane Hobbing

In Memory of Ruth Dalsky
Brilliant, loyal, and good on a horse

THE CAST OF CHARACTERS

THE PRESENT

Mary Minor Haristeen, "Harry"—She is in charge of Buildings and Grounds at St. Luke's Lutheran Church, which was finished in 1787. She loves working outdoors whether at the church or her own farm, where she nurtures crops, horses, and the house pets. She's pretty good to her husband, too.

Pharamond Haristeen, Dvm, "Fair"—A veterinarian who specialized in equine reproduction. He is a year older than his wife and they married out of college; for her that was Smith, for him, Auburn. People think Harry got her nickname through marriage but her first name is Harriet, which she dropped in high school because she liked the sound of Mary Minor. She has her ways, to which Fair is accustomed.

Susan Tucker—She grew up with Harry, Fair, and her own husband, Ned. She and Harry are cruising toward forty-four so it's safe to say they truly know each other. This does not mean they agree on everything, but they do love each other.

Ned Tucker—He is serving his first term in the House of Delegates in Richmond, about one hundred miles east. He never interferes in what messes his wife and Harry have created or fallen into. Dealing with the blowhards in Richmond is easier than dealing with these two best friends.

The Very Reverend Herbert Jones—The beloved pastor of St. Luke's Lutheran Church. As a combat captain in Vietnam, he realized he could lead. After the war he entered the seminary, as he chose to lead through the church. Solid, warm, watched over by three Lutheran cats, he is a man doing what he was born to do.

Janice Childs—One of two partners in Bottoms Up, a successful brewery, with Mags Nielsen. Tall, blonde, a good athlete, what you see is what you get. Like Harry and Susan, she is a member of the Dorcas Guild at St. Luke's, the women's group. If she says she's going to do something, she does it.

Mags Nielsen—Thrilled with the growth of the brewery. She is task oriented and can interfere in odds and ends with the Dorcas Guild, but she is generous with her time and money.

Pamela Bartlett—She is now in her mid-eighties. She is president of the Dorcas Guild and remains active in other organizations in central Virginia, plus she is physically active. Age is what you make it and she has made a lot of it by keeping going.

Sheriff Rick Shaw—He keeps order on an inadequate budget. Harry's nosiness drives him bats but she can be helpful and he can't help but like her.

Carlton Sweeny—An assistant horticulturist at Montpelier Estate, the house of James and Dolley Madison. It was home to Carlton's people, also owned by the Madisons. He likes walking where his ancestors walked and loves his work. If you can plant it in the ground, he's interested.

THE EIGHTEENTH CENTURY
Big Rawly

Maureen Selisse Holloway—Rich beyond imagination, she owns Big Rawly, still in the Holloway family today. Susan Tucker's maiden name is Holloway. Maureen's younger second husband, Jeffrey Holloway, not well born, works with his hands and is divinely handsome, which overcomes the above. She has a sharp business sense, is farsighted, and can be brutal and ruthless when she needs to be.

Jeffrey Holloway—A cabinetmaker not of Maureen's class. He likes working with his hands and Maureen finally gave in to it by building him a large shop and a forge where he can build four-in-hand carriages. The vehicles are beautiful and reliable, and his success makes him happy, so she's happy.

CLOVERFIELDS

Catherine Schuyler—Highly intelligent; assists her father in his business. Her passion is breeding and training horses. Impossibly beautiful, she is married to Major John Schuyler, a hero of the Revolutionary War. It is a good marriage.

Rachel West—A warmer personality than her sister, older than her by two years, the twenty-two-year-old Rachel is married to a former P.O.W., Charles West, a British Captain captured by Catherine's husband at the Battle of Saratoga. Both were involved in building St. Luke's Lutheran Church, which Charles designed, thereby finding his passion apart from his wonderful wife.

Ewing Garth—The owner of Cloverfields, the father of the above sisters, he is a sound businessman. He pays attention to our economy, nascent, as well as Europe's. He is a warm, kind man who greatly misses his deceased wife.

FREE MEN

Martin—In his early forties. He and his partner catch runaways. He is keeping his eye out for more lucrative work as the New World, like the Old, favors education as well as money. He is not well born and not educated, but he can read and write.

Shank—Younger than Martin, he likes their work well enough because sometimes there are good paydays for catching slaves. However, like Martin, he wouldn't mind a change of career if it means more money. The travel alone is exhausting.

ROYAL OAK, MARYLAND

Ard Elgin—Manages this estate for Mr. Finney. As they both came here from Ireland, they understand each other. He is a good manager and his boss, Mr. Finney, is a hard man but a fair man.

Miss Frances—The cook at Royal Oak, and she, too, is Irish. She takes no guff from anyone. She is the workers' cook, not the house cook, who does not mix with the workers, called "hands." Miss Frances has no time at all for the house cook snob, never even sees her, nor does anyone else, but they sure see Miss Frances.

Ralston—Now nineteen, he works in the stables at this Maryland estate. He escaped Cloverfields. He didn't much like his parents, really loathed Jeddie Rice, and felt if he could be free, he'd become a famous horseman and rich. All young people have dreams.

William—Escaped from Big Rawly but went back to steal jewelry, money, whatever he could, and he also went back for Sulli, a pretty girl of sixteen. He filled her head with stories. Maybe he even believed them.

Sulli—Easily convinced by William, she quickly came to regret that, but at least she was free and she works hard at Royal Oak, taking orders from Miss Frances.

THE SLAVES: CLOVERFIELDS

Bettina—A cook of magical abilities, she is also head slave woman on the estate. When Ewing's wife, Isabelle, was dying, Bettina nursed her, stayed with her. When Isabelle died, Bettina promised her mistress she would take care of Catherine and Rachel. She kept her promise.

Jeddie Rice—With good hands and a light seat, he has a sure touch with horses and soaks up everything Catherine teaches him. At nineteen he's a man, but he evidences no interest in anything but the horses. He is ambitious without being obnoxious, for a horseman can rise in the world, slave or free.

Tulli—He might be eleven but he looks about nine. Such a sweet little fellow, he works at the stables and tries very hard.

Barker O—Runs the stables, drives the horses, is splendid on the seat of the carriages. He enjoys a big reputation among horsemen, much deserved.

Roger—Being the butler, his is a powerful position. He must know most of the people who call on Ewing as well as how to treat them according to their station. He's a good, reticent man.

Weymouth—Roger's son, early twenties. He does a good job but he lacks his father's drive.

Bumbee—She's in charge of the weaving, buying yarns and fabrics. She's an artist, truly, and the ladies who work with her do as they are told.

THE SLAVES: BIG RAWLY

DoRe—Runs the stables; is Barker O's counterpart. As Jeffrey Holloway now builds sumptuous carriages, DoRe shows them off to buyers. He has been courting Bettina.

Elizabetta—As Maureen's replacement lady's maid since Sheba vanished with a fortune in pearls set amidst diamonds, hers is a nonstop position. She's lazy when Maureen is away. She's a decent sort.

THE CAST OF CHARACTERS PRESENT: THE ANIMALS

Mrs. Murphy—Harry's tiger cat, who often evidences more brains than her human.

Pewter—A fat gray cat with an inflated opinion of herself. She believes the world began when she entered it.

Tee Tucker—An intrepid corgi bred years ago by Susan Tucker, the sensible dog watches out for Harry and endures Pewter.

Pirate—Almost fully grown, an Irish wolfhound who came to Harry and Fair when his owner died. He is very sweet and learning the ropes from Tucker. Rule One: Never believe anything Pewter says.

THE EIGHTEENTH CENTURY: THE ANIMALS

Piglet—The corgi that started the corgi line still at Big Rawly. He endured the war and captivity with Charles West.

Reynaldo—A blooded horse, he has terrific conformation and is fast. He's young, full of fire.

Crown Prince—The above's half brother, calmer.

Black Knight—Stolen by William, he has come to Cloverfields, where he has been restored to health and happiness.

Chief—A bombproof horse who takes care of Ewing Garth.

Sweet Potato—A saucy pony for the children.

Penny—A half-bred newly purchased mare. She is kind.

Furmidable Foes

1

May 22, 2019

Wednesday

A fully opened peony, hot magenta, swayed slightly in the gentle breeze. Deep in its florid heart a few black ants moved about. St. Luke's Lutheran Church, completed in 1787, after a few years of construction, attracted photographers thanks to the harmonious balance of the church and its attached buildings. The church, a gleaming cross on top of a bright white steeple, sat in the middle of a perfect quadrangle of lush green grass. Two arcades, slightly set back from the church's front door, arched stone like miniature aqueducts, flared out from the east and west sides of the main church building to a two-story stone houselike building. These structures contained the pastor's office and a general meeting room. The women's groups met in the western building, the men's, the eastern. The style was simple Georgian, a style that had become grander as America recovered from the Revolutionary War, paid our war debts, and finally began to generate profits. A portion of those profits, or "thankful increase" as the pastor may have called them, had been poured into the landscaping, the solemn yet uplifting grave-yard surrounded by a stone fence, and the pastor's house, which sat fifty yards beyond that on the east side with a stable, also made of gray fieldstone.

The landscaping begun by the architect, former Captain of His Majesty's regulars, Charles West, reflected his deep learning simply from being raised in England. Captured at Saratoga, marched to The Barracks as a prisoner of war, he quickly divined that these rebellious people were on to something.

Captain West created three large quads, terraced behind the church. Each quad was one hundred yards in length and roughly seventy-five in width, although the width changed over the centuries due to the practice of shoring up the terraces when hard weather began to wear them down. On the edge of the last quad Captain West placed the graveyard, whose first residents died before the church was completed. A married couple, the Taylors, had been laid to rest in October 1786, victims of tuberculosis while relatively young.

Lush grass covered the ground. Captain West preserved gum trees, walnut trees, red oaks, pin oaks, and sycamores by a piddling busy creek to the west. Hickories stood firm as well as tulip poplars. Captain West liked the different bark surfaces as well as the various leaves. To these he added a double row of sugar maples along the drive to the pastor's house and in front of the stables. The occasional blue spruce dotted the north face. A gigantic *Magnolia grandiflora* commanded the soft rolling hill in front of the church. Captain West's wife, Rachel née Garth West, added annuals and some perennials, as she had been taught by her mother, a marvelous gardener.

Over the decades other shrubs and trees had been planted. The annuals, of course, created some work as they needed to be re-planted. And some generations of congregants evidenced more enthusiasm for weeding than others.

Now, May 2019, enthusiasm was high. Of course there weren't many weeds just yet.

The grounds also attracted photographers, not necessarily Lutheran photographers, but no matter. St. Luke's happily shared its beauty with all. The effect of the grounds—especially now as central Virginia approached high spring—was exquisite and peaceful. The light shining through the two-story stained glass windows added to the feeling of sanctuary. Even the brass doorknobs on the high double doors to the church itself caught one's eye.

Kneeling down to inspect the magenta peony was Mary Minor Haristeen, in charge of Buildings and Grounds. "Harry," as she was known, was the first woman to hold this prestigious position. In the past the consensus was that women couldn't operate the equipment needed for such a position, nor could they fix same. Harry could and did do it all. She loosened the soil around a grouping of the explosive bush, all magenta, pink, and white. She'd put them in herself last fall.

Next to her, also turning soil, knelt her childhood friend, Susan Tucker. Susan had graduated from William and Mary, which she had loved and still did, while Harry had graduated from Smith College. Now in their early forties, they still tussled over who attended the better institution.

"So, why don't we go down to Williamsburg to check those gardens?" Susan suggested, then peered into a pink bloom. "Have you ever noticed that peonies host black ants?"

"The pink peony is hosting the best party." Harry stood up and stretched her back. "Actually, I think the ants help with pollination, but don't hold me to it."

Susan rose, too. Too much time on her knees had finally gotten to her.

Harry called out to the two other members of the Dorcas Guild, the main ladies group, "We're about finished here. Going over to the grave at the red oak. How you two doing?"

Janice Childs, tall, well groomed, wearing a gardener's apron over her summery dress, called back. "Meet you there."

Mags Nielsen, on the high end of that quad, hollered down, "Me, too."

Harry and Susan walked to the red oak on the western side of the quad, which contained the graveyard.

"What are you doing?" she hollered to Pirate, her Irish wolf-hound, huge, over a year and a half now but still a giant puppy.

"*Stop running,*" Tucker, the corgi, ordered the big fellow.

Pirate did that. "*I wasn't near one tulip. I was not digging. I was stretching.*"

"*Make her happy. Do what she asks.*"

"*Weenies.*" Pewter, the fat gray cat, sauntered by, tulip in her mouth.

Mrs. Murphy, the tiger cat, now trotting alongside the three other animals, said, "*Pewter, drop the tulip. She hasn't noticed it. She'll be one step ahead of a running fit if she does.*"

"*Bother.*" But Pewter dropped the yellow tulip.

One lone grave with a modest engraved marker rested under the tall red oak, leaves murmuring in the breeze.

On the headstone engraved in simple roman bold was the inscription UNKNOWN WOMAN, DIED 1786. REST IN PEACE.

Underneath this an "α" and an "Ω" had been engraved, alpha and omega, beginning and end. Since this corpse, or really just her bones, had been discovered on top of the caskets for the Taylors, in November 2016 she could not be identified. Dating the bones revealed she had been a woman, but the absolute fortune in pearls—seemingly the size of pigeon's eggs, diamonds between each pearl, long enough for three long strands that had been found with her—bespoke gender as well as enormous wealth, riches beyond imagining. A pair of earrings to match along with pieces of a silk dress in an expensive mustard yellow were all that remained.

This was sent to the medical examiner's office, the jewelry deposited in the large secure safe at St. Luke's.

Naturally, the pearls and diamonds provoked a discussion about whether or not there had been drag queens in America in the late eighteenth century. For some reason modern-day individuals contest the obvious. There were bones that could tell the tale. What if this had been a man?

Unable to resist, Harry had said, "Of course. There were drag queens in fifth-century B.C. Athens."

To which Janice Childs, well educated, now walking to the grave, had replied, "Yes, but they were on the stage."

That conversation, begun over a year ago, remained unresurrected, unlike its cause. The real shock came from finding out that these bones belonged to an African American woman more than likely in her thirties. She had been healthy, murdered, her body hidden using what was then a fresh grave, the only grave. She was killed by a physically powerful person, most likely a man, and, given that men, rich or poor, usually worked hard, most men could have snapped her neck.

The mystery of who she was and who had killed her remained a mystery. But the Very Reverend Herbert Jones felt that, whoever she was, she deserved a Christian burial. Not being a parishioner of St. Luke's, she couldn't be buried in the graveyard, so this lovely spot under the red oak became her final home. A small gathering assembled for the service for the Burial of the Dead on April 2, 2018. She'd been found in November 2016. The time lag reflected all the work at the medical examiner's office, fascinated as they were, plus the legal details that needed to be settled before she could be laid in the ground again. Susan's husband, Ned, and Fair, Harry's husband, built a simple pine box, reflective of her time if not her position. Had she been a member of St. Luke's, her passing would have been noted in the meticulous records. Nothing about her appeared in the county records either.

Janice, Mags, Susan, and Harry looked down at her tidy grave, which Harry tended. The cats and dogs sat nearby but not on the grave.

"I was thinking about adding something a bit more here. I don't know. Shrubs are easiest." Harry glanced up at the downy woodpecker in the red oak looking down.

"Whatever it is, it needs to be of the time," Mags announced.

Susan replied, "Given all that's around us, Mags, all those gardens in their original state from Monticello and Montpelier and Williamsburg, I think I have a good idea."

"Don't you think the peonies are a bit showy? I mean, she doesn't need a peony." Mags, who spent money like water, feigned restraint, at least in plantings.

Harry bit her tongue, for she had fought for those peonies. Lutherans shy away from too much show, and peonies are the trumpets of the floral world. Then again, weren't the stained glass windows showy? She'd finally won her battle and didn't feel like fighting it all over again.

As it was, she placed the peonies in the back along the quads, not in the front of the church grounds. There she planted more boxwoods, to augment those originally planted, and thousands of white lilies between the buildings, behind the arcades, as a backdrop for the stunning magenta peonies edging those small grass swaths between the buildings.

"Actually, peonies became a big deal in English gardens, in Europe, in the early 1800s but we had them here," Harry said, quietly.

Susan, having lived through the peony palavers, mentioned, "They are native to the Northern Hemisphere. We had them here as well as in Canada."

Janice, not to be outdone, had studied peonies when all this came before the Dorcas Guild. Being a staunch Lutheran, she, too, felt uneasy with too much splash. This did not prevent her from driving an expensive Audi A6. However, this was her only concession to the booming success of her brewery business with Mags, her partner.

"Of course, but this peony was introduced to Britain from the Mediterranean in 1548. Something more discrete perhaps."

"Woody peonies?" Harry posited.

Susan, seeing the exchanged glances between Janice and Mags, quickly said, "We can't go wrong with white azaleas. A shrub is not as much work as flowers. What if we plant three white azaleas behind her headstone?"

Harry jumped on the suggestion. "Lovely. Discrete."

"I agree." Mags smiled, feeling she'd gotten her way, as Janice nodded.

"I'll take care of it. Thank you two for coming today and getting the early weeds." Harry was grateful.

"St. Luke's must be perfect for homecoming on June second. I wasn't sure it was a good idea—sorry, Harry—but now I see so many people have responded and truly are coming home. You were right," Janice confessed, then added, "And it is Reverend Jones's eightieth birthday. Aren't you amazed that no one has spilled the beans about the party?"

"Yes." Harry hoped the secret would hold. Then she looked down, realizing she was looking at a secret that had held for 243 years.

Pewter wandered off a bit, then leapt in the air, a grasshopper between her paws. "*I have a dangerous grasshopper.*"

"*Are grasshoppers dangerous?*" the sweet Irish wolfhound wondered.

"*Only if they darken the sky,*" Tucker answered.

"*He spit on me!*" Pewter complained.

"*Spit, spit, tobacco juice and then I'll let you go.*" Mrs. Murphy chanted the old promise to the bug.

Pewter opened her paws, and the grasshopper flew to freedom.

"Well, off to pick up Kevin," Mags said. "Car's in the shop."

"That new Range Rover?" Harry asked.

"Don't get me started." Mags grimaced.

The four stood there a moment looking at the grave, the red oak behind it, big denuded gum tree to the left, which at some point would need to come down.

"I think of her as a lost soul," Janice said, staring at the modest tombstone.

"And I think there will be the Devil to pay," Mags replied.

"You know, given that broken neck, I think the Devil already has been paid," Harry thought out loud.

"Let's hope so. It's a centuries-old murder but it's still murder." Janice turned but continued. "Somewhere, someone knows."

The two friends walked toward the parking lot up by the church. Harry and Susan stood a moment.

Harry looked up at the red oak and then to the gum tree. "Mother used to say that even a dead tree casts a shadow."

The slight breeze, sun behind the gum tree, and a shadow was cast over the grave.

Mother was right.

2

Thursday

Fair Haristeen, DVM, drove his Ford dually vet truck down the winding farm road, parking it next to Harry's beloved 1978 Ford half-ton. The blue on the old truck shone now, iridescent, while the silver siding surrounded by a thin bit of chrome had translucent spots that reflected the light.

Fair was worn out as this was foal delivery season for all non-Thoroughbreds and his specialty was equine reproduction. He sighed and eased his six-foot, five-inch frame down from the comfortable leather seats. As he did so, he glanced in the back of the old Ford.

"Honey," Fair called out as he opened the kitchen door.

"Hey. I know you're tired. Your drink is on the table and I'm making Mother's famous potpie. Will snap you right back."

Smiling, he dropped into a chair. "Your mother was a good cook. I often wish she could have lived to see us marry. Dad, too."

"Fate," Harry, not one to show emotion, responded.

Her parents were killed in a car accident her last year at Smith College. There wasn't a day since then, and she would be forty-three in August, or was it forty-four? Funny how one fudges the years and then forgets. Wasn't a day she didn't think about them.

Both Harry and Fair had been raised by upright people. Fair's parents had passed away in these last years. His father had been a radiologist and his mother ran a nonprofit organization for the hospital to raise money for those who couldn't pay the bills. Medical costs have never been cheap, no matter the century. But both husband and wife had been raised with discipline, high expectations, and love.

"How was your day?"

He sipped his restorative scotch, three ice cubes. "Good. Two deliveries. Easy. Healthy foals. Then one of Mim's youngsters bowed a tendon racing around the field. Low bow."

He cited the location as a low bow, a tendon injury, proved less troublesome than a high bow, but one could always see the scar tissue.

"How is the Queen of Crozet?" Harry asked.

"Good. She's worried about her aunt Tally, who is becoming quite frail."

"Given that she is, what, a hundred and five, or close to it, she will eventually leave us."

"I don't know." He laughed. "Aunt Tally is tough. Years ago I treated an old mare, a Thoroughbred, and she made it to thirty-nine."

"Wow. I know some ponies make it into their forties."

"Funny. Old age."

"Mine starts next Tuesday."

"Honey, you will never be old, no matter what the calendar says. How are the arrangements for Reverend Jones's birthday going?"

"Food's ordered. We've rounded up enough tables and chairs. The Dorcas Guild bought table covers, multicolored napkins, plastic cups with the date on it. And what has the St. Peter's Guild done?"

"Prizes. A raffle. Games for the kids, plus we're paying for the food." He paused, took another sip. "Your truck is blossoming."

"The small peonies I bought for us. The azaleas are for the unknown's grave. I am determined that the homecoming will be a horticultural display"—she paused—"as much as it can be."

"You'll succeed." He rose and turned on the TV, a large flat-screen on one wall of the kitchen.

Fair's excuse for the prominent placement was that he needed to see the weather every morning. Easier to see the radar on a big screen.

Harry, who paid little attention to any media, knew better than to protest. Whenever a man buys a piece of equipment, whether a backhoe or a large TV, his reason is always how useful it will be, how much money will be saved in the long run. No man will ever admit to frivolity. To Fair's credit, if Harry wanted to re-cover an old chair, he didn't complain, even when she doubted he thought it necessary.

The large farm shed housed one huge John Deere tractor, a smaller 50 HP tractor, implements everywhere, more stuff hanging on the walls, everything clean. Granted she used it more than he did, but he bought every single thing in that shed that she had not inherited. And his purchases were useful, although initially expensive.

"Hey, honey, look."

Harry did as instructed. "That's Mags and Janice's brewery and restaurant. Turn it up a bit."

Fair clicked up the volume. A brewery delivery truck had been pilfered at Bottoms Up, the brewery. All cartons were missing. The theft was assumed to have happened in the night. The brewery itself had not been broken into.

"Beer must be worth more than the money in the cash register," Fair mused.

"Having someone want your beer that badly is a good advertisement." Harry took the remote from him, turning down the sound. "Bet the girls are upset. It's funny—their husbands thought the

whole idea a middle-aged-crisis thing when they got started but they gave in, ponied up the start-up money. What was it, three years ago? And look how successful they've been." She thought a moment. "I'll call them tomorrow. Too much chaos now."

"They're intelligent people. Kevin has made a success of his nursery business. Mother Nature is a tough business partner." Harry spoke from deep experience as a farmer. "And Janice's husband certainly is successful as a stockbroker. I don't know how anyone can call the market trends, but he does."

"Why is it that so many women want to start a business in their middle years?" Fair's eyebrows rose.

"It's the first time they're free. His business is established. The kids are out of the house. The mom's no longer a taxi service, and by middle age you've lost a few friends. You wake up."

"I never thought of it like that," Fair honestly replied.

"Men don't." Harry playfully pretended to slap his cheek. "You can count your lucky stars that I've always had a job."

"You mean besides me?" he teased.

"You're not a job. You're an angel."

He looked up at her, leaning over the table, stood up to give her a big kiss. "You always surprise me."

"I try." She kissed him back as he sank into his seat again.

"Potpie will be ready in a minute. You're really tired. People don't realize how physical a vet's job can be."

"Some days. Other days it's easy." He glanced at the TV. "Now there's a wreck. Box truck carrying beer turned over and look at the cartons and broken bottles. I'm surprised people aren't out there with straws." He turned up the sound. "Booze is big business. Look at that mess."

"Booze, prostitution, drugs. Big money. Look at the cars backed up on 64 because of the accident."

A pileup on I-64, the main east-west corridor through the middle of the country, filled the screen. As 64 started in the southeast corner of Virginia, the traffic flowed heavily and fast. Someone was always smashing another vehicle or going off the road. Perhaps the interstates were a mixed blessing, although no one who lived before President Eisenhower had them built thought that—nothing mixed about it.

"Why would anyone steal specially brewed beer?" Harry wondered. "Or illegally brewed liquor?"

"Harry, I'm sure they can sell the stuff for three times as much in New York City." He smiled slightly. "Probably only Bottoms Up's truck was pilfered."

"How about the craze for hard cider?" he then added. "Ten years ago there was only one distillery. You couldn't give it away."

"Fads. But I give all these brewers credit, legal or illegal. Nothing like the water running off the Blue Ridge Mountains." She changed the subject. "Before I forget, is your tuxedo clean?"

"It is."

"Remember we have to go to that big fundraiser Saturday night for AHIP. I expect the whole county will be there, including the sick, the lame, and the halt." She used the old expression her grandfather used to use, a pipe, full of fragrant tobacco, jutting out from his jaw.

AHIP built houses for the needy, and renewed others. The "A" stood for Albemarle, the county. Albemarle Housing Improvement Program. In truth, the state needed to fund, really fund, such organizations in each county. Virginia, like all other states, had poverty, much of it hidden.

"If you see Bottoms Up beer, be suspicious."

"Why?" she asked.

"With the explosion of breweries in Albemarle and Nelson Counties, if the organizers had picked one, war. Death." He laughed.

3

November 14, 1787

Wednesday

"God put that woman on earth to punish me!" Ewing Garth held his arms back while his butler, Roger, removed his elegant, tightly woven wool coat.

Ewing then unwound his scarf, his gloves already in the pockets. The coat from London demonstrated why London was the center of male fashion. If any American brought up Paris, the listener sniffed. Paris did not impress English-speaking people as being worth imitating for men's furnishings. Even if we did go to war against them, Ewing had rejoiced when all was over and he could once again order gentlemen's haberdashery and much else.

Roger, twinkle in his eye, replied, "To punish us all."

Ewing slapped Roger on the back. The two, children together on Cloverfields Estate, knew each other inside and out. One owned the place after his father passed, the other, enslaved, had become the butler. Roger possessed a rare understanding of power, place, and intelligence, and had even at eight years old. He proved invaluable to

Ewing, who recognized his virtues. It never occurred to Ewing that Roger, whom he owned, might prefer another life. Roger kept his thoughts to himself.

Bettina, the head cook, bustled down the main hall, much of which she filled. "Mr. Ewing, hot Irish tea. I'll bring it into the library."

"Would you rope it for me?" He asked her to add a wee bit of spirits, whiskey.

"On a day like today, perhaps a bit more than wee." She turned her back, singing as she walked down the polished hall.

The medium-height fellow, a tiny bit overweight but not much considering he was in his late fifties, dropped into a brocade-covered wing chair as Roger briefly disappeared.

Bettina returned and placed the small silver tray on the Hepplewhite stand next to the chair. Scones rested on a plate along with the tea.

"Thank you. You know, of course, I was at Maureen Selisse's. Maureen Selisse Holloway. I can't get used to her new married name."

"Tell you what. She burnt the wind marrying that handsome young thing, Francisco not even cold in the grave." Bettina put her hands on her hips.

"Bettina, he was cold long before he was dead."

The two looked at each other, nodded in agreement.

"I do hope the Lord forgave his sins. I never will." Bettina now folded her arms over her ample bosom.

"Indeed." Ewing agreed.

She waited. He sighed. Roger returned.

Ewing took a deeply restorative sip for he had become chilled on the ride home, even though the carriage was enclosed. "She throws up one barrier after another. Now we all knew she would do that, but I must say that Gorgon betrays more imagination than I ever imagined. We are still negotiating over DoRe, as you might suspect, but now she wants breeding rights in perpetuity to Catherine's two blooded stallions. Says she needs beautiful horses to show off her husband's handiwork."

DoRe, Maureen's head of the stables, had proposed to Bettina, both of them middle-aged and widowed. It was a love match.

"Mr. Ewing"—Roger also addressed Ewing thus—"you will wear her down like water on rocks. Time. All in good time."

"Wisely spoken."

"Bettina." Serena called from the kitchen.

"That girl." Bettina had no wish to leave but Serena sounded in need.

She was. The pork roast had caught on fire in the large indoor oven built into the sides of the enormous brick fireplace in the large kitchen. A large pot hung on an iron pole over the fire, middle of the fireplace. Food preparation moved into the house when frosts came. Otherwise all roastings, frying, boiling pots were supervised outside in the summer kitchen.

Bettina grabbed a pan of sauce and tossed it over the pork, putting out the fire without subjecting the meat to water.

Back in the library, Ewing motioned for Roger to sit by the fire.

"Mail?"

"Two letters from France. One from Boston."

"Well, nothing good is coming out of France right now. I'll read them tomorrow. Maureen has so many ties to France and Spain. She asked me did I think the Treasurers would declare financial matters closed, since the state cannot pay its debts. I said I didn't know and I don't. There's enough to concern us there. God knows what the French will do."

"The way of the world." Roger shifted his weight as he sat to the side of the fire on a shining bench.

"Was Mr. Jeffrey with Mrs. Selisse?"

"No. I walked down to his workshop. He has three carriages under construction. Three. He is a good fellow. She bought him that title, well you know all that. He doesn't care but she says when they go to Europe he will. No one is anything over there without a title.

I don't see that working with one's hands reduces one in society, but then again we live in a new world, or we're trying to."

Weymouth, Roger's son, early twenties, came to the open door. "Bettina feels you need more tea." He held the teapot.

Ewing waved him in. "Did she offer anything else?"

Weymouth smiled broadly. "Forthcoming."

Serena, young, attractive, snuck up behind Weymouth with the whiskey decanter.

"Ah, please."

She poured a dram. "Sir?"

"Oh just a thimbleful, my dear." He smiled up at her. "Weymouth, bring a glass for your father. He's been out in the cold today almost as much as I have."

Sharing a bit of whiskey with Roger was not lost on either Roger's son or Serena. Watch the men, watch what they did, to whom they spoke, and if given direction, take it. Roger was the most powerful slave on Cloverfields. Ewing was one of the most powerful men in Virginia. By extension, Roger's power seeped out from Cloverfields.

When the two young people withdrew, Ewing took another sip, then asked about Weymouth's lack of a wife. "Any luck?"

Roger shook his head.

"Perhaps in time. If he meets the right woman. He's a good young man, Roger, but he lacks ambition."

"I thought he could take over for me someday but he has no interest. He doesn't memorize the names of important people who come here, the names of their family, their special interests. Their holdings are of no importance to him."

"Don't despair. Being a father presents many trials. And he is young."

"When I was his age I shadowed Chibee." Chibee was the butler before Roger. "I soaked up everything he told me. When we called on other landowners for gatherings or meetings, he would pull me to the side, tell me everything about everybody."

"Very intelligent man. As are you, Roger. Really, don't despair over Weymouth. Tell me what happened while I was at Big Rawly with the harpy."

Roger laughed. "Inspected Jeddie's cabin. He needs new boards on the porch. He's a tidy man."

"Catherine says he has wonderful hands on a horse. As does she. But don't you find it odd, Roger, that Jeddie is down there by the weaving cabin, with no interest in the women. Unless I'm missing something?"

"None." Roger sighed, for Weymouth had an interest, but in the wrong women.

"He seems manly enough."

"Yes," Roger simply responded.

"If there were anything amiss, wouldn't we know by now, or at least you would know? You know everything." Ewing laughed at Roger, who feigned ignorance.

"I don't know a thing."

"Would you tell me if you did?"

A silence followed this. "If a man's behavior compromised Cloverfields, I would. But I figure such things are people's business. But I truly believe Jeddie evidences no interest in women. Now remember, Catherine cared nothing for men."

"True. She met the right one and that was that. Well, for me, too. As I recall when we were young, Roger, you were more of a sampler of feminine beauty."

Roger laughed, as did Ewing. "Took me longer but I found a good woman in the end. She's still with me and every day she surprises me. Now she's not worried at all about Weymouth."

"Boys tend to be close to their mothers."

"And vice versa. Sometimes I think she knows me better than I know myself."

"Oh, my Isabelle was the same. I guess God gave us different gifts."

"Well, he forgot some people. One thing I did hear is that Maureen has set a bounty on William's head."

"She didn't tell me!"

"She wouldn't."

William, a runaway slave from Maureen's Big Rawly, had also seduced Sulli, a pretty house servant about sixteen. Maureen, never wanting to lose a penny, flew into a rage. She had beaten anyone on her farm whom she suspected might know of something. Finally, Jeffrey, who had never asserted a husband's assumed authority, stepped in and told her in no uncertain terms that that was enough and she was never to have anyone beaten again. Maureen, amazed at the transformation of her pretty boy, backed down.

"And what if the bounty hunters find him and Sulli, too? She'll have two recalcitrant people in her farm stirring the pot. No good can come of any of this."

"What if they find Ralston?"

This was a young man who worked in the stables with Jeddie. They hated each other. Then Ralston ran off with William. They succeeded in eluding their captors and crossed the Potomac, finding a place at a big horse farm owned by an Irishman who had made good in the new country.

As Ralston had started trouble and became aggressive toward the women, all were glad he ran off.

"He'll stir up trouble, too. Ever notice how some people have no sense? They never come to a good end."

True.

4

November 15, 1787

Thursday

The green and white Royal Oak sign, the letters in old gold script, swung on its hinges. The horses, snug in stalls, paid little mind to the increasing wind. The cattle huddled in their large barn. Thick red Hereford coats kept them warm.

The humans on this large working estate battled the elements, without the benefit of fur. Ralston, head down as he walked outside the stable to check on the gates, wore a hand-me-down leather jacket, a thick sweater, decent gloves, and an old skullcap pulled low. The farm manager, Ard Elgin, an Irishman like the owner, Mr. Finney, liked Ralston because he worked hard and thought ahead.

Ralston wrapped up the last chores of the day in enveloping darkness. He always checked and double-checked the horses before retreating to the unmarried men's bunkhouse. One of the reasons Ard liked him was because the young man didn't complain and learned everything he could.

Cloverfields, the stables well run by Catherine Garth Schuyler and Barker O, driver, head man, bred different kinds of horses than Mr. Finney bred. Ralston wanted to learn everything he could about horses, shoeing, catching problems early.

The wind now howled around his ears. He hurried to the bunkhouse, which should now be warm, as the other men preceded him by at least an hour.

Mr. Finney, and by extension Ard, hired men based on experience and ability. The younger you were, the lower on the ladder. Mr. Finney employed both white men, usually Irish or of Irish descent, and black men whom he never inquired as to how they reached him. Mr. Finney and Ard figured any worker not local, not born and bred on the northern shore of the Potomac River in Maryland, was most likely a runaway. Not only did they not care, they figured those men would be loyal. They were. The bunkhouse again was more divided by age than race, but mostly the younger fellows created their rules. The young men of color slept on the top bunks. A rough equality worked in this atmosphere. Chores for keeping the bunkhouse cleaned and warm were divided up. Shaving times also were specified; otherwise every man would be bumping another to stand in front of the mirror and scrape. Not that Mr. Finney forbade beards. He forbade sloppiness. If you were clean shaven, good. If you had a beard, tidy it up. The men's clothing was washed and ironed, depending on the item, by the women workers. Mr. Finney loathed any form of what he deemed "unkempt." This progressed to "bloody unkempt."

Mr. Finney, late forties, was a hard man but a fair one. He proved generous at Christmas and encouraged his "boys" to embrace the One True Faith. But if a worker did not become a Catholic, he forgave them. Mr. Finney, although devout, thought religion the cause of endless unrest, that and stupidity, which never seemed in short supply.

Maryland, founded by Catholics, pleased Mr. Finney. Although the Catholic Church fostered slavery, it being mentioned many times by the Bible, Mr. Finney did not. A small but influential number of landowners questioned the practice.

Ralston, quiet, walked to the fireplace to sit and warm up a bit.

An older man, Sean, walked to sit beside him. "Snow, I think."

"Yes, sir." Ralston addressed older men as "sir."

Sean offered Ralston a puff on his pipe, which the young man gratefully took.

"Eases the mind." Sean took his old pipe back.

"Does."

Slowly warmth crept into Ralston's bones. "Cuts to the bone that wind."

Sean nodded. "We're close to the big river. Always raw near a river. Don't guess you were raised near a big river."

"No, sir. Lot of strong running creeks, though."

"M-m-m." The older man took a deep drag, offered his pipe once more to Ralston, then took it back. "Boy, you keep on. Good hand with a horse. Don't pay that other boy no mind."

He was referring to William, who had earned the dislike of most of the men thanks to his bragging. The women loathed him because he had knocked around Sulli. William could have cared less about her but she kept him warm at night. She slept with him whenever he demanded it. The two of them lived in a cabin at a distance from the last stable. Had its own pump, which saved steps.

Ralston loved Sulli. She said she loved him, too, but if William ever found them together he'd kill them both. She swore this after they slept together the first time after William had knocked her around and left her for a few hours.

Ralston looked at the medium-built man, heavy muscles, bright blue eyes, light brown hair, and a lilting Irish accent. "Thank you, sir."

Sean stood up, put his hand on Ralston's shoulder, then walked to his bunk near the fireplace, where he'd sleep well.

Sitting there, Ralston thought about the people at Cloverfields. They were all he knew. He did not miss his mother or his father. All they did was tell him what to do and how to do it. Sometimes he missed Barker O, the powerfully built stable manager. Sometimes he even missed Catherine. She knew horses. He'd observe. He felt he would never see any of those people again. Fine. Apart from William, whom he now hated, he also didn't much care for Jeddie Rice, a far better rider than himself. The young women had spurned him, which infuriated him. Well, he was free. They weren't.

He put two more heavy logs on the fire, walked to his bunk in the rear, disrobed, climbed up the ladder attached to the beds, and crawled under the blankets, old wool blankets, but they kept him warm. He fell asleep immediately.

Down in Richmond, staying in an Ordinary, the weather there being ugly, too, sat the two men looking for William and Sulli. They knew a third slave had escaped but he didn't belong to Maureen Selisse Holloway. That didn't mean they couldn't trap him, too.

Once hired with the tantalizing carrot of a $500-apiece bonus if they found the escaped slaves, they rode on a mail carriage, cheaper and they knew the driver. Reaching Richmond in three days, lots of stops, they walked to the tobacco warehouses, the lower James River. Speaking to the captains of the various boats, they left papers with drawings of William and Sulli, as well as physical descriptions of each and a listing of their skills.

No one had seen them, and as the captains all knew information on the slaves would have earned a tip, both Martin and Shank believed them.

Sitting at a rough table, they listened to the wind outside. Although farther south, it proved as cold as up in Maryland. The whole mid-Atlantic was hosting the beginning of the first winter storm.

"I still say they made it to Philadelphia. Place is crawling with runaways." Martin held a hot whiskey in a glass with his left hand; his right held a biscuit.

"Money. Costs money to get up there," the thinner Shank responded.

"They stole some jewelry."

"Not enough."

"What if the girl had filched that pearl and diamond necklace Mrs. Holloway kept blabbering about? You know, took it and hid it."

Martin half smiled. "Two young kids, slaves, people would know that they would never be able to get away with that much money. A necklace like that would tip the whole thing off. They'd be dead, I think."

"She did froth at the mouth about that necklace. She smelled of money."

"And French perfume." Martin drank some whiskey. "They're on foot. Probably tucked up somewhere or even working. Unless they found a ride or had enough to pay for one, they aren't in Philadelphia. Might be on their way."

"Goddamned Quakers." Shank grimaced.

"Hey, they're doing us a favor. Lots of runaway slaves up there." Martin nodded.

"The trouble with Quakers is they won't tell us the truth, even for some of the reward Mrs. Holloway is offering."

"Now Shank, not everyone in Philadelphia is a Quaker and I expect even a Quaker can be bought if the price is right."

"Ha." The thought made the thinner man happy. "I say we head north and at every river crossing find the ferrymen. Never know but if those two are up north, they had to get across the Rappahannock; if they swung west, then they had to cross the Potomac. There are only so many ferries. If nothing turns up, then we head up to the Susquehanna. Sooner or later someone will remember."

"Not that I'm complaining, but those two brats don't seem worth the reward. A person with real skill, yes. But they are shy of twenty. Wet behind the ears. No real skills."

"Mrs. Holloway's a hard woman."

Martin thought, listened to a shutter still fastened wobble against the wind, rapping short taps on the building. "Maybe that's the answer. If and when we drag those two back, she'll make an example out of them. Scare the hell out of all the others. She won't kill them but I bet she'll come damn close."

"If she is paying all this money to find them, she isn't going to kill them," Shank sensibly said.

"Well, back to business. Everyone has his price."

Neither man could know that Maureen Selisse's right-hand woman, Sheba, had worn her necklace and earrings when Maureen would go on a long trip. In France, at a convent school sent by her Caribbean father, Maureen, very pretty, learned about fashion, saw spectacular jewelry on Countesses, Duchesses, and Princesses. Once married to Francisco Selisse, she expected great jewels and received them. Given his incessant infidelities, it seemed a fair trade to Francisco.

When Maureen returned from one trip, both Sheba and her most extraordinary necklace and earrings, among many, were missing.

Maureen told Martin and Shank, should they find the jewelry or the slave, they would be as rich as Midas.

Much as they desired this, both men thought if the jewels, intact or broken up to sell, had not turned up by now, they never would. They would concentrate on the runaways, real cash.

5

Saturday

A large work party swarmed at St. Luke's starting at eight in the morning. Harry supervised the planting of azaleas and more azaleas. As the hyacinths bloomed out, she put in hundreds of iris, the huge-headed purple ones, in the right square between the church and the right buildings, interspersed with the lilies. The great thing was that all she had to do once they bloomed was tie them over. On the left square she'd bought hundreds of white iris. If the effect didn't turn out as she wished, she'd reseed with bluegrass once fall arrived. The iris, not yet blooming, should open to full effect for the homecoming.

A few new English boxwoods provided a backdrop for the peonies, which were already wide open. She hoped they would not be past their prime come the festival. That depended on temperatures.

Mags and Janice volunteered to plant the white azaleas behind the unknown woman's grave. Mags, often generous, also donated more plants and shrubs.

The men of the church mowed, trimmed, and re-bedded those gardens needing it. Younger members of the church worked alongside the adults, measuring out yardage on the second quad in preparation for games, capture the flag being a special favorite. Inside the Dorcas Guild building, Jeannie Cordle commanded a cleanup, while her husband took charge of St. Peter's building.

Men climbed on the roof, cleaning out drain spouts. Garden beds were edged. The grass spilling over onto the parking lot was weed whacked. The flurry of activity impressed the Very Reverend Herbert Jones as well as everyone working.

Elocution, Lucy Fur, and Cazenovia, the reverend's Very Lutheran cats, played with Mrs. Murphy and Pewter, chasing one another under the Italian lilacs, blooming late this year, which was perfect for the upcoming event. The fragrance of lilac could lift a drooping spirit, enhancing lively spirits even more.

Harry, plugging in another white iris—she had some leftovers—commented to Susan, "Soon time for lunch, you think?"

Susan checked her beat-up old Omega. Each time she looked at her watch, she was reminded of how she couldn't afford one now. Prices escalated for everything, even sweet corn.

"Another half hour." Noticing Harry's sigh she added, "We can set up now. What's a bit early?"

"I am famished. Loading up the two trucks took so much time, I didn't make breakfast and neither did Fair. Hey, look at that."

Pewter, a triumph over gravity, shot straight up in the air to bat at a lilac bloom on which alighted a yellow swallowtail butterfly.

"If I hadn't seen it, I wouldn't believe it." Susan laughed.

Her dog, Owen, played with Harry's two dogs. The grade school children ran after them. The dogs would stop, turn, and return the favor, barking. Pirate's voice, already deep, scared one of the little ones. The giant puppy stopped, felt terrible, and licked the boy whose older brother also comforted him. The older brother picked up the little guy, putting him briefly on Pirate's back. The Irish wolfhound, so gentle, allowed it even though it's not a great idea to place any child on a huge dog's back because of the strain on the back.

Pirate lowered his large head and the child hugged him when his brother lifted him off, Pirate's tail now flipping back and forth.

"Good doggie. Good doggie."

Harry and Susan observed this. Then Susan said, "Same age developmentally, don't you think?"

"Dogs are ahead." Harry smiled. "Actually, they're ahead of us emotionally for sure. I'll go tell Pamela to put out the food."

"Okay."

Pamela Bartlett was always in charge of social arrangements for the club. She had been president of the Dorcas Guild since 1972. No one ever challenged her for reelection because every woman knew Pamela was the best. Truthfully, Pamela loved it, especially since her husband had passed away in 2005.

After talking with Pamela, Harry walked to her 1978 Ford truck and slowly backed it toward the rear of the church.

She's leaving me. Tucker bolted for the truck.

Pewter turned from the lilac frolic to observe the dog. *"She's so needy. Oh, there goes Pirate. Dogs"*—a pause—*"have no idea what they're doing."*

"No one has any idea what they're doing." Mrs. Murphy uttered an unwelcome truth, especially for humans.

Harry crawled into the back of the old truck and set up speakers. She dropped over the side, reached into the cab of the truck—no extended cabs or extra doors, a real true truck—and pulled out a fully charged CD player. Lowering the tailgate, she slid it on the bed, pulled down the two speakers, placed César Franck's wonderful composition in D Major for the organ, and let it blast.

"Lunch," Pamela called out while using a large metal spoon to smack the back of a metal pot.

All that commotion got everyone's attention. Toting their tools with them, the thirty-some people gratefully gathered at the long tables set together, chairs already in place.

The men had put all that out before starting their chores in the morning. Pamela used old-fashioned checkered tablecloths like the ones Harry used at home. Little pots of flowers sat on each table, plates, napkins, utensils at one end.

Within minutes a line extended nearly to the first quad. No young person hurried to be first in line. This was Virginia. The children stood with their parents, and the ladies, widowed, served themselves first, with the exception of Pamela. Reverend Jones walked up and down the line chatting with everyone.

Both Janice and Mags told the others, seeing them for the first time since the robbery, that there were no suspects and they had no leads. Mags teased that Harry had kept them all working so feverishly, this was the first opportunity to speak of it.

Harry asked, "I guess you will find out how good your insurance company is. All that beer has to be worth a couple of thousand dollars."

Janice replied to a nosy question, "Not quite that much, Harry. Remember the stores and restaurants buy our various brews at a discount."

Mags jumped in. "What makes it exhausting is you have to alter your schedule for the adjuster's schedule. Then they come out, ask all kinds of questions. They'd grill our drivers, grill us. The entire process is predicated on finding a way out of their responsibility and casting the blame on the client."

Janice added, "Then the trucks will be inspected, for this was one of our trucks. It's all a con."

Mags shrugged. "We said, 'The hell with it!'" She then covered her mouth with her hand. "Shouldn't swear on church grounds."

Susan, listening carefully, suggested, "Forget getting insurance through your computer. Go to a local agent."

Mags replied, "What good will that do? They'll place your account with one of the giant national companies."

"The difference is you know where your local agent lives." Susan grinned.

This got a laugh from the surrounding people, some of whom worked for local agencies.

After fifteen minutes, they bustled along. Everyone was seated and eating after Reverend Jones said grace.

Pewter wedged next to Harry's leg and grumbled, *"Why do they do that?"*

Cazenovia asked, *"Do what?"*

"Prayers."

Elocution, on Harry's other side along with the two dogs, answered. *"Bless the food. You know, give thanks."*

Pewter reached up to pat Harry's thigh. *"Wouldn't it make more sense to give thanks after you'd eaten? Then you'd know if the food was good."*

Mrs. Murphy, not adverse to a treat, replied, *"They do what they want. Or what they think they should do."*

"Too time consuming." Pewter got a piece of fried chicken, so then Harry had to give everyone chicken.

"Harry!" Susan chided her. "Now I have to give Owen food. Why'd you start?"

Janice looked down at Pewter. "That cat hasn't missed too many meals."

"She'll pay for that." Pewter eagerly took another piece of chicken. *"Revenge is sweet."*

Lucy Fur, daintily accepting some turkey from Reverend Jones, quoted the Bible. *"Revenge is mine, saith the Lord."*

"You know, Lucy, you spend too much time with the Rev when he writes his sermons." Pewter dismissed the quote.

As the four-legged contingent ate and blabbed, so did the two-legged.

Pamela finally sat down where Fair had saved a place for her—she was one of his favorite people.

Someone uttered the buzzword "polarization," which fired up the group. Opinions flew like flies.

Ned, Susan's husband, elected to the House of Delegates, couldn't help it. He leaned toward the pastor. "Oh, Reverend Jones, I think millions of people all over the world are desperately scanning the horizon seeking someone on whom they can blame their problems."

That started it all over again. Soon the entire group lobbed one idea, one opinion after the other, but it was respectful as well as educational.

"I don't see any Hispanic people here." Mags challenged them.

"Mags, Spanish-speaking people are usually Catholic." Harry stated the obvious.

Reverend Jones, a little smile on his face, said, "We can hope they see the light and embrace the Lutheran faith."

At that moment, Father Vargas appeared.

"Speak of the Devil." The Reverend Jones roared with laughter, got out of his seat, and walked over to the young priest who had taken over at St. Mary's after the elderly father finally retired.

Everyone laughed and the young, tall, thin priest threw up his hands in wonderment.

Reverend Jones motioned for Fair to squeeze a seat in for the good father. Then the pastor loaded a plate for Father Vargas as Pamela rose to fetch him something cool to drink, something perhaps with a hint of spirits. No one was looking really.

"You need fat on your bones. Come on." Reverend Jones filled the fellow in on the discussion.

Everyone talked at once until finally Harry ordered them: "Let the poor man eat. We can all bless one another afterward."

More laughter since "bless" has a variety of meanings in this part of the world.

"The grounds are beautiful." Father Vargas complimented the group once his plate was empty.

"You know, Father Vargas, we're trying to stay as faithful to 1787 as possible, but occasionally we stray in the name of beauty," Susan said.

"Seventeen eighty-seven." He thought a moment. "That's the year the Constitutional Convention was convened in Philadelphia."

More talk as Janice rose to select a dessert. Walking to the food tables, the heel to her gardening shoes, as she described them, broke. "Darn. I'll never find another pair."

Harry, behind her on the same mission, consoled her. "There's no problem that a new lipstick can't cure."

Janice laughed. "If only that were true, I'd buy cartons."

"It is. Imagine if you had a lipstick the color of the magenta peonies?"

"You know, you might have a point there." She pointed to the cobbler, dropping some on Harry's plate.

Walking back to the tables, Janice asked, "Did women wear lipstick in 1787?"

"Pamela will know."

And Pamela did. "Not as we know it, but they crushed berries. People have been improving themselves since the earth was cooling."

"Think magenta." Harry cooed.

Janice, thinking that, said, "Don't you wonder about the bones we buried? Planting those azaleas makes me think even more about her. She must have been uncommonly beautiful. The remnants of the silk were smashing even after being underground. I can't imagine them in full color with those jewels and perhaps berries rubbed on her lips."

"Magenta." Harry teased her.

"Actually I was thinking about the necklace that few of us have ever seen but you and Reverend Jones."

A pause followed this. Then Reverend Jones said, "It's extraordinary." He waited a moment. "I've been remiss. I haven't attended to the necklace and earrings."

"It's not like you have nothing to do." Harry tried to steer the conversation a bit away from the necklace.

"Well, I still say we should sell it and put the money in the church's treasury." Mags might have kept her mouth shut.

Reverend Jones, voice deep and mellow, amplified her position.

"Yes, parishioners think that. Most believe the Virginia Museum of Fine Arts would be interested. Others think we might find a blood relative of that poor woman, which seems unlikely as we do not know who she was. All in all, it is an extraordinary situation. Until we have more information, we should protect it."

6

Sunday

"Aren't those pink and white dogwoods lining the driveway of the old hunt club smashing? I wish Farmington Hunt Club was still there. Although all things change, I guess." Harry looked out the window as they drove on Garth Road east.

"Yes, they're gorgeous. I think the work being done on the schoolhouses outside Crozet is impressive." Fair, driving the Volvo station wagon, mentioned the old schools being rehabilitated.

"What a long haul that was to put the county commissioner's feet to the fire." Harry turned around as Pewter wanted to come up from the backseat. "No, if you come up, then the others will want to come up."

"The dogs can stay in the back. I need to help drive." With that, Pewter started to step onto the center console.

"I said, 'No.'"

"Spoilsport. You don't have to sit with these lowlife dogs."

Mrs. Murphy upbraided Pewter. "*Everything's been fine until now.*"

Tucker, curling her lip, snarled, "*Shut up.*"

Poor Pirate drooped his ears, being the youngest and very sensitive.

Pewter narrowed her eyes, hissed, then returned to the center console. Harry smacked her front paws, which forced no retreat but did stop her forward motion.

"Tazio Chappars testifying at an open county meeting along with the people she organized did the trick." Harry mentioned a young, talented, mixed-race architect who had also presented plans and the cost. She had been impressively organized.

The schools, called the Colored Schools, a grammar school to eighth grade, and the identical, if slightly larger, building for ninth through twelfth, plus a third for equipment, deteriorated when it closed down in the seventies. The word "colored" had been started in 1911 to lump together children of tribal heritage, mostly Monacans and some Appomatti, with children of African blood. This sleight of hand by Walter Plecker, head of the Virginia census from 1912 until 1946, was one of the worst things ever done in Virginia in the early twentieth century.

The buildings—frame with wonderful floor-to-ceiling windows, narrow oak plank floors, and a potbellied stove in the middle of the room—served generations of children. Served they were, for they had good teachers, not one of them white, also by design. Those were bad times, but those children learned. Their teachers devoted their lives to the young.

Tazio, pushed into this by a lady who had passed now, gathered Harry, Susan, all their friends, and the husbands, too. History teaches us that if we are willing to actually embrace the truth and not the ideology du jour, things are more easily accomplished.

So finally the county released funds and Tazio, with her team, was breathing life into the buildings and our past, which would be visited by students throughout the county. Each class would have a day or two to learn firsthand about former times.

"Think we'll ever know the truth about anything? Like Caesar's death? Who was in on it? We know some, but don't you think there were silent participants? Or what about the rebuilding of Paris under Napoleon II? Will we ever know what they found in those medieval streets and where the people really went?"

"Whoever is in power writes history. Somebody always has an ax to grind. Probably why I didn't much like history in high school. A bunch of battles and dates," Fair responded.

"M-m-m. Honey, you forgot to turn at the Beau Pre sign."

"See, you fascinated me." He reached over to squeeze her hand.

"Oh, bull. But don't let that stop you." She smiled at him. He drove down the quite steep hill to Ivy Creek, even steeper back in the eighteenth and nineteenth centuries. The road on which they drove, named after the Garths on the north side, housed the Holloways on the south. Both estates impressed, although Cloverfields, more restrained, heading toward high Georgian, paled before the splendor of Big Rawly, tons of money spent on it by Francisco Selisse. As his wife had studied in Paris at a convent school for well-born young girls, she being filthy rich from the Caribbean, the house looked like a marvelous French château. Reputed to be brutal, Maureen Selisse, later Holloway, reflected high aesthetic values.

He turned right at the bottom of the hill, turned around, no traffic this Sunday, nosed out on Garth Road, and turned left again at the small Beau Pre sign. The area somewhat reflected the French influence and Big Rawly commanded the rise it had commanded since the 1760s. A high view is a good view.

Passing the ferocious angel who guarded Eden in the family graveyard, they pulled into the estate itself. Susan, her mother, and her grandmother, along with Owen, the corgi, came out to greet them.

"Ned's already in the back," Susan informed Fair, which meant, "Get to it."

This he did as Harry walked into the house. Mrs. Holloway's old dog slept impervious to the commotion.

"A libation?" Grandmother Holloway asked.

"Thank you, no. I'm going out to see if I can salvage anything from your old shed."

"Well, it's not as old as the estate"—Susan's mother smiled—"but it's older than Mother and I."

At this, all three of the Holloway women laughed.

Out the back door followed by Mrs. Murphy, Pewter, Tucker, Pirate, and Owen, Harry walked the twenty yards to the crumbling clapboard structure. Susan followed in a few minutes after bringing her clippers to cut back some vines. Harry reached for a pair of gloves her husband handed to her.

"Ned, you've been busy," Harry noted, observing the crumbling shed before her.

"Time has done a lot of it for me. The roof is shot. All I had to do was tap what was left and the tar paper covering fell."

"Beams held," Fair observed. "Look at the size of them."

"Think any of this building can be salvaged?" Susan asked.

The four of them looked up then down at the wooden floor, part of which also had fallen in.

"Well, once we pull the old siding off, I'm willing to bet the sides of this storage building are also large beams. We could, you know." Ned felt positive.

"Well, let's get to work. A four-man or, well, what can I call us? A four-person demolition derby." Harry picked up a heavy hammer from her husband's toolbox—he had everything—and started swinging at the siding.

"Four-person, Harry?" Susan lifted an eyebrow.

"I'm trying. So dearie"—she lifted her tone—"how are going to fill out your license? Do you want an X, meaning 'no gender'?"

"With two grown children, I don't think I could get away with it." Susan pulled out ancient nails—some looked hand forged. She placed the nails in a tin can in case they were hand forged.

The friends bantered back and forth, casting aspersions on gender, the temper of the times, and anything else they could think to provoke one another. It wasn't so much that they were politically correct more than that nothing was correct. They flung one silly jibe after another at each other, as only beloved old friends can do.

The animals, outside, heard the laughter.

"*They're in a good mood. Means treats,*" Pewter predicted.

"*Greenies.*" Tucker, like Owen and Pirate, loved greenies.

"*I am not eating a greenie,*" Pewter announced.

"*Of course not, Pewter, you'll eat mouse tartar.*" Tucker put her nose to the ground to see who had been there and when.

"*Steak tartar*"—the gray cat's whiskers swept forward—"*I'm not eating some tiny wormy mouse.*"

"*Of course you aren't. You're too fat to catch one,*" Tucker let fly.

Fat she was, but even a fat cat is quicker than a corgi. Pewter raced over to the dog, who tried to move away, but Pewter, enraged, put on the afterburners.

Howls filled the air.

"Sounds like someone's getting murdered." Susan listened.

"Damn those two. All they do is fight." Harry knew exactly who was fussing with whom.

Hurrying outside, issuing threats for they easily outpaced her, Harry heard a crash. One wall came down, pushed by the three inside. Dust and wood bits flew upward.

As Ned thought, the beams were very thick. They'd stood for centuries.

"One more squeak, one more growl, and you all are being marched to the house and shut in the porch room. I mean it."

"*She started it.*" Pewter glared at Tucker.

"*Oh la.*" Tucker lifted her head.

Pewter lashed out, smacking the side of Tucker's face. "*Vermin.*"

"Pewter. Enough." Harry turned as they were calling her back to the now three-sided shed.

"Look." Ned proudly pointed to the beams, all of them hand shaped, the ax marks visible.

"Wow."

"Ready for the next side?" Fair was already pulling nails, wedging a crowbar into a crevice.

Harry picked up her hammer. "Hey."

"You all right?" Fair turned as his wife put one foot through the floor, which gave way.

"Well, yes, but we might want to tear up the floor before more of us go through it."

Ned peered at the hole as he helped Harry out. "She's right. Come on."

Working from the edges, they lifted the old oak boards, which would have been fine if the roof hadn't fallen through on one spot, allowing the floor to rot over the decades.

After a half hour, they had pulled it all up and stacked the wood outside with the removed siding.

Susan, staring at the packed-dirt ground floor, stood with mouth agape. Harry, alongside her, also took a deep breath.

"Let me get Mom and Gran." Susan ran to the house.

Fair, towering at six five over Ned, a mere six footer, saw Susan running, put down the wood he was carrying, and came to stand by Harry. The men, too, looked down.

"Graves. Has to be." Fair noted the sunken earth, side by side, each the size of a coffin.

Walking quickly for a woman about to bust ninety, Gran, with her daughter at her one side and her granddaughter at the other, reached them. Her hand flew to her neck.

"So, it's true."

"What is, Gran?" Susan thought she knew everything about Big Rawly, but then one rarely did.

"Most of the slaves are buried on the north side of the graveyard, as you know. There are small flat headstones. But the stories were that a small number were buried near the house, slaves who died in the house."

"House slaves?" Ned wondered.

"Well, usually house slaves would be buried in the cemetery but it could be they were hastily interred due to sickness. People back then knew that some diseases transferred from person to person. The rumors always were that Maureen Selisse Holloway was cruel. It's also possible some unfortunate slaves died from mistreatment."

Susan reached for her grandmother's hand. "What should we do?"

"Notify the county historical society," Gran replied.

Ned, brushing back his sandy hair, still thick in his early fifties, added, "Mrs. Holloway, the graves will need to be identified and the bones carbon-dated. As to DNA testing, well, I really don't know but the remains might be able to be identified. Maybe these people have descendants. The county is full of Holloways and Selisses who are mixed race or African American. If these are their people, then they must decide what to do."

"Well, we know if they were white servants, they'd be in that small graveyard near the big oak," Gran informed them.

"Good God," Harry blurted out.

"Harry"—Susan's mother spoke—"you and Tazio Chappars are close from working to save the old schools. Why don't you start with her. Go through the old school records to track the names. We need to write down names from the main graveyard and cross-reference. Same with the graves of indentured servants," she sensibly ordered.

"Yes, ma'am." Harry had been saying that to Susan's mother since she was tiny.

She remembered always how good Susan's mother, grandmother, and grandfather had been to her when her parents were killed in the auto accident.

"More old bones," Pewter moaned, for she had heard quite enough about the nameless bones at St. Luke's.

"Our human said when they found the bones at St. Luke's that no good can come from disturbing the dead." Mrs. Murphy remembered how upset Harry was at the time.

"That may be so," Tucker replied. "But in this case, I think it's like finding the remains of a man who fought in World War II or Vietnam and returning them with honor to the family. So this might be the same kind of exception."

Owen, her brother, thought about that. "They've rested here for centuries maybe. I think they should stay home."

Pirate, encountering such things for the first time, asked, "Is that how humans think of their dead, as being home?"

"They think home is with God," Mrs. Murphy told him. "The ritual at the burial is very important to them. But I still think you shouldn't disturb the dead."

"If they go to their descendants, it's not being disturbed." Pewter had been listening despite her flippancy.

"True, but that doesn't mean the humans won't find out things they'd rather not know," Mrs. Murphy prophesied.

Later

The afternoon sun was gliding to the top of the Blue Ridge Mountains, the soft slanting rays intensifying the spring colors. In an hour the sun would set, a magical time, for twilight had begun to linger once on the other side of the spring equinox.

The cats and dogs, glad to be home, chatted with the horses in the pasture.

"We haven't gone up into the walnut grove since last fall. Let's go," Tucker encouraged the others.

"The way to get into the walnut grove is a hard climb. I'm not punishing my legs," Pewter declared.

"Fine." Tucker had already turned her back on the gray cat.

"I'll stay with you," Mrs. Murphy said to Pewter. "Haven't caught up on the horse gossip in a while. They are always up to something."

The two dogs trotted through the back pastures, then along the edges where the sunflowers had been planted, finally reaching the edge of the woods. A dirt farm road went straight up the lower grades. As the incline increased once in the large walnuts, the road needed switchbacks with large turnarounds to be serviceable.

Rock outcroppings became more numerous, with trickles of water spilling into streams that ultimately found their way down to the pastures to become a deep, swift running creek dividing Harry's land from her neighbor Cynthia Cooper's, currently on vacation. Coop rented from Reverend Jones, as this was the old Jones's homestead.

"*What's that?*" Pirate noticed a small shed protected, somewhat hidden by trees.

"*Wasn't here in the fall.*" Tucker noted the last time she had been walked this way.

The two dogs, one so big, one so low to the ground, pushed through the undergrowth.

Tucker pushed open the knocked-together wooden door of a shed, with a slanted roof, wood with tar paper over it. The two dogs inhaled.

"*Whew,*" Pirate exclaimed.

Tucker, scrutinizing the glass apparatus and the wooden shelves, the strong odor of old fermented corn, said, "*Still.*"

"*Still what?*" The Irish wolfhound did not step inside.

"*Humans make whiskey, rye, liquors. They do it in secret. The water here is so pure.*"

"*Tucker, we pass those breweries on 151. Why is that okay but this is secret?*"

"*That's beer. This is strong stuff. Mom says the federal government hits them up with nasty taxes.*"

"*What's a tax?*"

"*Pirate, let's save that for another day. It's just about impossible to understand. I think you need to be human to believe in it.*"

"*Oh.*"

"*Let's get out of here.*" Tucker backed out. "*Look up. See the farm road down? Not far from the crest but most people don't know paths off the ridge. Also, they're frightened of the bear, bobcat, and coyote. Especially at night. Whoever built this is a cool customer.*"

They moved a bit toward the south for their descent. There was less undergrowth there, which had obscured some of the farm road. Harry might clear these roads about every five years. Hard to do even with a Bobcat. A big bulldozer would lurch, possibly tip over, on this grade.

Perhaps a quarter of a mile down, Tucker lifted her head. *"Smell that?"*

Pirate sniffed. *"What is it?"*

"Smells like a long dead animal but there's something else." She veered off the deer path to a shallow depression, large boulders looking over it. *"Ah."*

Pirate stared at bits of human remains. The rib cage, completely exposed, had been stripped clean of flesh. No arms or legs could be seen. Torn, shredded pieces of cloth lay under the rib cage. Part of a skull, hat intact, some hair under the brim, had been wedged against the rock.

"What is that other smell?" the Irish wolfhound asked.

"I don't know. Smells like nuts, kind of. Pirate, a dead human means trouble. When we get home, don't tell Pewter."

"Why?"

"She'll find a way to get Harry up here. That will be nine miles of bad road."

"Are we really nine miles away?"

"No. It's an old saying." The corgi headed down.

"The bones at Old Rawly didn't smell awful."

"Those were old, old, old. These bones aren't old."

"They talk about the bones at St. Luke's," Pirate remarked.

"Again. Those are really old. Just don't tell Pewter."

"I won't."

Death be not proud, though some have called you so. Death may not be proud but it certainly seemed prevalent.

7

Monday

A light dusting covered the ground, making Ewing hungry for a sugar cookie. Walking with him for a bit of exercise, Yancy Grant swung his cane out then back. While it lent him a jaunty air, it also helped his stability, for his knee had been shattered in a duel with Jeffrey Holloway. Pieced together as best as could be, he could move around but not quickly. He needed help mounting a horse, but he could ride.

"The King left them high and dry," Ewing announced.

"Why would anyone trust the French right now? The Prussians shelled Amsterdam with howitzers. The defenders had but two hundred and fifty men, but they acquitted themselves with honor, without French troops for relief."

Ewing nodded. "From time to time I receive a letter from my friend, Baron Necker. He confirms your report. Does it not occur to you, Yancy, that pieces are being moved on the checkerboard of Europe? Alliances ignored or broken. New ones begun. I thank God every day that there is an ocean between ourselves and our supposed betters."

"Just so." Yancy nodded. "Well, this is the end of the Dutch as a free people."

"It's the end of the Dutch Patriots. Not for all time, I think, but given the squalor we are seeing in France, the shameful abandonment, it seems to be the curious way of the world."

"Perhaps." Yancy stopped to look at a horse he once owned frolicking with Reynaldo and Crown Prince, two of Catherine's finest stallions. "Black Knight looks full of beans." He laughed.

"Catherine dotes on him."

Yancy smiled. "A gift, your daughter has a gift. Ah, don't tell me."

A brief burst of wind sent tiny flakes swirling in their faces. The two old friends turned their backs to the west, headed east toward the main house. Given Yancy's pace, they wouldn't reach it for another fifteen minutes.

"The weather mystifies me." Ewing pulled his scarf tighter. "I think it will be sunny, the clouds roll in. I think the flurries have passed and after a respite a bit more."

Yancy tapped the farm road to test a spot that might be slick. "Firm. Well, look at it this way: The weather is the salvation of many a conversation speeding toward boredom."

Laughing, the two finally reached the back door of Cloverfields. Roger, keeping his eye on the back window, opened the door, quickly helping Yancy up the steps.

As the two men repaired to warmth, Jeffrey Holloway tested a thick corner pole, heavy wood, that had been set in the ground. Big Rawly needed another woodshed closer to the house. Maureen also had extended the roof over the kitchen door as well as newly constructed wooden siding to stockpile wood there. Everyone felt this would be a deep, hard winter.

DoRe, powerfully built, strong hands from handling leather as he drove the horses, held the large, thick pole that had been squared.

"We're lucky the ground isn't frozen hard." Jeffrey picked up a shovel to fill in the dirt.

"Master, I can do that," a growing young slave offered.

"I, well, yes you can." Jeffrey stepped away.

If Maureen heard he worked at a slave's task, she'd hit the roof. Jeffrey enjoyed physical labor. However, his wife enjoyed exalted status. Best he not push it.

"Ground is level here." DoRe motioned to two other young fellows to test the three already settled corners. Those big timbers held firm.

"Level because Sheba's mother's buried here," Pete, a bit older, said as he moved shovels outside the large square.

"Her mother and two brothers," Norton, the young man who took over for Jeffrey, added. "That's what my momma told me and she told me that the Missus was so angry when Sheba ran off with her pearls and diamonds and what else that she knocked down the markers, leveled the ground. I thought she was just planning a new building."

"Caribbean. They were all Caribbean like the Missus. They came up with her when Francisco moved to Virginia," Pete growled.

"The brothers couldn't have been old." Jeffrey was curious.

Pete offered, "'Bout the same age as Sheba, high prime, I guess. Damn fools, well Momma said they were damn fools. Wanted the same woman. Got in a knife fight, killed each other."

"The woman was Sulli's mother. Beauty runs in the line"—DoRe coughed—"as does no sense."

"You know if we can get a roof on, the sides will be easy tomorrow. I've built the struts for the roof. On the wagon over there. Two of you can haul one. I'll drive the wagon in the middle, we can lift them up, you can nail them down, and then we can put in support posts. Not enough weight to sag. I know." He smiled at DoRe. "I'm doing it backwards."

"Mr. Jeffrey, you can do anything." DoRe climbed into the cart with Pete, a young man already on each of the heavy beams that would be the supports on the outside edges. The men had done quite a lot of work as they'd started at sunup, and it was late now, with sunset about two hours away.

The swirl of light snow kept them all moving as fast as they could. The roof supports were fixed as the sun dipped below the Blue Ridge Mountains, turning indigo.

"I'll hand up these tarps. We can finish the roof tomorrow and the sides as well, I think," Jeffrey advised. "Don't want anyone working on a roof in the dark. If we can finish this by the end of the week, have the wood shingles on the roof and the clapboard on the side, we can load it with wood and refresh the woodpile by the door. Everyone got enough wood at home?"

"Do." DoRe spoke for all.

"Seems like we spent half the summer cutting wood." Norton wasn't exactly complaining as much as noticing.

"Gonna be a hard winter." DoRe looked skyward. "Had enough hands to get up the corn, the oats, the wheat. You're built for timber." He smiled at Norton, muscular.

Tarps secured, the young men headed to the barn to bring in the horses. The three worked with DoRe. No one was much of a rider but they could keep a horse fit. Cheerful fellows, DoRe thought them a lot easier to work with than William, who he had found to be a vain braggart.

"DoRe"—Jeffrey started toward the barn, as that was where DoRe lived in special quarters to be close to the horses—"need more blankets?"

"No. Bettina gave me a heavy one that Bumbee wove."

"You've asked a good woman for your hand."

A big, broad smile covered DoRe's face. "Yes, sir."

"My wife never talks about Sheba to me. Do you think she stole that necklace?"

"I do. I think she'd been planning her escape for years. Sheba doted on the Missus and the Missus would tell her all about Francisco. Women talk. Sheba thought she should be as grand as her Mistress. She could lie and smile at you. She would tell the Missus on all of us. Truth is, we all hated her."

"I can understand that. What about her mother?"

"She filled Sheba's head full of how powerful they'd been in whatever island they lived on. She lived, I don't know, long enough to have gray hair and then she dropped. In the house carrying that big silver bowl."

"And she's buried near where the woodshed will stand?"

"Oh, Sheba cried, threw herself down, said she didn't want her momma far away." DoRe shrugged. "The Missus gave in. Sheba would lie down on her mother's grave and then her brothers', cry. Course she made sure the Missus saw her doing it." He shook his head. "A cobra in a skirt, that one. She'd shine on Francisco but reported everything he did to his wife. Sheba had hidden power. She was a woman to be feared."

"Glad I didn't know her. While I'm here, let me look at the horses so I can tell my wife how good they look."

"Thank you." DoRe meant it, for Maureen could turn on anyone in a second.

The young fellows pulled blankets on them. A few were blooded. Others were good riding horses, as both Jeffrey and Maureen liked a bracing ride.

"No horses were missing when Sheba ran off?" Jeffrey quizzed.

"No, sir. I think she had someone helping her. Someone who met her on the road. The Missus was gone. But I don't believe Sheba could have walked far, as she was wearing a gown. Always was. Had to be someone in on it."

"A lover?"

"No. I expect she promised whoever some of those jewels. She was shrewd. Everyone wants to get to Pennsylvania or Vermont. I figure Sheba headed that way or used some of the money to pay for passage to France. Missus always talking about France. Bad as Sheba treated all of us, she figured a way out of here. She'd talk French to her mother and brothers and the Missus, too, so we wouldn't know nothing."

"How much do you think the necklace and earrings were worth?"

"Lord, I don't know. Francisco was rich. Liked to show that off. More money than I can imagine."

Jeffrey was glad of the bricks underfoot in the aisle and in the stalls. Herringbone laid, the bricks added symmetry, keeping the chill from coming up off packed earth and made it easier to clean the stalls and the aisles.

"Sure you're warm enough?"

"Yes, Mr. Jeffrey."

"Think Sheba will ever turn up?"

"Not in our lifetime." DoRe opened the door to his living quarters so Jeffrey could feel the warmth.

8

Tuesday

Books piled on Harry's desk in the tack room of the stable. She preferred her office there rather than in the house. The quiet of the tack room, interrupted by the sounds of the horses snorting, snoring, eating, helped her concentrate.

Large, the glorious smell of oiled leather filling the air, clean saddle pads piled neatly on the floor, and one old tack trunk pushed against the wall added to the allure for her. The saddle rack against one wall held her two saddles and Fair's one. The gleam from polished bits in bridles reflected the overhead light. On the desk, an old, heavy schoolhouse desk, squatted her computer. A pullout section for writing turned the desk into an L. The pullout was small, meant she didn't need to move the desk computer. Most times she pushed the computer back. So much of what Harry needed could be found in old books.

With the computer moved to the rear of the desktop, Harry

crossed her legs in the large padded chair, rollers underneath. A notebook, opened to her right, meant she was serious.

"Not a peep." Pewter, sprawled on the fleece saddle pad, lifted her head.

Mrs. Murphy, curled up next to her on the inviting fleece, yawned. "You know how she gets."

Two large gardening books sat to Harry's left elbow, while a smaller book concerning gardens in the colonies was opened before her.

Murmuring as she read, Harry lifted her head, speaking to her pets. "Who would have thought that gardens could be political?"

Bursting through the dog/cat door, Tucker stopped, poked her head back through, facing into the aisle. "Ha."

"No fair," Pirate, too large for the door, complained.

"Please, my repose." Pewter glared.

Harry rose, walked over, opening the door so the ever-growing Pirate could enter.

"I can outrun you." Tucker was full of herself.

Pirate plopped down. "You can outrun me? You can't outrun me."

Pewter giggled. "Better watch out, Bubblebutt. The puppy is starting to talk back."

"He's at that age. You never got out of it."

"Tucker, if I weren't so comfortable, I'd get up and bloody that nose you stick in everybody's business."

"Pipe down. I can't hear myself think." Harry returned to the smaller book. "Climbing roses. M-m-m, patriotic colors. Makes sense. Dolley Madison liked roses twirling around her columns. She must have been so much fun." She looked down at Pirate, who seemed very interested in what his human was talking about. "It does make sense. Your garden signaled your political leanings to friends and passersby but a British soldier walking by would have no idea."

"What does a British soldier have to do with anything?" Pewter, irritated, grumbled.

Mrs. Murphy, who often read over Harry's shoulder, answered, "It takes time to change people's minds. To organize change. The English ran the show."

"English?" Pirate's ears lifted up. "What is an 'English'?"

"A form of human. Don't worry about it." Tucker thought that an excellent answer.

"How many forms are there?" the innocent fellow inquired.

"I'll see if I can get Mother to take you to Walmart someday," Tucker replied, putting her head on her paws.

Making notes, Harry flipped pages, studied photographs and drawings.

Picking up the phone, for she'd rather talk than text, she dialed. "What are you doing?"

Susan's voice came over the line. "Sitting in the sunroom with a cup of coffee to start the morning. Did you finish your chores?"

"I did. Can't believe we passed Memorial Day. Where does the time go?"

"Goes fast. What are you doing?"

"Looking at gardening books. Janice and Mags talked about eighteenth-century gardens."

"Right."

"I don't think we should tear up the plants added after the building of the church. I can't think of a way to be totally eighteenth-century without moving much of what we have. What we have is beautiful. St. Luke's is under no obligation to uproot the work of generations."

Susan, voice firm, said, "I agree. It's disrespectful. But neither of them has suggested uprooting."

"But I need to be reasonably well educated on the period, you know. The last thing I want is some kind of uproar because there's no way to go backwards, my thinking, without destruction."

"What's your idea?"

"Will you call Kat Imhoff and ask if we can visit the Montpelier gardens?"

Mrs. Imhoff was the director of Montpelier.

"Of course."

"Thanks. You know everyone better than I do."

"Ned. Helps to be married to a delegate."

"Yes, and it helps to be the granddaughter of a governor."

"Miss him. There are so many questions I wish I had asked."

"Funny, isn't it? We all feel that way about mothers, fathers, relations, dear friends who have gone on. Stuff pops into your head and you think, 'Dad will know.'"

"Any special time you want to go over there?"

"No. You pick or let Kat pick. Hey, what's going on with the graves under the shed?"

"We can't do a thing. The sheriff's department has to come out. If this doesn't look like a pressing crime, then Grandmother and Mom can call the historical society and they can determine how they want to date and possibly identify the bones. It may well be that, even though these are probably one or two hundred years old, the medical examiner must still be contacted and take charge."

"Red tape."

Susan sighed deeply. "Tell me about it."

"Aren't you surprised anything gets done?"

Susan laughed. "Maybe that was by design. Our Founding Fathers figured those legislators would argue, slow down the entire process. Government by paralysis."

"Ha." Harry reached over to pet Mrs. Murphy, who had leapt onto the desk. "Those brakes seem to be wearing out."

"Seems to be." Susan changed the subject. "I wish we hadn't found those skeletons. Big Rawly's had enough turmoil over the centuries. It's unfortunate they didn't keep better records."

Harry took a breath. "There must be three bodies at least. I only saw three depressions. Three people were laid peacefully to rest. All with burial. However, if I don't fortify myself with study, including any notes in St. Luke's files of, say, bulb purchases, I may have a fight on my hands. Sorry, my usual non sequitur."

"Do you really think that many people will care about eighteenth-century authenticity?" Susan shrugged, long accustomed to Harry jumping from one subject to another.

"Give anyone the chance to express himself and I truly believe no problem is so small it can't be blown out of proportion."

9

Wednesday

Looking over the horseshoe flower garden in back of the big house at Montpelier, Harry was struck by how simple yet elegant it was. A party was usually held on this lawn surrounded by the flowers on Dolley Madison's birthday, May 20. The beloved lady was born in 1768.

The kitchen garden in the distance testified to how practical President Madison had been. Distinguishing themselves from English garden imitations, he created semicircular terraces for vegetables and fruits.

Carlton Sweeny, the young assistant gardener, stood with Harry and Susan, pointing out shade and sunlight, how the sun moved around the food garden and the more formal garden.

"Dolley, like so many people, relaxed by gardening. Obviously she paid a great deal of attention to the sun, as did her gardeners."

"Odd. She was a Quaker, opposed to slavery, yet married a slave owner," Susan, who loved history, replied.

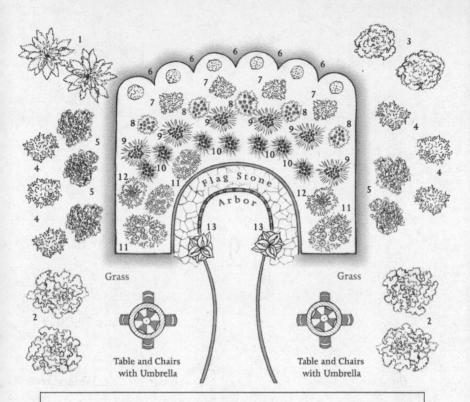

PLANT ID NUMBERS

1   hemlock tree

2   English yew (*poison seeds in the berries; 3 berries can be poisonous*)

3   black locust

4   rhododendron (*produce a honey-type substance—poisonous*)

5   azalea (*produce a honey-type substance—poisonous*)

6   English boxwood (*not poisonous*)

7   jimsonweed (*all parts poisonous*)

8   foxglove (*seeds, stems, flowers, leaves—poisonous*)

9   bearded iris (*nonpoisonous*)

10   Siberian iris (*nonpoisonous*)

11   coreopsis (*nonpoisonous*)

12   salvia (*nonpoisonous*)

13   American false hellebore (*all parts are poisonous*)

The handsome fellow, maybe early thirties, nodded. "He wasn't happy with the situation either, but like so many, including in the North, they needed labor. It was the way of the times." Carlton scanned the garden, which he adored.

"Mr. Sweeny, what got you interested in horticulture?" Harry asked.

"My mother and grandmother lived in our garden. Ever watch two grown women fight over begonias?" He laughed. "But I didn't really know there was a future in it. I went to Tech, found my way to the forestry department. I wanted to dig in the dirt, I guess. So I was accepted at a horticultural college in England. If there's one thing the English know, it's gardening." He beamed.

"They've been at it longer than we have." Harry smiled.

Smiling back, he said, "Yes. Have either of you ever seen Versailles?" Both nodded so he continued. "The ultimate expression of our dominion over Nature, false though that idea may be. It's stunning, but I belong with climbing roses, you know?" He grinned. "Dolley's climbing roses."

"There are revolutions in every activity and gardening began to change thanks to Inigo Jones and Capability Brown down to Gertrude Jekyll." Susan, as always, knew her history. "And here we are."

"Did you really study with the Duchess of Rutland?" Harry remembered what she'd been told.

"She graciously endured me. Finding Capability Brown's plans, his last big commission before his death, is one of those extraordinary moments. I learned so much. The duchess wrote a book, *Capability Brown and Belvoir*. It's very good."

"Mr. Sweeny . . ."

"Oh please, call me Carlton. I'm happy to be with two people who are serious gardeners."

"You must come to Big Rawly. There's a lot remaining from the original plans." Susan, who had met him in passing when at Montpelier, had not had the chance to really talk to him. Plus he was handsome. Of course, she loved her husband, but looking at a handsome man is ever so pleasurable.

"Thank you. I'd be curious. Didn't you all find skeletons in the last few days? I'm sure I read that, but it's high spring here so a lot slips away. Intense work. Everything is waking up but, hey, no nematodes, no rust. Life's good." He felt a cool breeze cross his face. "Allyson, my boss, will be happy." He mentioned Montpelier's curator of horticulture.

"We did find bones," Susan answered. "Don't know a thing yet and probably won't for some time. I expect the Original Thirteen are filled with secrets. We must be walking over them every day."

"True enough. Religion was so important in those days. Giving someone a proper burial, no matter how poor, was the thing to do, which means an unattended grave, or one we don't know, is a red flag."

"You never know what will happen next," Susan rejoined, "or who will do it. Well, to change the subject, when do you think Dolley's roses will open?"

"M-m-m, another ten days at the most. Even though it's the end of May, we can't discount a cold snap. It's the nighttime temperatures that really cause the delay. Are your roses open yet?"

Susan answered, "My tea roses are."

"Now, there's an old, old rose." He smiled.

"Me, too," Harry replied. "My lilacs were fabulous this year. Have both the old kind and the Italian. And last year they barely bloomed."

"You fertilize, I'm sure." He spoke as though to a fellow gardener, which she was, but not at his level.

"I use compost. Have horses."

"Ah." He crossed his arms over his chest. "We try to use only what would have been available to the Madisons, but given the amount of people who visit here from all over the world, sometimes I'm tempted to dip into modern fertilizers. They do the job, no question, plus you don't battle as many weeds. Let me take you all to the dependencies." He started walking, then stopped to clarify. "Slave quarters."

They smiled at him. "We're all Virginians. 'Dependency' is the eighteenth-century word." Harry walked on his left side while Susan took up the right. "Were your people slaves here?"

"They were. I think it's one of the reasons I love it here. I feel close, I see their handiwork, and, to be fair, I see what the Madisons accomplished as well. Plus Montpelier has a gifted director in Kat Imhoff. She sees the big picture. The programs here include all manner of subjects, of people. Allyson leads twilight trail hikes in our Landmark Forest. Madison was our first environmentally alert president. It's one of the reasons Montpelier differs from Mount Vernon and Monticello. Not that those men degraded the environment, but Madison truly thought about it. There isn't a day that I don't learn something new, and often from a visitor."

"It's still a jolt for me to visit Montpelier with the wings taken off," Harry confessed. "God bless the duPonts for saving Montpelier. Those were their wings."

Susan chimed in. "But to return all this to the time of the Madisons, well, it was probably the right thing to do, destroying the additions. Gives people an idea of what life was like."

"Yes, it does." They walked behind the big house, still imposing without the wings. "When you see how people lived then, whatever their station, you realize how spoiled we are." He laughed again. "We walk into a room and flick a switch. We open a refrigerator, food. We turn up or down the thermostat and if the house is high tech, the thermostat takes care of itself. Anyone living then would think we live in paradise today." He paused. "When I visited Belvoir, where the castle was originally built in the 1180s, I think, and rebuilt twice since then, that's when I really grasped how young we are. Kind of overwhelming."

"Yes, it is." Susan agreed, then stopped. "The stone quarters are so symmetrical."

"They had clear ideas about practicality and beauty. It's simple. Again, it reminds me of how young we are as a nation, the simplicity." Harry wondered, "Don't you think simple is better?"

"For us, yes. But even one hundred years from now people will look backwards. We'll probably seem a bit primitive." He stopped. "Here's the end of the more organized planning." He swept his hand outward. "From here just native species."

Both Harry and Susan stared at the expanse, then considered the amount of study and work that had gone into bringing Montpelier back to life.

"Incredible!" Susan exclaimed. "Beautiful."

Carlton Sweeny had proved an engaging guide, a young man who knew his stuff and loved his work. By the time the two dear friends drove back down to Crozet, their heads were stuffed full of facts, future plans, and new tips on how to maintain plant health.

"You know, I now realize I've been cutting back my hydrangeas too early," Harry said.

"An enthusiastic young man. It's one of the things Ned and I talk about, how many young people should study forestry, agriculture, horticulture. Critical areas. So many who go to college are focused on money. Someone needs to talk to them about a lifetime of fulfillment. I'm not sure pots of money are as fulfilling as what Carlton does."

"Well, Susan, your two kids made the right choices. But I know what you mean. Seems like everyone wants to start a computer something, be a lawyer, or be a doctor." She turned her head as they passed the drive into the GE Building north of Charlottesville. "Speaking of going into business."

"The pendulum swings. Always will. Can GE recover its position? I don't know. The mantra that companies are too big to fail is so much bull, you know?"

"I do." Harry agreed. "But think about it. Including you and me, most Americans have never known want, violence, or savage repression. Is repression still with us? Of course, but not anything like what our grandparents observed or experienced. My worry is we're soft. Everyone thinks that life will always be easy, at least so far as the basic needs are concerned."

"Ease can often lead to bad decisions. Ned, a man who has never known want, tells me what really goes on in Richmond. Being a delegate has opened his eyes. He talks about the hidden poverty in Virginia. Is this a comfortable state? Sure, for most of us, but there are people here who have never seen a dentist."

"Good Lord." Harry inhaled.

"Speaking of how hard life can be, you know people lived up near the ridge behind your house. Not a lot, but families lived all along the Blue Ridge until the 1930s."

"FDR removed all of them to make the Skyline Drive, the Parkway. Cruel, really."

"You and I haven't been up there since fall. Let's go check the timber. Especially the hardwoods."

"Sure."

10

November 28, 1787

Wednesday

Tidbit, a light chestnut mare, nickered when Ralston entered the stable. He adjusted her blanket, rubbed her ears, and put out fresh hay for her, as he did for the other six mares in the eight-stall stable. The one empty stall gave a tiny bit of relief. Caring for horses in the cold took longer. One's hands froze; buckets of water spilled on one's legs and shoes. Ralston stuffed his gloves in his pocket. He preferred mares. For whatever reason, they seemed to like him.

Ard came into the stable, the packed earth crunching underfoot. "Good?"

"Yes, sir."

Hands jammed in his pockets. "Why don't you sleep in the stable tonight? I'll have one of the boys bring wood and start the stove. It's better sleeping in here than the bunk room. Keep an eye on the girls."

Ralston nodded. "Is. No one snores in here but the horses."

Ard laughed. "Mr. Finney's wrapped up in his guests from Baltimore. Ship captain and his wife. Quite a peach, I'd say. A pretty girl lightens your heart. Now, don't get me wrong, I love my missus. A good woman. But I do like to look at the young pretty ones."

"Yes, sir." Ralston smiled. "Anything special you'd like me to do with the mares?"

"No. They're in for the night. Going to be a cold one. They'll be happy."

"Yes, sir."

"Mr. Finney says Baltimore is growing. The port brings in goods, people. I suspect he's thinking about investing in a ship or cargo." He shook his head. "Not me. Worst time of my life coming over the water. I'll never go back." His face softened. "I'll never see my mother. If she could see me now." He smiled. "Royal Oak is grand."

"It is. Mr. Finney built a beautiful place. The stables have everything."

"That they do." Ard walked down the aisle and returned, opened the door to the tack room. "Personally I think every stable should have a man sleeping in a tack room or stall. I bring it up, but Mr. Finney says the boys like living together. Do you?"

"Ah."

"Ralston, I'm not a snitch."

"No, sir. I like being alone."

"Is your mother still alive?"

He paused again. "Yes, sir, but we never got along. I'm happier on my own."

"Yes." Ard liked the young man, curious about him for he was so closemouthed. "You and William are like chalk and cheese."

"Yes, sir."

"Why did you travel with him?" Ard knew better than to say "run away," but that was obvious.

"Well, he promised all manner of things." Ralston took a breath. "Most of which was bull, but not finding Royal Oak"—a long pause—"a good thing. Good horses."

"I like you, Ralston. You're a good hand with a horse, a good rider, and you keep your mouth shut. William talks against you."

"Yes, sir."

"No one much listens. I'll give him credit—he has courage on a horse. But he beats the hell out of his woman. She's a sweet thing."

Ralston felt his face burn. "Mr. Elgin, no man should hit a woman."

"Oh, I agree. But as my sainted father used to say, 'A woman can pluck your last nerve.' Carried away by coughing, he was. Well, I'll get the wood over."

Ard started for the door, which he had closed against the cold, wet wind. "Ralston"—he stopped—"I've seen you look at Sulli and I've seen her look at you. Watch your back, boy, watch your back."

"Yes, sir. Thank you, sir."

Ard lifted his hand, then opened the door, closing it quickly.

Ralston checked each stall, his face still burning.

Two hours later, the night clear, the stars cold like brilliant chunks of ice, Ralston mended a pair of broken reins sitting by the potbellied stove. He heard the outer doors open and close. He didn't move.

A light knock on the tack-room door, then Sulli's voice. "Ralston."

He put down the reins, vaulted to the door, opening it. "How'd you get away?"

"William's drunk. The boys found or bought liquor somewhere. Passed out."

Ralston wrapped his arms around her, kissing her. "I can't live without you, baby."

Sulli kissed him back. She had no answer but she felt the same way. They took off each other's clothes, going to the firm straw pallet, covered with a thick blanket on the bottom and one on the top. With the stove crackling away, the room kept them warm as they kept each other warm.

Afterward, she rested her head on his shoulder. "I have to go back. He'll wake up from his stupor eventually."

"I know. Been drinking a lot?"

"When he can get it."

"M-m-m." Ralston sighed. "At least he hasn't been beating you lately."

"No. But he nags at me. I wish he hadn't told Ard we were married. I can't get away from him."

He nodded, stroking her hair—she'd braided it tightly. He thought she looked like a queen. "Sulli, we'll figure something out."

"He'll never let me go. He doesn't love me. He uses me."

"If he won't let you go, then I'll have to kill him. And if he lifts a hand to you again, I will kill him any way I can."

"You can't go killing people. Someone will tell, you know? We're free now. Won't be free for long if you commit a murder."

"I'll find a way."

11

November 29, 1787

Thursday

"I think of the mountains as feminine." Ewing swung out his gold-topped cane as he and Catherine walked west on the east-west farm road, one of his favorite walks. "The curves, the hollows filled with ground clouds like froth. Your mother loved the mountains."

"They certainly put things in perspective." His beautiful older daughter, at twenty-four, agreed. "More snow. Look at the clouds backing up behind the spine."

"Winter. Ah well, Mother Nature keeps her own calendar. You know, my dear, it started early this year. The fall color painted the trees in what, early October?" He walked more briskly. "I have not heard anything from our friends in France."

"Perhaps no news is good news, Father."

A long sigh met this common expression. "Not this time. Baron Necker usually writes me once a month and I him. And those to whom we send tobacco, always a much-awaited crop, but I haven't heard from him."

"Well, if Europe once again went to war, we would know."

"Oh, I think this is the calm before the storm. Remember the line from Tom Paine's *Common Sense*? Where he declared if God believed in absolute monarchy, would he have given people an ass for a lion?"

Catherine laughed. "True. You know, when you insisted that Rachel and I read pamphlets and such, Rachel was bored. I liked it as much as I could at twelve. Those readings made me think."

"Your sister possesses your mother's artistic impulses. But when I would ask her questions, she did answer with a distinct lack of enthusiasm." He smiled.

"Let us say the French imitate us—not that they would admit it—but let's say they, too, threw off a king's yoke. I do not believe it will make one bit of difference. Feudalism runs in their blood, no matter how they dress it up."

"Ah." He thought about this, happy to be in his daughter's presence. "So there must always be a king or a queen or some sort of solitary leader, like Cromwell perhaps?"

"Yes. Now, you have visited those countries. I have not. I defer to you, Father, but then I usually do. You are one of the wisest men I know."

"Oh tosh." He loved it. "When your grandfather packed me off on my Continental tour plus England, Scotland, and even Ireland, I was overwhelmed by the architecture, the art, the dress, the wealth. Then I realized this is wealth accrued for centuries and often on the back of serfs who became servants. That is the way of the world. There will always be people on the bottom."

"Yes."

"But my dear, I met such intelligent, educated people like Baron Necker, both of us young men. And yet"—he paused—"and yet I knew I was a new man, a different kind of man, a man from the New World. I was young, perhaps a bit full of myself."

"Father, that's not your way."

"Well, you flatter me, but I was in their countries and I did it their way, but I thought it all rather suffocating, this essentially pulling one's forelock when meeting one's so-called betters. You know, I am glad your sister married an Englishman, a highborn Englishman. Who knows better than Charles what we have to offer?"

"He has often said had he remained in England, he would have been expected to marry, not for love, but to replenish the family's fortunes as his older brother, Hugh, who inherited the title, had to do. I cannot imagine not marrying the man I love. John is not a reader; he's a doer. Lafayette saw that."

"Your husband is a brave man. I think too much bookwork is not always the answer."

"Then why did you make Rachel and me endure those tutors?" She teased him.

He looked at the ground, then up at her. "Sometimes you can be sly as a fox."

"Where do you think I learned?"

He laughed, wiping his nose with a kerchief. It had begun to run in the cold. "Catherine, you and your sister lighten my heart. I forget to tell you how much you mean to me and I fear sometimes I forgot to tell your mother. One of the reasons I accomplished what I have is due to her wisdom."

"She loved you. She would always tell Rachel and me that she hoped we would find a man as good as you."

"I worshipped the ground she walked upon. Isabelle could see things I could not. I once asked her if she felt overshadowed, pushed aside because when we men would talk about the troubles, about should we break with the King, of course, she would leave the room. She said something that stuck with me. 'I can get more done when no one notices.' And she did."

"If the women, the wives and the daughters, had not supported the cause, I don't think we would be free of the King. And yet, I wonder. You know, Father, how we women have been told we are citadels of virtue, the civilizing force."

"I believe it. I believe men without women descend into brutality."

"Then how do we explain the brutality of Maureen Selisse?"

A snowflake twirled down. Ewing peered at the western sky, darkening. "Let us turn for home, my dear. Maureen, I have no idea. Cruelty seems to be her byword."

"She's beating slaves again for the merest infraction. Bettina told me and DoRe told her. She pretends this is the overseer's idea, but she's determined to find Sheba and her magnificent necklace. Jeffrey put a stop to it but she continues behind his back."

"Those two deserved each other, Sheba and Maureen."

"I don't doubt that, but it does appear that Sheba outwitted her. The necklace and earrings are worth a fortune." Catherine slipped her arm through her father's.

"She's been gone for a year, since October last year. Given the jewelry, her command of French, I assumed she returned to the Caribbean or went to France or perhaps even Quebec. Sheba is cunning," he said.

"You would think we would have heard something. She possessed something of such value, worth more money than most men make in a lifetime," Catherine wondered.

"It's possible she has taken up with a rich man. I often wondered if she didn't dally with Francisco, but then I thought no, she had Maureen in her power. She wouldn't risk it. He could be a brute, too, I fear."

Catherine added, "I heard that Jeffrey built a fancy woodshed over the graves of Sheba's mother and two brothers. Packed the earth down and even built a floor over it. No record of anything to do with Sheba or her people."

He waved his hand. "The dead can't hurt you."

Catherine leaned on him slightly. "I don't know about that."

12

Saturday

"How many stops is she going to make?" Pewter complained. "The back of the Volvo is full of plants. What if I wanted to sit back there and look out the big window?"

"You never want to sit back there. You always want to be in the passenger seat." Tucker rested her chin on her front paws, which poked into Pirate's rear.

As the Irish wolfhound puppy grew, Tucker refused to scrunch up, so the corgi would lie next to the big dog, push her legs into Pirate's sides, or simply flop on top of that deep gray coat. Pirate never minded, but then Pirate hadn't a clue as to how big he was becoming.

As it was, the fat gray cat commandeered the front passenger seat with Mrs. Murphy squeezed next to her.

"Everyone okay back there?" Harry glanced in her rearview mirror.

"Yes," the two dogs answered.

Harry pulled into the ABC store, the state liquor store. Virginia swept up a lot of income from these state stores but they were not inspirational in their choice of alcohol. However, the bourbon, whiskey, and scotch were pretty good. Still. Harry, oblivious to booze anyway, put the car in park and left the windows open, for the late afternoon air was pleasant.

Both cats strained to see what Harry was up to since this was not one of the usual destinations.

Twenty minutes later, accompanied by a portly man in an apron, Harry rolled out a cart, as did he. She clicked her key fob and the back door clicked open.

Lifting it up, Harry ordered in no uncertain terms, "Nobody move." She turned to the middle-aged man. "We can put it here. There's room. Doesn't look like it as I picked up azaleas, but I know we can."

With care the two put in twelve huge bottles of cheap gin. Harry thanked him, tipped him, got behind the driver's seat, fired the motor. Singing "Beautiful Savior," she drove to St. Luke's.

Why she chose a hymn was anybody's guess, but she carefully drove the station wagon to the back, parking on the side of the road by the second quad.

"All right. Behave yourselves."

Potting soil, a small spade, plus a few handheld gardening tools were unloaded first. These she carried to the shrubs around the lower quad. Returning, she carried the azalea pots one by one. Harry was on an azalea tear. She placed these strategically in front of the peonies, some of which miraculously still luxuriated in full bloom. They were late bloomers; Harry could tap blooming dates. Of course, she read the information on tags. Having plants continue to bloom so there's always something of interest open tests any gardener. Having played on these grounds since childhood, she knew St. Luke's peculiarities with soil, shade, and wind.

On her knees, she stuck her fingers in the soil. Moist. Digging wouldn't be too hard. Picking up the spade, she dug all the holes first. Then she placed each azalea in its new home, carefully covering the hole, smoothing out the top, pulling over a bit of the mulch from the other plants. They looked good. This labor took an hour. The sun moved farther west. Another hour to sunset. She knew tomorrow the parking lot would be jammed for the Sunday service and then the homecoming afterward.

Both the Dorcas Guild and the St. Peter's Guild would be there long before the service, to put out tables, chairs, everything needed for the big day. Baskets filled with game items would be at either end of each quad, although everyone knew the big game would be capture the flag, which never failed to arouse everyone. People even played in wheelchairs pushed by whoever could run the fastest.

The azaleas, white and palest pink, set off those late-blooming peonies, themselves deep pink, purest white, or magenta. A few of the magenta bushes glowed so dark, they looked black in certain light. Harry felt her magenta peonies were spectacular.

Carrying the tools back to the Volvo, she then unraveled the hoses—each quad had a hose coiled at the end. The higher quad's water came from the side buildings of the church. The lower water ran from the old stables at the pastor's house, which had been turned into a garage. She watered all her plants, newly planted, plus the rest.

By the time she'd finished with that, another hour passed. She then dragged the hoses back to the buildings. She'd hauled them out yesterday, but somehow dragging them back, wrapping them around next to the faucet, wore her out. She knew she had to get hose holders with a handle to roll and unroll. But there wasn't time before the big do.

Looking around, seeing no one, she walked to the vehicle, carried a huge gin bottle in each hand, and made it to the farthest plantings. She opened the bottles, carefully pouring the liquid into the roots of the plants, but especially the peonies. By the time she had soused every peony and newly planted azalea, the sun nudged the horizon. Walking back for the last two bottles, she

hastened to the grave of the unknown woman, where she juiced those plants.

Her next problem, how to dispose of the gin bottles? She'd need to take them home, bag them up, and stuff them immediately into the garbage cans outside.

She wanted no one to know her secret, including her beloved husband.

Gin blossoms didn't apply only to humans.

13

Sunday

The light spilling in from the two-story stained glass windows shone on the Very Reverend Herbert Jones as he read the Antiphons. The trinity vestments, a middling green almost like wet palm fronds, the embroidery exquisite, picked up the light. Impressive under any circumstances, the Rev, as he was known, seemed especially intense today, the day of homecoming.

Every pew overflowed. People stood in the back. The ushers found chairs for the elderly as well as for pregnant women. The men, as was only proper, stood.

Harry, upon entering the church with Fair, nearly burst into tears seeing who had come from as far as California to be together on this extraordinary day.

The reverend's deep, rich voice, his rhythmic hypnotic cadence, spoke the centuries-old words, "Unto Thee do we call. Thee do we praise. Thee do we worship: O Blessed Trinity.

"Glory be to Thee, Co-Equal Trinity: One God before all worlds began, and now, and forevermore.

"Holy, Holy, Holy, Lord God Almighty: Which was, and is, and is to come."

The three Lutheran cats, under the altar, hidden by the cloth, stayed put. Usually they liked to go up to the balcony, edged in gilt, the white paint not original but the original color, setting off the gold. But this Sunday they wanted to be close to their human as they had felt all week his rising emotion, his care with his sermon, which would follow soon enough.

"I will never understand the Trinity," Cazenovia whispered.

"Doesn't matter. Humans believe in a human god. We believe in a cat. I know there's something," Elocution, the eldest, posited.

Lucy Fur immediately rejoined, "Not a dog!"

The other two nodded as the reverend moved along in the service.

The organist, a longtime lady parishioner, hit the keys for hymn 561, written by Charles Wesley in 1712. "Gentle Jesus, meek and mild, / Look upon a little child." On they sang as the reverend had especially selected this hymn for the children.

Once the service ended, the Very Reverend passed down the center aisle the gold crozier before him. Then he stopped as he always did at the doorway to shake every hand, speak to each person, and, if allowed, bend down and kiss the cheek of a tiny Lutheran.

So many people waited, this took forty-five minutes. Some of those who came a long way kissed his hand, for this former Vietnam captain had saved many a life, not only in combat by thinking ahead but by his openness to others, his ability to listen to problems as well as doubts. If ever a man was born to serve, it was the Very Reverend Herbert Jones.

The ladies of the Dorcas Guild waited for the onslaught, for many would like a refreshment. The big luncheon would be served after capture the flag. Who can run with a full stomach?

The men of St. Peter's Guild had laid down the lime lines for the dimensions of the field, about the same as a football field. They even put down ten-yard lines and the goal line was green on one end, bright gold on the other. The flag waited for all on the fifty-yard line.

Not everyone played. Many of the ladies in their fancy shoes did not, although Susan threw off her shoes to run, to the squeals of the children.

Fair and Ned acted as referees. Harry took those not playing on a tour of the grounds.

"I have never seen such peonies," Belinda Yost, down from New York City, exclaimed, to Harry's delight.

"Fortunately, we had a late spring. Made everything perfect for homecoming and the Rev's birthday."

Diana Flynn, with whom Harry had studied her catechism, now living in Traverse City, Michigan, whispered, "He still doesn't know, does he?"

"No. Wait until you see the birthday cake." Harry, blissfully happy to see old friends and blissfully happy that her idea of a homecoming birthday surprise proved successful, grinned.

Twenty women walked slowly with Harry, each of them a passionate gardener.

Brie Gidney, now Los Angeles–based, a producer no less, paused in front of a row of thick, extraordinary azaleas. "There's no way I could grow these in California. I'd have to use up half the reservoir."

"Is hardscaping catching on?" Diana asked, referring to landscaping with rocks and cacti, to preserve the ever-dwindling water supply.

"Yes, but it doesn't look the same. What irritates me, forgive me for complaining, is that we get smacked for watering our garden, but the golf courses are emerald, every one."

"Look at the quads, speaking of emerald." Belinda paused. "Once you adjust to the winters, the shorter growing seasons, you can create a wonderful garden in New York. Tom and I have pots in the city but our weekend home all the way up in Skaneateles, well, I can do a lot. Lots of blueberries." She laughed.

They walked along, happy in one another's company as the kids screamed and the adults urged one another on. Many a father grabbed the flag, passing it on to a child, which made the game that much more fun. Ned and Fair, perspiring, ran their butts off on the sidelines, too, for the game rocked back and forth between the two teams.

Pamela Bartlett, age notwithstanding, kept up the pace with the gardening crew. Her silver hair gleamed. She, too, among old friends who came home, felt how extraordinary the day was.

Mags Nielsen watched from the tables, for when the time was up, her task was to ring the big dinner bell that Big Mim had lent from her farm.

Mags's sidekick, Janice, shod in three-hundred-dollar sneakers, was playing capture the flag. Janice could run, which surprised homecomers, but anyone who played tennis against her knew that, so the St. Peter's men assigned someone to defend the swift woman.

Reaching the grave under the red oak, Harry paused so the ladies could read the simple marker.

"She was buried properly with a service on April 24, 2018. The Rev insisted we do this." Harry stepped aside so all could crowd around. "The Dorcas Guild felt simple flowers and shrubs should grace her resting place. We have no idea who she was. Not one lead."

Belinda peered up at the red oak. "A majestic guardian."

Brie, thinking as only a producer can, remarked, "What a sentry. She was on the Taylors' caskets? I remember when we were walked back there as children to read the old tombstones and remember those who went before, what they did for us. The Taylors were the first people buried in that cemetery, right?"

Pamela's cultivated voice immediately commanded attention. "Yes. We think they died of tuberculosis within hours of each other. Can't be sure, but the description in the church records gives us a pretty good indication. People recognized cancer, heart attack, tuberculosis, even diabetes. They used different names. But why this woman was placed on top of the Taylors, no casket, wearing what had to be a beautiful mustard silk gown and those huge pearls and diamonds, it's beyond our comprehension."

Janice added, "And she was African American. The medical examiner's office, the best, by the way, determined that."

"Patricia Cornwall knew what she was doing when she wrote about Virginia's medical examiner," Brie said.

"Unbelievable," Diana exclaimed.

"Virginia had a strong population of free African Americans as well as thousands of slaves once we really got into the eighteenth century. Is it possible she was an early entrepreneur like Maggie Walker?" Belinda cited the woman who started the Penny Bank not long after 1865.

"Maybe she was an ambassador's wife? She could have been French, you know, someone from the Caribbean of impossible beauty." Brie was writing the movie script already.

"I think she was a mistress, kept by someone with wagonloads of money." Janice spoke with authority.

"Then why did she wind up on the Taylors' casket?" Belinda shrewdly asked.

"Maybe the wife found out. You never know." Diana already felt a tingle thinking about a long-ago mistress and an outraged wife.

She wasn't far from the truth, but the details were wrong.

"Will we ever see the necklace and the earrings?" Brie wondered.

Harry, nodding to Pamela and Janice, moved aside so they could come forward.

Pamela took charge with Janice as her second. "The Dorcas Guild, after a year's worth of thought and discussion, has decided to preserve the jewelry as part of St. Luke's history."

Beaming, Janice added, "There were some who did not want to sell the jewels, thinking a relative could be found. Impossible, of course. It will be in our vault."

"We all strongly believed the exquisite workmanship should be on display, at least once a year. Now mind you, over the years this could change. Who knows what we will find, or uncover?" Pamela folded her hands together.

"It really is extraordinary," Janice added.

"A great story in the right hands." Brie's mind spun.

"Ladies." Harry smiled, holding out her hand to direct them back up over the quads to all that food.

Janice walked with her and Harry stopped at the magenta peonies. Fishing in her pocket, she pulled out a lipstick. "Match. Found it."

"Ha." Harry reached into a small silk purse that hung across her body. "Mine's better."

They both held their lipsticks up to the open bloom.

"H-m-m." Harry squinted.

Janice twisted her lipstick until the tube was almost all the way up in its black plastic case. "Better."

"I'll get you for this."

The yellow team had won the game. Those who played were thirsty as well as hungry, but the eldest parishioners went first in the line.

Once all were seated at the tables, the talk ratcheted up. Elocution, Lucy Fur, Cazenovia, under the tables, snagged a piece of ruby red dropped roast beef. *"The best."*

The cats loved the celebration as much as the people.

Once the hot food was devoured, the conversation paused as Fair and Ned rolled out the huge multitiered birthday cake up to the Very Reverend Jones, who blinked. Was there ever a cake that big, and then three more? Herb's had a big birthday script in blue across his cake.

Everyone stood and sang "Happy Birthday."

The reverend couldn't help it. He cried.

"Cut the cake," a six-year-old called out, to be instantly shushed by his embarrassed mother.

The reverend, cake knife in hand, figured this was not the time for a speech. He looked over these people whom he had baptized, married, helped to bury their mothers and fathers and even a few children. Those to whom he had taught catechism.

His sonorous voice rang out. "Thank you. I am eighty years old and I have no idea how I got here. I quote William Butler Yeats, 'Think where man's glory most begins and ends, and say my glory was I had such friends.'"

After the luncheon, the men of the St. Peter's Guild invited everyone down to the grave of the unknown woman, where two Brinks guards stood, armed for effect. One held a polished wooden box.

Once all were there, the story of the woman was again told. One man opened the box and held up the pearl necklace while the woman guard held out the earrings.

Fair said, "We thought those of you who have come home would like to see this."

The gorgeous jewelry took away people's breath.

The guards smiled as Fair then said, "Reverend Jones, Happy Birthday again."

"This gift is for you alone." Ned stepped forward, handing the overcome reverend a set of car keys, then pointed to a new Tahoe sitting in his driveway. "Your old jalopy was on its last legs. The congregation has all purchased this for you."

That night, home at last, Harry and Fair cuddled in bed.

"What a perfect day." Harry put her head on his shoulder.

"Any day with you is perfect, baby doll."

"You." Harry laughed at him.

"*Gross.*" Pewter sniffed on the end of the bed.

Brie, staying with Susan Tucker, sat in the living room with her hosts as they, too, reviewed the day. "If someone stole that necklace, now that would be a movie."

"Brie." Susan's voice rose.

"Hollywood." Ned laughed.

"But what a film. A gorgeous woman, mistress to a powerful man, dispatched by the wife." Brie nearly licked her chops.

"How would you update it for today?" Susan wondered.

"Oh, someone descended from either the wife or the victim. Murder sells, you know."

Indeed.

14

Saturday

Occasionally bounty hunters got lucky and found their runaway slaves quickly. Martin and Shank, hired by Maureen Selisse Holloway, slogged along Virginia's coast. They had contacts there in the shipyards. No one had seen Ralston, William, or Sulli. Plus, no captain would have carried them anywhere without a fee. So after ten days of slow going, they reached the Potomac River as they headed west. The ferrymen, always ready for a tip, hadn't seen three young people matching the descriptions of the runaway slaves. If any had, they would have eagerly mentioned it. They didn't lie because they knew Martin and Shank, and the two knew them. Shank, in particular, would get even. Martin's vengeful streak proved more sophisticated, whereas Shank was physical. He'd lay you flat on the spot.

Along the way they bought a nice draft mare, Penny; a beat-up wagon; and a harness.

Patient—a necessary quality in that line of work—the two finally reached the Point of Rocks Ferry. The ferryman, Arch Newbold, recognized them as he reached the Virginia shore, discharging only two passengers.

"Arch, it's Martin and Shank." Martin greeted him.

"You look the same as you did last time I saw you." He flicked his hand under his full beard. "Not me."

"If I lived on this cold river, I'd cover my face, too," Shank joked.

"It comes off in the spring. Winter started early this year. Not many travelers." Arch frowned.

"Do you recall seeing three young slaves? A pretty woman and two fellows, one tall and thin, the other medium-sized. No telling when or if they reached the river, but this would have been before winter set in. We don't know how they're traveling."

Tying up the ferry, no passengers on the dock, he motioned for the two to follow him to his shack. Sturdy, a small fireplace, a couple of chairs, it beat staying out in the cold.

The two sat in the chairs by the fire as Arch beckoned. He threw in another log.

"Feeding the fire. Helps."

"Does, Arch." Martin nodded, offering Arch a sip of liquor. Along with the horse and cart, the two bounty hunters bought crocks of liquor as well as thimbles, odds and ends.

Smiling, Arch swallowed, his eyes watered; he handed the crock back to Martin as he coughed. "What the hell do you have in there?"

"My secret." Martin leaned back in the chair. "In my business I meet many people."

"Guess you do." Arch wiped his eyes.

"Don't drink too much. Your legs will lock up on you," Shank informed him.

"One draw will keep me." Arch moved his booted feet closer to the small but vigorous fire. "Three young ones, worn out and hungry, I can tell you that much. They got here, counted out their money. I didn't say nothin'. Didn't have enough for all three.

"Fellow came down with a stubborn horse. Couldn't get the animal moving and wanted to take horse and cart across the river. The shorter fellow turned out to be good with a horse. He crawled under the cart, saw the wheel was froze up, something in it, I think. He asked the woman for a thick stick. She found one and the tall, thin fellow tipped up the cart while the other one underneath dislodged it. The man, never saw him before or again, paid their way. Whatever he had in the cart he wanted to get over to Maryland. Didn't seem like produce. The cart wasn't too heavy for the tall fellow to tip so I figured it was something light, wool maybe. Lot of people got sheep, cattle. I'm not for anything I have to feed." He laughed.

"So you'd say at least the shorter one could handle a horse?" Shank asked.

"Seemed like a good hand. Runaways?"

"Yes."

"I don't ask." Arch shrugged. "If they can pay the fare, I take them."

"I would, too," Martin agreed.

"You know people over there?" Shank relaxed in the warmth.

"Couple I do. Couple of big farms. The farmhands might come down for an errand but mostly I stay to myself. Got a few regulars who cross once a month, but the people I see usually, I only seen them crossing once or twice."

"What about back at the crossroads? Dry goods store. Think any of those folks are moving people through?" Martin saw the golden rays on the water outside the small window.

The sun was setting.

"No. Not any money in it," Arch replied. "Be dark pretty fast now. If you go back, not but a mile, a small inn is there. Like I said, not many people traveling. You won't have trouble getting rooms. Food's good. Good stew."

The two stood up, as did Arch. Martin shook his hand. "Thanks. If we do find those three, there will be a little something for you. Keep your eyes open, Arch."

Arch felt a coin cool in his hand. "I will, I surely will."

When Martin and Shank left, closing the door, Arch looked at the silver. "One dollar. Those three must be important." He doused the fire, spread the ashes around with a fireplace rake, stepped outside, pulled up his collar, and headed for home. Only half a mile from the river on a small rise, he was glad to see it: Light shone from the front window. The wind was raw.

He opened the door. His wife, a well-padded woman, was stirring something in the pot over the fire. He walked up, taking off his worn coat, kissed her on the cheek, then held out his hand. The silver dollar shone among the coins.

"Arch."

He smiled and sat down. Running a ferry proved hard labor and Arch wasn't getting any younger.

"Two fellows, known them some, looking for runaways."

"And they gave you a silver dollar?"

"And I'm going to get you that shawl you want."

"Now, Arch, honey, it's going to be a long, hard winter. All the signs are there. Wait until spring."

"I want to see your pretty face against that color. What do you call that color?"

"Sapphire blue."

He shook his head. "You'll look"—he thought—"like the girl I married."

She turned from her pot, laughing. "I will not."

"You don't have one wrinkle."

Now she truly laughed. "Because I'm getting fat!"

They laughed together. Two people who didn't have much but they had each other.

15

December 2, 1787

Sunday

Mr. Finney's impressive carriage rolled down the long drive of Royal Oak as he and his lady were going to mass.

Ralston, in the mare barn, watched. As few Catholics lived in Albemarle County, Virginia, he found the ritual fascinating. Not that he had ever attended a service, but Ard told him about the candles, the votives, the big baptismal font, all the statues.

Each breath Ralston and the mare he was grooming took came out in puffs of smoke. Ralston knew it wasn't smoke but that's what it looked like. He finished the careful grooming, slid on the mare's blanket, and moved to the next stall.

Working abated some of the cold. The notion that Sunday was a day of rest applied more to the humans than the animals, who needed food and water. Ralston was happy to oblige. If he took on the three barns, caring for all the horses, somewhere along the line he would call in the time he did this for the two other fellows, each assigned a barn. They took off on Sundays.

Fortunately, William had not been put in charge of a barn. Ard used him more for riding but also for odd jobs, which allowed Ard to keep an eye on William.

He wasn't keeping his eye on the young man this Sunday morning; old Dipsy Runckle was. Hammer in one hand, kneeling down, Dipsy tapped the large wooden wheel of a newly built work cart.

William, on the other side of the cart, kneeling by the wheel, held his hand on the center of the wheel, the inside of which held the axle.

"Anything?" Dipsy asked.

"No."

Dipsy tapped again harder. "Now?"

"No."

"Switch with me," Dipsy commanded, so the two men changed places and Dipsy now tapped the wheel center where William had been. "Anything?"

"No. Dipsy, what good does tapping do? This axle is solid, the wheel well full of grease. Spokes solid."

"I got my ways and you don't know shit." Dipsy found most young people tedious and stupid.

William fumed but he shut up. Dipsy stood up, having performed the same ritual for the front axle and wheels, and he climbed into the cart. An eight-foot bed, while not overlong, could fool an inexperienced driver. Getting around any corner can be difficult depending on the road surface, and most roads were mud. The longer and heavier the vehicle, the more difficult the task.

Built for light hauling, this deep blue cart would see a great deal of use. On any farm much of the hauling involved lighter items: a few square bales, maybe a barrel or two of oats or wooden boxes of corn for the cook. Light wagons and carts worked every day on most farms, so a breakdown could be costly. Better to have a few smaller ones than one huge one.

Dipsy walked front to back, then again. Stopping in the middle, he jumped up and down. As his knees were shot, this was not a high jump but still his weight pounded the weakest part of the bed at the center.

"Solid." The old man smiled.

William, leaning over the side of the cart, observed, "Should be, the time spent building it."

"You can do something in a hurry or you can do it right." Dipsy knelt down, running his ungloved fingers over the top of the sides. He moved up to sit in the driver's seat, a butt-width plank with a backrest. Running his fingers over the top surfaces, he grunted. Ran them in the other direction, then leaned back against the backrest.

"Looks good." William passed an opinion, which carried no weight with Dipsy.

"A fresh coat of paint makes anything look good. This will get used and used hard. No point making someone's job harder by filling their fingers full of splinters. The one thing I can't do is fashion an axle as good as the one in the Studebaker carts Mr. Finney bought."

"Those people must have a big forge," William remarked.

"Bet they do. It's their business but we can come close."

"Guess so."

Dipsy continued sitting on the driver's seat, pulling his gloves back on. "Mr. Studebaker figured out no one could use the number of carts Mr. Finney was buying." He smiled. "Mr. Finney's smart. He was buying carts to resell for more money. They put a stop to that. Mr. Finney was doing them a favor by my lights. I don't know, I'm not a moneyman."

"Why?"

"People bought a top cart, heard the Studebaker name. They stamped it on the undercarriage. Word gets out. People would go to the source. Anyway, Mr. Finney decided he could build carts, too, so this is our first. It will last."

"Who's bought it?"

"Rosemont."

This was a farm three miles east of Royal Oak. Owned by Edward

McBain, young, ambitious, he was expanding. McBain wanted everything that Mr. Finney had.

"Lots of cattle," William laconically remarked.

"Mr. Finney will want this delivered tomorrow or next day. Weather might turn." He slapped his hands on his thighs, no real slap due to his fingers. "It's a good strong cart. Bet Mr. Finney gets more orders."

"Right." Evidencing scant interest, William, work finished, left, walking back to his cabin.

When Ard hired William, Ralston, and Sulli, William lied, claiming Sulli as his wife. Ralston was moved to the single men's bunkhouse. Mr. Finney believed marriage a great benefit to a man. Husband and wife deserved privacy. However, if they ate with the other workers they paid six dollars a month instead of three dollars. As Sulli worked in the communal kitchen for Miss Frances, they paid five dollars, a bit of a discount for wonderful food.

Mr. Finney believed a well-fed worker was a better worker. The Irishman, fair to a fault, expected a good day's work. He got it.

As William walked over the frozen ground, Martin and Shank, now on the Maryland side, observed everything. If the three runaways remained in Maryland, they would find them through questioning, observation, and studying the roads. The bounty hunters figured the three stayed on foot. If they intended to reach Philadelphia, they would need to pick up jobs, perhaps staying for months, especially in winter.

Enticing as Philadelphia was, so was a good job. Marylanders owned slaves, as did many people in the Original Thirteen, save Vermont. Pennsylvania, thanks to its Quaker roots, never encouraged the practice. But if a resident of the large state chose to own slaves, they were legally permitted. If shipowners carried slaves, they were also permitted.

Confident that the runaways had passed through this area, Martin and Shank felt they would soon pick up the trail. If the slaves had passed themselves off as freedmen, who would care unless a large reward was offered for their return?

The two threw wide their net. Little by little they would tighten it, then close it to strike like rattlesnakes.

Often a search would consume months. Every now and then the pursued would fall into their hands.

Finding simple lodging at a small inn in Doubs, they once again began their search.

Both Martin and Shank excelled at picking up and sifting bits of information, at finding a lead or hearing of an offhand comment. Greasing palms aided the process. They'd seen people turn on one another for two dollars.

Neither man held a high opinion of the human race.

16

Monday

"Took longer than I thought." Harry dropped into a chair.

"Did." Janice sat next to her in the women's building of St. Luke's.

"It was a huge success thanks to you, Harry. You had the idea and convinced the rest of us." Pamela smiled.

The Dorcas Guild had returned at 10:30 A.M. to double-check, pick up anything they missed yesterday, and enjoy a "girls' lunch" of the leftover food. Why does food always taste better the second day?

Sitting around one rectangle table, the workhorses of the Guild chatted, compared notes.

"We actually surprised the Rev." Mags laughed.

A scratch at the door made Harry rise to open it. "Beggars."

"*Smells good*," Elocution declared as Lucy Fur and Cazenovia marched in.

Susan laughed as she picked up three paper plates, piling chicken and ribs on each one. "Well, girls, they helped yesterday. I consider them members of the Dorcas Guild."

Tazio, Renie, and Libby, young members, listened more than talking themselves. Tazio cut some of her fried chicken for the Reverend's cats.

"Weren't the necklace and those earrings spectacular? I have never seen anything like that short of royal displays in European museums." Mags thought the food delicious, especially since she didn't have to cook.

"Funny you should say that." Harry cut open a baked potato she had put in the microwave.

Given that Harry worked off every calorie, she could eat whatever she wanted. Not one Dorcas member joined her in a baked potato but they all watched her pile butter, sour cream, and bacon bits on it.

"That's got to be one thousand calories," Janice exclaimed.

Harry looked at her. "So what?"

"I can't believe you eat like that," Janice replied.

"I'm a farm girl. What can I say? Back to royalty. Fashions in jewelry change like clothing. Think of Tiffany's designer, Jean Michel Schlumberger. And you can always pick out Cartier's design from the 1930s."

"Maybe you can. I can't," Renie, bright red hair, confessed.

Susan, consoling, focused on Renie. "Harry goes on research jags. Never go into any library with her or sit next to her when she turns on her computer."

"Oh, Susan."

"Harry, it's a function of your notorious nosiness." Her best friend giggled.

"I am not nosy. I am curious."

"Yeah. Agreed." Susan put down her fish. "But you were going to force us to listen to your idea about jewelry fashions. Here we are, a captive audience."

"*You know, some cats wear jeweled collars,*" Elocution, between mouthfuls, announced.

"*Why would any cat wear a collar? It's awful.*" Cazenovia flipped her longhaired calico tail.

"*No one wants to, of course.*" Lucy Fur jumped in. "*It's so their humans can show off.*"

"*Why don't the humans wear a jeweled collar? Why put one on us?*" Elocution demanded.

"*Because they have no sense. Maybe the rich lady puts a collar on her cat identical to her own choker.*" Lucy Fur, like Elocution, thought the whole thing absurd.

Harry, not understanding the cat conversation, food dripping out of their mouths as they talked, answered Susan. "If you put up pictures of Mrs. Vanderbilt, Alva Belmont, those grand society madams near the end of the nineteenth century, beginning of the twentieth, look at the jewelry."

"Okay." Janice was interested. "I remember one photo of Alva Belmont with a pearl necklace, three strands of pearls, hanging below her waist."

"If you go before photography there are drawings of queens in full regalia. The jewelry for Queen Isabella II, wife of Edward I, is different from what Elizabeth I wore. English royalty. Factor in other countries and there is a lot of variety. Different stones, colors meant something; the jewelry was a statement."

"But isn't jewelry always a statement?" Mags interjected.

"Yes," Pamela simply said.

"What I'm getting at is that our nameless woman's jewelry is a bit more complicated than what an American woman at the time would normally wear." Harry pushed on.

"Like Martha Washington?" Janice wondered.

"The first First Lady possessed good, understated taste. Abigail Adams, of course, would find such display frivolous. Dolley Madison liked color and display but she, too, was careful not to display too much wealth. It wasn't considered American."

Everyone was thinking.

"Do you really think we were that self-aware?" Tazio asked.

"I do. The last thing we wanted was to look or act like royalty or aristocrats. Think of what our leaders wrote about before we fought, while we fought, and after we fought." Harry finished her delicious potato, picking up the skin and eating it. "Sorry, I should have cut the skin."

"It's easier that way." Libby, with a cute round face, smiled. "I was a history major at Chapel Hill. You know we never studied or discussed fashion."

"No one does." Susan shook her head. "How stupid. The fastest road into the past is through sports, the arts, fashion. Just think of whalebone corsets."

"Dear God. It's a wonder our foremothers could breathe." Pamela laughed.

Susan, wise to Harry's ways, said, "What are you driving at?"

"Well." A pause followed this. "I don't think the owner of that necklace and earrings was an American."

"Really?" Mags was now completely fascinated.

"Too ornate. Too flashy. All those diamonds and pearls. Way too flashy."

"In other words, Mrs. Washington would not have worn them." Pamela cut a small square of cherry cobbler, passing the plate.

"Nor would any other woman whose husband had political designs?" Tazio questioned.

"That would be rubbing people's noses in it." Harry continued. "Even a successful businessman, hoping to parade his wealth through his wife, had best be careful, even after the Revolutionary War. The vulgarity came in the last half of the nineteenth century."

"You know, Harry, you just might be on to something." Janice rested her chin in the cup of her hand. "Like maybe those bones belong to a diplomat's wife?"

"Or the mistress of someone from Spain, say, or France, or Spain's colonies," Mags added.

"But then if she disappeared, wouldn't someone have noticed?" Pamela wisely noted.

"You'd certainly think so," Janice replied.

"Well, Harry, what do we do with what we've got?" Tazio wondered.

"Just hear me out." Harry held up her hand. "We secure the jewelry in our safe, where it is already. We write up the discovery, the time, the building of St. Luke's, our history. We know when she was dumped on the Taylors', pretty much."

"Why do we?" Mags eyebrows raised.

"Think, Mags. If their grave was opened even two weeks after their deaths, that would have been obvious. She had to be placed on their coffins within a day or two of their joint burial. Someone could dig up the freshly dug earth, toss her in, replace the earth."

This really got them.

"You're right!" Janice nearly clapped her hands.

"So if we write our history, each year on our anniversary, which I take to be when the organ was first played, we hand out a booklet with photos of St. Luke's, the gardens, the original architectural plans, the history of Charles and Rachel West, of subsequent pastors, and our big mystery. On that day we open our church to all, which we pretty much do anyway, and we display the necklace and earrings."

No one said one word. Minutes passed. The cats looked at one another, feeling this an excellent opportunity to steal more food, which they did.

Finally Pamela, smiling broadly, added, "With armed guards. Drama."

"Yes! Once a year." Harry beamed. "I don't think St. Luke's has ever received our historical due."

"Hear. Hear." All the ladies rapped the table.

"Now what?" Mags asked.

"We talk to Reverend Jones. We secure his approval. We begin writing St. Luke's history, which will take time, lots of work, digging up photos, all that stuff."

"Like Katherine Butterfield's history of St. Anne's-Belfield." Libby mentioned the late historian of the fashionable private school of Albemarle County.

"If we could produce something half as good, we'd be in deep clover."

Harry smiled, as she had much admired Mrs. Butterfield.

Susan tapped her spoon on a glass. "All in favor of securing the jewelry and displaying it on our annual foundation day, say 'Aye.'"

"Aye." In unison.

"All in favor of a history with drawings and photos of St. Luke's, say 'Aye.'"

"Aye." In unison.

Then Janice piped up. "You didn't ask for all opposed."

"Janice, the vote was unanimous." Susan threw up her hands.

"Oh. Okay," Janice agreed.

Lucy Fur, full, said to her two friends, "Do you think Poppy will go for it?"

Elocution replied, "I do."

Cazenovia added, "As long as the history is accurate. Doesn't hide anything. He'll like the idea."

"Given the necklace, well, that's a mystery. Humans love a mystery." Lucy Fur thought a moment. "That means they have to write about the cats, dogs, and horses of St. Luke's."

"Harry will see to that." Cazenovia cleaned her whiskers.

"Maybe they'll find the answer to the bones," Lucy Fur said.

"Given that her neck was broken, it can't be a good story." Cazenovia raised her voice. "You know, we don't kill one another. Maybe once in a blue moon but cats don't kill one another. Humans do."

"We know that." Elocution lifted a long, silky eyebrow.

"Talk of old troubles might bring on new," Cazenovia said with authority.

17

Tuesday

The early corn pushed up shoots already over a foot tall. Harry had organized her fields by projected harvest data. Corn could be harvested into late September some years. The sunflowers would usually be in full bloom mid-August. The rest of her flatter lands hosted various mixtures of orchard grass, clover, timothy, and alfalfa. Alfalfa seed, expensive, guaranteed it would be paired usually with timothy. Whether two-footed or four-, everyone had preferences.

Harry walked through the fields abutting the mountains, where she planted fescue. Fescue could cause a pregnant mare to spontaneously abort. However, fescue could tolerate heat and cold. It was a native Virginia plant, made good hay. As this part of her farm received a bit less light due to the mountains and a bit more cooling temperatures, fescue thrived, but she never put a pregnant mare in these pastures.

Walking with her, ever-present notebook slid into her jeans back hip pocket, was Susan.

Mrs. Murphy, Pewter, Tucker, Pirate, and Owen sniffed delightful odors: bobcat, deer, Canadian geese. The geese resting on those pastures closest to the fast-running creek paid no attention to the little convoy. The animals had learned the hard way as youngsters that geese can be aggressive. Tails had been hurt by those beaks. Tucker wouldn't even look at one in the eye.

"Come on. You've dawdled over your hay, your corn, your sunflowers. Let's get up there and measure some of the timber," Susan grumbled.

"You've been a good egg."

"I have. I am always a good egg." Susan began the climb using the farm road.

A quarter of a mile up, the grade still easy, Harry fetched a measuring tape from her other hip pocket.

"Good thing we marked some of these last year." She moved to a fine hickory, wrapping the tape around the trunk.

"Number one. Thirty-one inches. Right on the silver line."

"Yeah. A bit higher now. She's growing. M-m-m. Just a hair below thirty-three. Good growth."

Susan wrote down the figures. "Given almost eight months of rain last year, she should be getting a bigger waistline."

Every hundred yards, give or take, for the two had not measured distance that precisely, they would measure a tree with silver painted around the trunk. Spray paint proved so easy to use.

The climb steepened. Progress slowed. While in good shape, both breathed a little harder. Susan, who ran daily, felt a twinge in her calves that surprised her.

On and on they toiled until near the top of the lower ridge of the Blue Ridge Mountains. At fifteen hundred feet, it set against the taller mountain behind it.

Westerners mocked the Blue Ridge. "Hills. These aren't mountains."

To which a Virginian would reply, "These were once the tallest mountains in the world. You are looking at the power of time."

That usually shut them up. Harry loved mountains, any mountains, but her heart rested with the Blue Ridge. Right now her heart was beating.

"Five minutes' rest. The closer we get to the top, the more it gets me. Once when I was in Sheridan, Wyoming, I drove up the Big Horn. As I didn't know the terrain, I figured I'd better drive. The high meadows are beautiful and as I parked and sat there, up came a herd of cattle being driven by cowboys and women, too, to their summer pastures. The only way we could do that here is to fence them. Too close to 250 or 64. Damn roads."

Susan, glad to sit on a cut trunk for a moment, nodded. "That was the trip where we split at Salt Lake City. We don't do that anymore."

"Only if we plan. At twenty, summer vacation felt like heaven."

"It was heaven," Susan reminisced.

The dogs stayed with them. Mrs. Murphy and Pewter, noses almost as keen as dog noses, caught a whiff of those not so old bones.

Moving east to the rock outcropping, they found the rib cage after passing the well-hidden still.

"Not much left." Mrs. Murphy observed the whitened ribs.

"Hey, look at this." Pewter headed for the partial skull, baseball hat still in place. "Let's tell Harry." Off she shot.

Tucker's ears drooped. She knew exactly what had happened, as did Pirate.

"What's wrong?" Owen licked his sister's face.

"Damn cats. They found what's left of that human," Tucker answered.

"Follow me!" Pewter hollered as Mrs. Murphy came up behind.

"Pewter, don't take them there. It will start a mess," Tucker warned.

"A dead person. I found it! Wait until you see what's left. Dead. Dead. Dead," Pewter gleefully announced.

Pirate, confused, inquired, "Why is Pewter so happy about a dead human?"

"Because she found it. Harry and Susan will follow her."

"Yes?" The Irish wolfhound's ears lifted.

"Pirate, if they are still fussing about the bones in the old grave at St. Luke's, think how they'll be now. They have no sense."

"But the person is dead," Pirate rightly said.

"They will have to find out why, if possible. Was it a natural death or murder? And don't forget, Pirate, the still is not far from the remains. That will set them right off."

Owen chimed in. "Pirate, you haven't seen these two, um, on the case."

Puffed up like a broody hen, Pewter would run forward, run back, claw Harry's jeans leg, and run off again, with Mrs. Murphy by her side.

"A still!" Harry spied the small shack-like building.

"Damned if it isn't," Susan agreed.

Being country girls, they had seen stills, none of which resembled the high-class apparatus for beer Mags and Janice used at Bottoms Up.

The cats kept going. The dogs followed, too.

"Here!" Pewter triumphantly stood by the opened rib cage.

"What the hell!" Harry exclaimed.

Then Pewter ran to the skull under the boulder. "Heads up!"

"Very funny." Mrs. Murphy did laugh, though.

The two women came over.

"Black hair. What's left. You'd think some animal would have torn the cap off," Susan noted.

Over the years both Harry and Susan had seen a few corpses or skeletons. Again, being country girls, death did not offend them. It was part of life. Cause of death did provoke them, though.

"A man?" Harry half asked, half declared.

"Don't know that many women with hidden stills." Susan plucked her cellphone out of her shirt pocket.

"Ned?"

"No, the sheriff."

Within thirty minutes Sheriff Shaw and a deputy, Dwayne, drove over the high meadow, stopped, and walked over to them. For once, GPS had routed them correctly.

The two women told their story while Dwayne inspected the still.

"It's intact," he announced.

Sheriff Shaw, kneeling down, touched nothing. "Hard to say but I'd bet whoever this was died early fall." He stood back up. "Get forensics out here. We need to photograph everything undisturbed, then send this to Richmond."

"Not much left," Harry said.

"Those folks are the best. You'll be surprised at what they deduce."

"*I found this! Me! Me! Me!*" Pewter crowed.

"*She's going to be impossible,*" Tucker predicted.

"*She's impossible now,*" Owen remarked.

"*There are police dogs. I should be a police cat!*" Pewter bragged.

18

Wednesday

"A bit of cheer." Shank held up a brown bottle at the main stable at Royal Oak. "Lift your spirits."

Martin, standing in the back of an old wagon bought with Maureen's down payment, beamed. "Here, gentlemen, a sip to tantalize your taste buds."

"Don't mind if I do." Ard smiled broadly, taking the bottle from Martin's outstretched hand. "Great Day!"

"Your eyes are watering," Dipsy howled at him, grabbing the bottle. "A real man can take a drink."

So he did and about fell over coughing, which made the other men roar.

"Gentlemen, these are potent waters." Shank grinned as one by one the male workers at Royal Oak crept into the main stable.

Ard, clearing his throat, wiping his eyes, said, "Boys, we can't all be in here at the same time. Those of you with brave hearts, pay up and go back to work. Don't want Mr. Finney thinking we're slacking, especially with Christmas up ahead."

A murmur passed through the men as one by one they fished coins out of their pockets to pay for the bottle, not cheap at three dollars for a full bottle and half that for a half bottle but, oh, so desirable. Now, where to hide the bottle? Can't let the wife find it if a man had a wife. And the bunkhouse, your best buddy would drain your bottle dry if he found it. You'd find him passed out or dead.

Excited talk filled the air while the horses ignored it all.

William, all braggadocio, handed over his money.

Martin lifted a bottle from the banked hay. "Here you go, young man. Best country waters in the States."

William uncorked his bottle, sniffed, took a swig. He was smart enough to take a small sip, but that still packed a punch.

Ralston, curious, tried to sniff William's bottle, but the slightly taller William cuffed him.

"Young fellow, come here. A small, restorative sip. A man's mouth can only get but so dry." Martin beckoned to Ralston.

Ralston gingerly sipped the contents, gulped, stood still, rooted to the spot. Then he passed the bottle back up to Martin in his green, broad-brimmed hat with a jaunty pheasant feather in it. Naturally, Ralston didn't want to appear weak or unmanly so he, too, fished out the requisite amount, a bit of money for him, but he did it.

"Hurry up, boys. Back to work," Ard barked, then enjoyed a tiny drop of the magic.

Giggles alerted the men that women approached.

Miss Frances strode in. "And what might you be selling?"

Shank nodded to her, respectful to a female, grabbed the bottle from Martin, and reached out to her. "Madam, these are very strong waters but you might wish a small lift."

Eyeing him suspiciously, she tilted the bottle to her lips, took a swig—not a small one—licked her lips, and handed it back.

"Madam," Martin exclaimed, "you possess a formidable palate." He figured no one would know that "palate" wasn't the correct word but it sounded high-class.

Glaring at him, she put one hand on her hip. "I'm Irish. We all possess formidable palates." She put the accent on the "p."

Sensing he had the men over a barrel, for how could they be shown up by a woman, Martin leaned down, smiled big. "Merry Christmas, you *Alainn Bean-vassal.*"

She stepped up on the side step, grasping the bottle he had given her, kissed him on the cheek, and stepped down, staring at all the workers. "Never miss the chance to kiss a handsome man."

He had called her "beautiful lady" in Celtic. She rarely heard her native tongue anymore.

The men rushed the cart, coins jingling in hands as Miss Frances turned to leave the barn. One kitchen worker had snuck out and Sulli did, too, peeking into the barn.

Shank noted Sulli as he had noted William and Ralston.

Shank and Martin sold a lot of strong spirits made with crystal clear mountain water. Given their product, they found ways to get onto farms or into homes, loosen tongues. They had beads, children's toys, a few small items of silver like thimbles, for every woman sewed. A silver thimble presented by one's husband, son, or beau delighted a lady and a fellow could afford it. Silver impressed. Gold even more, obviously.

Dipsy, two swigs in his gullet, walked up to Shank. "If you two peddlers want a cart that will outlive you both, we make them here. Noticed yours is rickety."

"'Tis," Shank agreed.

As the people filtered out, Dipsy persisted. "Leave your horse and cart here for a minute. Follow me."

The two, eager to observe all they could at Royal Oak, followed the older fellow to the small but well-organized shop where the blue cart stood waiting to be delivered to Rosemont. He held out his arm in an expansive gesture. "The best."

Shank and Martin circled the cart. Martin knelt down to look under the bottom, "Heavy axle."

"Takes an elephant to break it," Dipsy bragged.

Shank knelt down, too. "You know, sir, you might be right. What would a wagon like this run?"

"This one is sold but I'll see if Mr. Finney would take an order or sell one we use on the farm, at a lower rate, of course."

"What would this cost new?" Martin stood up.

"One hundred and fifty dollars. Two hundred if you want a ten-foot bed and you want special paint. We can make any length you want. Our axles will hold the weight."

"Let us consider this, Mr.?"

"Dipsy Runckle. Call me Dipsy."

Martin, rubbing his chin, said, "Mr. Runckle, we travel. Many people would see this piece of handiwork. We could sell some. Actually, I believe we could sell a lot. If you lower the price for us, we might be able to swing it."

Dipsy crossed his arms over his chest. "Mr. Finney can be a hard man, but I'll talk to him. He's a shrewd businessman and would be able to consider your offer."

"And what would you like, Mr. Runckle?" Martin smiled.

"We can discuss that if I convince Mr. Finney."

Once back out on the road, Martin and Shank drove five miles to their lodgings. The horse, a decent enough half-breed, trotted, for the cold enlivened her.

"Fit the description."

"Did." Shank agreed. "Girl is a pretty thing."

"Is." Martin felt the heavy coins in his pocket. "You know we made over sixty dollars. If our line of work ever fails, I think we have a new one."

Shank laughed. "Ever notice how people close to mountains make good liquor? When we met with Mrs. Holloway, I figured there had to be some fine distillers in the region."

"You think ahead." Martin smiled at him, holding the reins loosely.

"If we can lure those three off Royal Oak, our job will be easier. If not, we'd better be careful. The owner is a powerful man. His people don't talk."

"We're retrieving stolen property."

"Well, Martin, they aren't stolen exactly, but Royal Oak is tight, well run. Don't think anyone would turn on anyone else."

"You're right. My mind's running ahead. Mostly, I'm glad we didn't need to keep fishing throughout Maryland and wind up in Philadelphia." Shank grunted.

"Yes, but they're thirsty there, too."

"Ha!"

"We have a way back onto the farm. To buy a wagon." Martin put the reins in one hand, placing the other in his pocket. "But that doesn't help us grab those two. The third isn't Mrs. Holloway's. I still think we should sell him."

"We might not be able to take them all at once. The two fellows are young. They'll be quick. They don't look that strong but they will be quick." Shank studied his quarry as would any hunter.

"True."

"Martin, look up." Shank grimaced.

Martin did as a twirling snowflake lazed down onto the mare's mane. "We're not far, thank heaven."

"No. Not a bad little barn the inn has, but I'm thinking about the roads. Be good if we could bag our quarry while people are occupied with their dinners and celebrations. Not too many would be in our way. If we can find out the Royal Oak schedule, that will help."

Martin nodded, clucked as the mare increased her trot. She didn't want to be out in the snow in her traces either. "We've got rope, gags. We need to cut out each fellow, then grab him."

Shank said, "Well, if we can lure them off the farm, ought to be easy. It's the girl I'm worried about. Be hard to get at her. She's not going to be working outside."

"Oh now, Shank, where there's a will there's a way."

19

Friday

Soft light filtered into the mare barn on this winter solstice. While this was the shortest day of the year, the light shone with a unique soft quality.

Ralston finished up feeding the horses a warm bran mash, put out hay, checked each mare. The midday bell would ring soon for everyone to eat. He was hungry today.

Sulli, having finished the corn bread, put out the old plates, ran a bit ahead of schedule. Miss Frances hummed while she worked. Sulli kept her apron on but reached for her heavy shawl.

"Miss Frances, let me bring in more wood."

Eyes darted to the pile as she stirred a big pot of porridge. "Is a little low. Go on."

Sulli dashed out of the common kitchen, running toward the mare barn. "Ralston."

Hearing her voice, he stepped out of a stall. "Sulli."

No time to talk, they fell on each other.

"I miss you so much. He watches me like a hawk. Ralston, I can't stand it."

Kissing her, holding her, pressing his body against hers, he said, "I can't either."

Without any warning William ran inside and grabbed Ralston, throwing him on the floor.

Ralston crawled fast on all fours to the whips, reaching for one as William reached him. Nimbly hopping to his feet, Ralston swung, catching William full in the face.

Enraged, William looked for a heavier tool, backing up, arm over his face.

Sulli wanted to scream but caught herself. Bringing the other men would make this worse. She knew enough to let men settle their own problems, even if she was the problem. Turning, she ran back toward the kitchen, having the presence of mind to pick up hardwood logs.

Miss Frances turned as Sulli placed the logs next to the fireplace. "Your husband came in here. Told him you were at the woodpile. Dipsy let him off a few minutes early. A first." Miss Frances chuckled to herself, not thinking much of Sulli's flushed face.

Back in the mare's barn, the two slammed each other with fists, feet. Ralston tripped William as the taller man lunged for him. Then he kicked him while he was down.

Nimble, like Ralston, although bigger, William scrambled onto his feet and ran toward the end of the barn where a pitchfork with thin sharp tines stuck in a small hay pile. Pivoting the instant he had that pitchfork in his hand, he advanced on Ralston.

The smaller man stood his ground, figuring he could duck the thrusts. He underestimated William's reflexes and his own.

The tines of the pitchfork ripped into his old work coat. William kept thrusting, finally tearing the cloth to pieces while Ralston dodged. William then swung the pitchfork at shoulder height, catching Ralston on the side of the head.

Ralston went down. William became a blur.

Hurt though he was, he tried to get up, but William kicked him under the gut and, as he tottered, slammed his foot into his side. Ralston went down again.

William kicked him in the head, then rammed the pitchfork into his back, close to his side, with all his strength. Ralston lay pinned on the floor, the pitchfork standing straight up in his back, his coat shredded.

William dusted off his hands. He put his hands in the cold water, washed his face, squared his shoulders, then walked to the common feeding room.

Looking a bit worse for wear, he sat down and said nothing. Neither did anyone else. Occasionally men fought each other or injured themselves on the job. Then he walked to the kitchen.

Sulli avoided him, which Miss Frances did notice.

Martin and Shank appeared at the kitchen door, stepping inside, knowing the workers would be there. "Dipsy, sorry to bother you. We can come back."

"Sit down. Take a load off your feet. Sulli, put down more plates," Miss Frances ordered.

As the two ate Miss Frances's hot food, they spoke to Dipsy loud enough so others could hear.

"We've been thinking about the wagon you built," Martin started. "We think it would hold up. We cover many miles. Rough."

"Mr. Finney doesn't tolerate half-assed work," Dipsy replied to a few nods from the other men. "I've got one nearly finished, too."

"No need to go off the farm, but would you mind hitching up the sold wagon? You could use our horse, and we could drive it here. Get a feel, you know? Our hind ends sit a long, long time."

The other men laughed while William deliberately avoided looking at Sulli, whom he wanted to throttle. In time.

"I was hoping you'd ride along with us, Dipsy. Point out a few things."

"Of course."

As they finished up, Martin reached in his pocket to pay Miss Frances for the food. She waved him off.

Outside, the men walked toward the work shed. Once inside, they noticed wheels, axles, boards, parts for future wagons.

"William. Come on. Help me hitch up the horse," Dipsy yelled.

"We can do that." Shank had known Dipsy would insist on William. Dipsy had called on William to accompany him. That meant the young man had worked with him. He did want this to go smoothly and William knew the wagon, knew the harness. A fast hitch impresses.

Martin took their horse, Penny, by the bridle. Once at the shed, Dipsy quickly wiped down the cart while the salesmen, his idea, unhitched their mare and William guided her to the traces. William and Dipsy tricked her out in no time, as Shank closely observed.

Dipsy held out his hand and Martin took it, stepping up.

"Dipsy, come along with us," Martin said.

"You know this farm. We don't." Shank smiled.

Dipsy nodded, then ordered William, "Sit in the back, boy."

The four walked along the main road, passed the stables and the barns, down to the main entrance. Martin gently stopped the mare, turned the wagon around.

"Ah." Martin appreciated the turning radius as well as the obedience of his mare.

"Pick up the pace," Dipsy suggested, so the group trotted up to the stables and barns again.

"Go around the back. A couple of farm roads there. Rutted. You'll see how she handles." Dipsy leaned against the backrest. "You know, if you like, I can pad the backrest on the other cart. Not much money at all. Got stuff lying all over this farm. Don't have to buy a thing, only the labor. I can have it finished and painted by tomorrow."

William saw Sulli hurrying to the stable. He put his hand on the side of the wagon and swung over, sprinting toward her.

"William!" Dipsy bellowed.

"Pay him no mind," Martin soothingly said. "That's a pretty girl."

"Damn fool." Dipsy cursed, knowing he'd let him have it after the two men left. Might even get Ard to fire him.

The cart bounced along the bad farm roads but the wheels evidenced no strain.

"You can turn around here." Dipsy watched clouds lower.

"That's a long building there. A bunkhouse?" Shank asked.

"Warm. Beds are decent. Plenty of blankets."

"Married men have other places?" Martin swayed in the seat.

"Well, there aren't too many of us that are married. Ard is. I am. Two of the younger fellows and William, the fool."

"Mr. Finney sure takes care of his people," Martin approvingly murmured.

"See those cabins there? Lots of space between them. If there's a fight, you don't hear too much." Dipsy laughed. "The last one is William and Sulli's. Fight all the damn time. Don't know if you two men are married." Both nodded they were. "Well, women have their sphere and men have theirs. Don't step over that line. In either direction."

"Wise words." Shank studied William's cabin.

Once back at the shed, Martin and Shank wanted to unhitch their mare. "Straightforward."

"Is," Dipsy replied to Martin. "When day is done, the last thing you want to do is wrestle with your harness, which might be cold, wet. Heavy."

The two hitched their mare up to their old cart, shook hands with Dipsy. "You've sold us, Dipsy. How much to pad the backrest and how long will it take?"

"I can do it in a day. I'll stuff it with horsehair, too. Would you rather have a cowhide or thick wool?"

"Cowhide. Water won't destroy it," Martin quickly responded. "Then we will come back day after tomorrow." He handed Dipsy half the asking price. "Rest when we pick it up."

"I thank you. Mr. Finney will be pleased. What color would you like?"

"A dark yellow if you have it, or green. And I hope Mr. Finney knows what a good man he has in you and shares some of this money."

"He's a fair man. Five dollars for the backrest. You'll be riding on a cloud."

They shook hands again. The two drove off while Dipsy returned to the shop. Not much tidying to do but he noticed William, hand under Sulli's arm, propelling her to their cabin. He shook his head, walking to his own cabin, smoke curling out of the chimney.

Ralston came to, crawled to the tack room. Struggling to his knees with the pitchfork still in his back, the tines sunk in maybe an inch. The old coat saved him. He pulled himself up, hugging the side of the door. Shuffling into the tack room, the little potbellied stove pouring out the heat, he tried to pull off his coat. Couldn't do it. As the pitchfork stuck on the right side of his spine, low down, he grabbed the handle and yanked it out while he screamed. Then he sank in the sturdy wooden chair, older than he was. Shaking, he breathed hard. He didn't think he could make it to the bunkhouse. He slowly turned sideways and got out of the chair, hand on the wall. Some horse blankets folded on the floor beckoned. He made it. Then he realized he needed to feed the fire so he crawled over to the potbellied stove, opened the door, carefully slid in round hardwood, closed the door. Shaking hard again, he crawled back to the blankets, opened one up, collapsed on it, and pulled the other one over him. His teeth chattered from pain, not cold.

He would live. He knew he would live, and he would live to kill that son of a bitch.

20

Thursday

"That's why I tried a horseshoe garden." Mags stood in the open part of the horseshoe, clipped bluegrass filling it.

At the round end Harry, Susan, Janice, and Pamela admired Mags's design and hard work.

"Edging it in English boxwood, that dark green with foxglove in front of that was a wonderful idea." Harry praised her.

"Boxwood stays green, too." Pamela wore her garden shoes, a nice espadrille that helped cushion the ground.

"Well, I wanted color contrast, hence the foxglove and the iris in front of them. Trying to organize the height. My spring garden is by the house, so I can see those snowdrops come up and the crocuses from the warmth of the kitchen. This I'd like to be late spring, some summer." Mags expansively swept her arm over the large area, which showed off her magic engagement ring from way back when.

"Love those salvias. You've really thought this through." Susan complimented her.

"*Look at the robins over there. I'll grab one.*" Pewter dreamed on, for any robin could see that fat cat crawling through the grass.

"*You can't kill a bird when visiting.*" Mrs. Murphy knew Pewter couldn't catch a bird, but she went along with the illusion.

Pamela glanced from the horseshoe garden to the English yews, on each side of the garden entrance. A five-foot-high plant under each yew set off the trunks. Three-inch white flowers, impressive, hung down from toothed leaves like trumpets.

"Your jimsonweed is spectacular."

"Oh, I can't kill it so I decided to enjoy the flowers." Mags shrugged.

"You do need to be careful with jimson," Susan warned.

"Of course she is, Susan. The stuff grows all over the place. I don't worry until the seed pods burst. There's some way at the back of the pastures at home before you get into the walnut groves. Fenced off and far from the fence," Harry advised. "Why am I telling you? You know."

"It can make you crazy." Janice laughed.

"Oh, Jan, you don't need any help." Mags teased her. "So you think this, some shade, mostly sun, will work?" Mags asked.

"I don't see why not. You have a good watering system. And I see roses about to bloom back up at the house. Roses really are tough." Harry admired this flower.

"How about the climbing roses on the pillars at Montpelier? I've studied the maps of Madison's gardens. I expect Dolley had a lot to do with the planning." Mags loved Montpelier.

"Allyson Whalley would know." Pamela named the curator of horticulture at the preserved home and grounds. "Or Clayton."

"Which reminds me. Pamela, congratulations," Harry said to the elegant, older woman.

"What did Pamela do?" Janice wondered.

"Her work in the Piedmont Environmental Council put another one thousand twenty-four acres under permanent conservation easement."

"Pamela, why didn't you say something?" Janice exclaimed, not realizing as she was not born and bred in these parts that you didn't brag. It just wasn't done.

"Many of us worked to preserve the land. The agricultural resources alone are vital to our understanding of the times," Pamela demurred. "The National Trust for Historic Preservation, a dynamic partner, worked with us. Everyone worked very hard and now Montpelier has almost two-thirds of the original property under protection."

"Remarkable." Mags folded her hands together, diamonds again gleaming.

"Did Kevin pick out that engagement ring?" Harry admired it.

"He has always had good taste. Even when we were young."

"He married you." Susan smiled. "Ned needs help. So I tell Harry what I want. She tells Fair, who tells Ned. Helps to have a best girl friend."

"We know," Janice and Mags said in unison.

"Took each of us working on our husbands to get the start-up money for Bottoms Up." Mags looked down at her ring. "Janice told Olaf who told Kevin I was considering selling my ring to get the cash."

"That got the first olive out of the jar." Janice laughed. "And now Bottoms Up makes more than Kevin's nursery."

"Not more than Olaf's investment business," Mags filled in. "I guess no one makes more money than those guys. Hey, before I forget, tell us about finding more bones. I swear, there are too many skeletons around here."

"And that isn't counting what's in people's closets," Pamela remarked.

"*I found the bones!*" Pewter bellowed.

"Pewter." Harry looked crossly at her, then matter-of-factly described the discovery.

"Susan and I share a timber tract. She owns it, I manage it. We climbed up the side of Taliaferro's Mountain, the one immediately behind my farm. It's overgrown. Anyway, a still was tucked up in a brambly area."

"Whatever for?" Janice innocently asked.

"Looking inside, we saw the apparatus for making home liquor." Harry shrugged. "This part of Virginia is famous for country waters, what Yankees call moonshine. Susan and I happened to stumble across a still."

"*I found bones!*" Pewter squalled.

"Pewter." Harry shook her finger in a determined face.

Susan watched her dog, Owen, sit next to the gray cat while he curled his lip. "The skull and rib cage shook us a bit."

Mags's eyebrows rose. "Small wonder." She took a breath. "Those moonshiners will kill one another. I think the theft of the beer in our truck might be their work. Deflect attention."

Janice crossed her arms over her chest. "Like the authorities were getting too close? Get them off track?"

"Works for everything else," Mags cynically but truthfully noted.

"No idea who the dead man was?" Pamela inquired.

"Not yet," Susan answered. "Might not be anyone from here. Ned says there is a network for moonshine and marijuana."

"They'll make weed legal," Mags predicted, "but never moonshine."

"Why?" Janice thought the whole thing foolish.

"It's easier to hide a still than acres of marijuana. So legalize weed, get more taxes. No way are those country boys going to pay taxes on their liquor. They've eluded the feds for generations. It's a matter of family pride for some." Mags seemed resigned to the status quo.

"Every now and then someone gets caught," Susan added. "But in the main, not many. A country boy will always outsmart a city boy."

"Well, I, for one, am upset that this was on our timber tract. We'll be questioned even though Sheriff Shaw knows we know nothing." Harry sounded confident.

"Harry, to protect Ned's reputation, the feds will need to wear us out." Susan sounded dolorous.

"*I'll take care of them!*" Pewter promised.

"*I'm sure the Alcohol, Tobacco and Firearms marshals will be terrified,*" Tucker quickly added. "*What would work would be to get Pirate to pee on them.*"

"*I couldn't do that!*" The youngster was horrified.

"*If someone threatened our mother, you could,*" Mrs. Murphy sternly replied.

"Anyway, I didn't mean to belabor this, but I'm going back up there to snoop around. I know that land better than any federal agent, better than Sheriff Shaw. If there's something there, even a dropped bottle cap, I'll find it."

Pamela advised, "Harry, be prudent. Those people kill. One man is dead already. He may have been killed or not but you don't know."

"She's right." Mags seconded the thought. "Let the sheriff do it."

Harry did not argue, but she didn't agree to stay away either.

This was not lost on the animals or Susan.

"You know, there's supposed to be a ghost at Castle Hill in the house. People have seen it. Sara Lee Barnes told me." Susan informed them all and all of them knew Sara Lee, a reliable source.

Pamela, as an afterthought, said, "I wonder about the ghost. Do you all believe in ghosts?"

A silence followed this, but as they sat in the rattan chairs on the screened-in back porch, tea at the ready, their host spoke up. "I do."

"I do, too," Harry agreed, then shrugged. "We don't know but so much."

"Such as?" Janice pushed.

"Well, if you think about it, we aren't even certain about male and female."

"Oh, I am," Janice roared.

They all talked at once. Good talk. Good ideas. Invigorating arguments. What friends do.

"The ghost at Castle Hill is supposed to be a woman from what, the Revolutionary period?" Janice threw that out.

"You know, okay, this is whoo whoo, but I wonder if there isn't a ghost where we buried those bones, under the red oak? Is she hanging around?" Harry lowered her voice.

"Well, what would she want?" Mags challenged Harry.

"Her necklace." Harry came right back.

This gave them all a moment.

Then Susan said, "Harry, that's creepy."

"Susan, the whole thing is creepy. Think about it. She's got a broken neck for starters."

"Maybe she wasn't rich. Maybe she stole the pearls or maybe she was a mistress and the wife killed her," Mags pitched in.

"Have to be a strong woman to break a neck," Janice posited.

"They were stronger back then than we are now." Susan clearly stated a fact. "Look how they worked."

"Even the rich?" Janice wasn't giving up.

"Some. Probably others were not, but take a cook, slave or free. Think of how big her forearms would have been from kneading all that dough. Or a laundress. The women who had to work had powerful bodies. And the women who drove coaches to show off, or rode, had to have some strength. So a woman could have broken her neck."

"But a woman would have taken the necklace and earrings." Janice was close to the truth.

"You're probably right." Susan nodded. "So she wants her pearls and diamonds back?"

Harry held up her hands, palms upward. "I don't know. It was just an idea."

"And those bones at the still, well, maybe there's another ghost," Susan wondered.

Janice dismissed this. "It's all too creepy."

And it was.

21

December 25, 1787

Tuesday

Early light reflected off the thin snow. A golden sheen made the hills and rolling pastures look as though Midas touched them. Martin and Shank drove along, the back of the new yellow wagon they picked up at Royal Oak filled with straw and three large tarps. Despite the cold, neither man felt a chill, blood pumping in anticipation of capturing William, Sulli, and perhaps Ralston.

Driving into Royal Oak, every chimney sent up spirals of smoke. Chores finished early, all could enjoy a day without labor. The only chores left would be bringing the horses back into freshly bedded stalls, checking the water, and giving more hay.

When they picked up the wagon, a good buy, they slipped Dipsy silver coins, asking him not to pay attention to their pulling into the barn farthest from the house. Dipsy was smart enough not to ask questions as well as smart enough to know these two weren't looking to steal tack.

Closing the doors behind them, they rubbed their hands, having taken off their gloves. Martin petted the mare's nose.

"We'll be back in no time."

Opening the back doors a crack, they squeezed through.

"Let's get what we can. We're paid for William and Sulli," Martin whispered, although no one was around to hear him.

"Can sell the other one to the cane cutters. Those Delta men pay good money. Good money," Shank repeated.

"If we see him, yes. If not, it's not worth taking a chance. Get what we can. He doesn't come from Big Rawly. You stand behind me when I knock on the door. Whoever opens the door, leap. I've got the gun. I'll level it at the other one. Ready?"

"Yep." Shank carried a heavy rope wrapped around his waist, handkerchiefs in his pockets.

"Merry Christmas." Martin sounded jovial, knocking.

They heard footsteps and the door opened. Martin stepped aside as Shank grabbed her, placing his hand over her mouth.

"One move and you're dead. One word and you're dead." Martin leveled his flintlock at William.

Shank stuffed a handkerchief in Sulli's mouth, began wrapping the rope around her hands behind her back. "Come here, boy."

William stood still.

Martin stepped up to him, smashing him across his face with the flintlock. William bent over from the waist, his hand going to his bloodied mouth. Then Martin, with all of his force, smashed the gun on his head. William crumpled like paper.

"Grab a coat for her. On the hook," Martin ordered as Shank propelled Sulli to the row of pegs.

Smiling, Martin dragged William by his hands. "Never waste time arguing with a man who doesn't listen."

Without bothering to grab a coat for William, Shank walked next to Sulli, who offered no resistance.

Martin, powerfully built, heaved the unconscious William over his shoulder while turning to close the door to the cabin. They moved silently and swiftly to the far barn. Shank stepped into the bed, pushing hay to the side. Martin dumped William onto the wagon bed. Then he lifted up Sulli, who was laid next to her tormentor/so-called husband. Shank moved ahead and opened the doors as Martin drove through. Then Shank closed the doors behind him and stepped up into the bed, pulling hay over the two captives and throwing a tarp over them. Then he stepped over the backrest to sit next to Martin as they drove out, no one the wiser.

At the Royal Oak sign, they turned left toward the Potomac, which would take twenty minutes.

Martin laughed. "That son of a bitch will freeze."

"Can't let him die." Shank focused on the money.

"Oh, I won't, but I guarantee you if I say walk backwards, he will. Sun's coming up higher. Feels good."

"Does."

They reached the ferry. Arch Newbold almost at the shore grinned, for this would be a big business day. People wanted to be with their friends, their family. He'd be crossing and recrossing this river until sundown, then home to his wife, a fire, and her cooking.

Many of the travelers were on foot, and Martin and Shank saw the wagons and carriages lined up on the Virginia side of the river. People were waiting for their friends.

Driving on, Arch commented, "Fancy."

At that moment Sulli tried to sit up. Shank spun around and knocked her back with one wicked swipe. Then he pulled the tarp back while Martin handed Arch their fare plus some.

"For the holiday." Martin nodded.

Arch, knowing this was for more than the holiday, said not a word. It was doubtful the two were reenacting the rape of the Sabine women. He figured out they were slave catchers the first time he dealt with them. As far as he was concerned, he didn't have a dog in that fight.

The other passengers evidenced little interest in the back of their wagon, their eyes securely on the Virginia shore and their waiting friends. Excitement ran high.

Once on the other side, Martin and Shank allowed everyone to disembark before they did. Then Martin clucked and the mare calmly walked off.

Two miles south of the ferry, Martin pulled off the road. "Check them."

Shank swung his legs over; feet hit the cart bed. He pulled back the tarps. "She's wide awake. He's still out." He knelt down to feel the vein in William's neck. "Alive."

"When we deliver him, he'll wish I'd killed him," Martin remarked causally.

"She can sit between us," Shank said.

"No, but she can sit up. She can't really run anywhere. Pull the handkerchief out of her mouth. Sulli, stay quiet. Try to run and I'll break your legs. Do you understand?"

She nodded that she did.

"And when we find an inn, we'll get you food, maybe a blanket. We have to tie you and stupid there to the carriage or tie you up somewhere where you won't create attention. Then I'll put the handkerchief back in William's mouth. Obey and you won't be hurt. Disobey and I will break your legs, but I will deliver you to Maureen Selisse one way or the other."

Tears rolled down her cheeks. She said nothing. Martin clucked and the mare stepped out.

Shank, next to him again, said, "Thought you were crazy when you paid twenty dollars for this mare. She's a good 'un."

"Yes, she is. I've been thinking once we collect our money, maybe we should sell this wagon. We could turn a nice profit and we can use about anything in our work. Sometimes, in fact most times, we don't need a cart. What do you think?"

"I think we wait and see what it might bring." Shank leaned back on the padded backrest.

———

Back at Royal Oak no one noticed William and Sulli's absence. They would tomorrow when neither one showed up at work. Ralston, having crawled outside from hunger, was moved to a lower bunk bed by the fire, hurt each time he breathed. Miss Frances, long practiced at binding wounds and diagnosing problems, had washed him down when he showed up on all fours to the bunkhouse. Ard hurried for Miss Frances, as the men had called him when they had discovered Ralston injured. No one wanted trouble, to be accused of hurting Ralston. Ard would know what to do.

The two managed to peel Ralston's shredded coat off him. Ard lifted him up while Miss Frances and a bunkhouse fellow, Young Leo, as he was known, removed what was left, blood spurting from where the tines pierced his back near the backbone.

Washing him, Miss Frances noted the wounds reached about an inch in depth. Could have been worse, but any wound can become infected. She felt all over his back, identifying two broken ribs. Then she wrapped him in clean torn blanket bandages and washed his battered face. She tried to get some food in him. He swallowed a little bit but even though hungry, he was too tired to eat.

Ard tried to get out of him what had happened, but Ralston wouldn't say anything. He feared that if he did, William would take it out on Sulli and God knows what he had done to her already. Ralston feared William's wrath should he hear of anything. He didn't know they were missing nor did anyone else.

Young Leo dipped a cloth in cold water to wash Ralston's face. Ralston was grateful for the young man's gentleness. He asked Young Leo if he had seen Sulli. He said only in the kitchen working with Miss Frances but he hadn't seen her since. Ralston took comfort from that, for if she'd been badly beaten all would have noticed.

Ralston needed to heal. He needed to figure out how to kill William without getting caught. The shock of their disappearance would register soon enough. He might as well rest for what little Christmas he had.

22

The screen door squeaked when Harry pushed it open, the two cats and dogs squirting through it to nudge in front of her. She then opened the door to the kitchen.

"You're home early." She walked over to kiss her husband on the cheek.

"Two easy deliveries." He kissed her back.

Foal delivery for Thoroughbreds crowded around January first, as all Thoroughbreds are registered as having been born January first. The other breeds, following a more natural cycle, were delivered in spring and early summer.

"Are you making supper?" Surprise filtered into Harry's voice.

"Well, yes." He held up a long fork. "You didn't notice the grill smoking outside?"

"What a treat."

"It's almost ready. Everyone's out. Will be a mild night and I figured you'd get home somewhere between six and six-thirty because Susan has to pick up Ned at the train station. How was the garden?"

"Mags has done a good job. They were curious about the still, the bones. Just enough in the paper to arouse questions. Who is that missing person? Mostly we studied the garden."

Carrying plates to the small square wooden kitchen table that they used when it was the two of them or two dear close friends, Harry moved slowly because Pewter wove in and out of her legs.

"Pewter."

"Put my plate down first. I barely ate anything today. My blood sugar is falling."

The plates clinked softly as Harry set them on the checkered tablecloth.

"I feel faint." Pewter plopped on her side.

"American Academy of Dramatic Art." Tucker sniffed.

Pewter quickly recovered from her plunging sugar level as she sprang upright, launching onto the corgi.

Harsh words were spoken.

"That's enough!" Harry swatted at both of them.

Mrs. Murphy didn't move a muscle. Her ringside seat was too good. Why spoil the show?

Pirate, disturbed by the yowls and hisses, lowered his head to gaze intently into the tabby's deep green eyes. *"They'll kill each other. What can I do?"*

"Pirate, don't fall for it. Pewter will roll away, leap up on the counter, puff her tail the size of a bottle brush, and curse. Tucker will sit below the counter, cursing back. The truth is, they'd fall apart without each other."

"Is this normal?" the gray-coated wolfhound wondered.

"For them it is. But she'll get her way. She knows exactly how to manipulate Harry."

True. Harry, hands on hips, stared at the cat. "You are awful." Then down at Tucker. "You, too."

She did, however, put out the animals' bowls, washed this morning. Each bowl, speckled white china, had a blue rim plus each animal's name on the side. Pirate's was big, which meant if Pewter ate very fast she might grab a bite of the wolfhound's, who never protested. He was uncommonly sweet, whereas the gray cat was anything but. She didn't even like dog food. She just liked to steal it.

Fair, pushing open the door with his foot, carried in a plate with handles on which two steaks, basking in juice, bore evidence to his grilling skill.

Fair had started corn on the cob in a pot, which Harry plucked out with pincers. He also made two small salads.

Once seated, they caught up about their days.

"And?"

"Oh, it's delicious. Every woman should have a husband who grills."

He grinned. "Ever notice when a woman prepares food, she's a cook. When a man does it, he's a chef."

"There are a lot of things like that. We've still only progressed so far." She popped a crunchy carrot into her mouth. "But better half a loaf than no loaf at all."

"You'd think more people would grasp that." He expertly sliced his steak.

"Yes, you would." She glanced at Pewter, who had eaten every morsel and was now down on the floor sticking her head under Pirate's. "That youngster is the nicest dog in the world. He could bite her head off."

"She'd have it coming," Fair added.

"I resent that. It is the function of every cat to put a dog in its place."

"Pewter, you are wildly successful." Mrs. Murphy sounded sincere.

As the animals batted one another, running from bowl to bowl except for Pirate, the two humans talked about their days, about the impending fundraiser at Castle Hill, all the tiny mosaic pieces of daily life. They enjoyed most of the same things, knew the same people, and had reached an age where they truly knew each other. They each accepted the wonderful traits of their partner as well as what Fair would euphemistically call "Harry's peculiarities." Her version of this was, "He's just being a man."

"Did you listen for the weather on the way home?" she asked.

"No, but I think it's supposed to rain. You didn't listen either?"

"Oh, channel 48 on my Sirius radio was playing an old Barry White song."

"Trip down Memory Lane?" He smiled.

"More like a gallop." She rose, walked to the big flat-screen TV on the wall, clicked on the local news channel.

Standing there transfixed, the remote in her hand, she moved to the side so her husband could see better.

Fair exclaimed. "Another still found in Tippett's Hollow! That's not far from here. Just the other side of the ridge."

The two listened and watched the report.

The phone rang.

"Harry, did you see the news?" Susan asked.

"Fair and I are watching it now. Is this area becoming the mecca for moonshiners?"

"At least no bones or bodies were found," Harry rejoined. "Hey, look at the barrels stacked by the wall. Whoever found this got there before the goods were moved."

"No one will ever stop this. It's been going on for centuries."

"Human nature doesn't change. If someone can make a bigger profit, they'll try."

Susan laughed. "True. Maybe we should look the other way."

"That's not always possible," Harry said, "not when it's on your land."

"You went back up there, of course," Susan stated.

"I hate to admit it but I couldn't find a thing. I'll go back up again. I'm not satisfied that I was thorough. Once we get permission, we should dismantle the still."

"Harry, that shed will still be there next year. You know this will drag on."

Harry agreed. "I guess that's the point of the process. Gives the accused time to clean up or clear out."

"Cynical," Susan said.

"It's hard not to be cynical these days," Harry sadly replied.

23

Wednesday

Snow swirled around the bunkhouse. All of Royal Oak appeared filled with white wind devils. Men walked with their heads down, whether going into the wind or with it at their backs.

Ard stamped his feet in front of the bunkhouse and opened the door. "You're sitting up."

"Yes, sir," Ralston answered, although he sat listing to port so no weight would press on the tine wounds. "Feel some better."

"Nice by the fire. Thought I'd look in on you."

"Thank you. Miss Frances brought me hot biscuits and another blanket."

"Cold seeps through the cracks in the wall, under window frames." He exhaled. "Hard season. Always is." Pulling up a stool, he sat next to Ralston. "Need to give you the news. Maybe you know something I don't."

Ralston looked at him. "Can't imagine knowing anything you don't."

"Well, William and Sulli are missing. A few embers in their fire-place, but they've been gone maybe half a day, maybe more. You and William butted heads. Was he the one who smashed you up and stuck the pitchfork in your back?"

"He was."

"Did it have something to do with Sulli?"

Ralston took a deep breath, thought a moment. "William beat her. He treated her like dirt and he didn't want anyone else to be good to her. As for me, he never liked me."

"Then why were you traveling with him?" Ard held up his hand. "You're escaped slaves. No one around here is stupid, but no one cares. If you tell me you're freemen, that's good enough for me. What Mr. Finney cares about is a good day's work and an honest man, one who won't steal from him."

"Yes, sir."

"So why were you traveling with those two if you didn't like William?"

"He planned our escape and he and Sulli had some money from the plantation where they lived. I had a little bit, but not much. He said he knew how to get out of Virginia. I didn't, so I listened to him and then we put what we had together and we left."

"You reached Arch Newbold."

"Sir?"

"Arch Newbold. The ferryman. You headed west instead of to the Atlantic."

"We figured most people would head for the ships, you know. We'd go away from them. Sleeping on hard ground, ducking into any building we could find. Once we got on this side of the river, we believed we could make it."

"Maryland's not a free state. Only two really are and even in Philadelphia, if you bring your slave with you, he is still your slave."

"Yes, sir, but if we could find work, work hard, we figured we'd be as free as we ever had been. You gave us a job. You didn't ask questions so I thought you wouldn't sell us back, know?"

Ard inhaled the aroma of the burning hardwood. "Mr. Finney doesn't believe in slavery. He says the Irish are worse than slaves to the English. He wouldn't do that to another man. And no one came looking for you. We saw no leaflets about runaway slaves."

"Would you have sold us back?"

Ard shook his head. "No. As I said, Mr. Finney is against slavery and Mr. Finney is a rich man. Made every penny of it himself. He doesn't need reward money."

"But other people might."

"Would you have sold William?"

"What?"

"If you knew the headhunters wanted him, would you have sold him out?"

"I hated his guts, Mr. Elgin, but I wouldn't do that. What I would do is kill him for what he does to Sulli. I'll find him and I'll kill him." Ralston addressed Ard by his last name.

"If you find him, he'll be back where he started. The bounty hunters caught both of them, I'm pretty certain."

Tears slid down Ralston's face. "Not Sulli. Maureen will torture her. That's the woman who owned her. Cruel. She has so much money, she can do what she wants to pretty much anyone. Even white people. If she wants to get even, she can. Oh, my poor Sulli." He dropped his face in his hands.

Ard put his hand on Ralston's heaving shoulders. "I'm sorry."

Lifting his tear-stained face, Ralston asked, "How did it happen?"

"I reckon it was the two men who bought Dipsy's coach. They knew the lay of the land. They'd seen both William and Sulli, and you." He stretched out his feet toward the fire. "In Virginia now. If you were on their list, they didn't know you were here."

"I come from a different place." Ralston straightened up even though it stung. "I don't know if they wanted me back or not. I didn't, oh, I didn't fit in. Not with my people or anybody."

"I see." Ard stood up.

Looking up at him, Ralston promised, "I can go back to work tomorrow."

"If Miss Frances says you can, fine. You're young. You'll heal quickly."

Ard left, but he wasn't sure if Ralston's inside wounds would heal quickly. It was obvious Ralston was in love with Sulli.

Reaching Leesburg, Martin and Shank looked for any kind of lodging with a decent stable.

Sulli and William, propped up against the back of the wagon, leaning under the backrest, felt the cold. One blanket wrapped each of them; the straw was piled up around them to hide the bindings but also for warmth. Both of their heads shone white with snow, now falling faster as sundown approached. Long, slanting rays turned the main street houses golden.

An inn appeared. Martin pulled up while Shank dashed inside. Maybe five minutes later he reemerged, smiling.

"Room in the back for the horse and cart. I paid in advance. There's pallets there, some old horse blankets. I also rented a room inside. Figured we could take turns as we go sleeping in the barns with our catch. So I'll take the first night, then the next night it's yours."

"Fine." Martin hopped out of the seat, grabbing the bridle to lead the horse inside the well-organized stable.

A few other horses stood in stalls.

The two men helped Sulli and William down. Shank watched them as Martin unhitched the mare, wiped her down, and threw a heavy rug over her, leading her into a stall with hay and water.

"Let's check the pallets." Shank walked to the end of the wide stable aisle. "You'd think they'd put the tack room or a heat stove in the middle. Ah." He opened a door at the end of the aisle.

"Ah, what?"

"There's a little stove. Maybe it is better on the end. Safer. I'll fire it up." A neatly stacked woodpile rested outside the room, which was fourteen by fourteen.

It took him a while to get a spark, but finally he did and the straw under the wood caught. The innkeeper had thoughtfully stacked kindling as well as hardwood. The room would warm up in no time.

"Bring them in here," Shank advised.

Martin, behind them, flintlock in hand, glanced around to see if anything could be used as a weapon against him or Shank. "How many pallets?"

"Six. Grooms must sleep in here all the time. Who can afford a room for a groom? Washbasin over there. We'll get by."

"I'll bring you all some food." He looked for beams or anything sturdy so they could tie Sulli and William. "We could tie their feet on this center beam. Keep their hands tied. Untie them in the morning so they can eat.

"That ought to work. Untie them tonight for dinner. You two pick your pallet," Shank ordered.

Both, chilled to the bone, selected packed straw pallets halfway to the stove. They couldn't be far from the center beam, but the room was already warming. Sulli stopped shaking.

"If you two sit down and behave, I won't tie you to the beam until after you eat."

"Yes, sir." William spoke.

Sulli kept quiet, sinking onto the pallet, raising her tied hands toward the heat.

The horses' munching sounded soothing. The odor of cleaned leather tack also added to what little pleasure there was.

Twenty minutes later, Martin appeared, carrying two baskets. He placed them in front of Shank. Four bottles of ale, cold, nestled in the corner of one basket. The other contained cold ham sliced, bowls of potatoes. That was all there was but it was nourishment.

Shank had untied Sulli and William's hands. Their sore wrists and stiff fingers made for clumsy eating and drinking, but they managed. Martin leaned against an old trunk.

"I say five or six days. What do you think?"

"Depends on the weather. If snow piles up, we'll need to stay here for a while."

"I sure hope not." Martin liked the warmth pouring out of the little cast-iron stove.

"Are there any people here?"

"No. Just two."

"Where are they going?" Shank asked.

"Don't know. They're well dressed." He sighed, feeling drowsy. "Cold sucks the life right out of you, don't it?"

"Yeah. My mother used to say one cold day could steal a year's warmth from your body. Well, let's secure these two. I'll see you in the morning. We can decide what to do then."

"Right." Shank pushed himself off, using his hands. He walked over to William first, tied his hands together, then tied one foot to the center beam. He repeated the procedure for Sulli. "Is that too tight?"

"A little," she demurred.

"I'll loosen it." He did while William glared, eyes searching the square space.

"I'll see you in the morning." Shank nodded as Martin left, closing the door behind him as well as the doors at the end of the aisle to help keep some heat in. The horses threw off heat.

"If you lie down, I'll pull a horse blanket over you. You'll fall asleep in no time," Shank instructed the two.

Old blankets were neatly piled on another trunk, a few holes in them, but they felt good after the nasty cold day in the back of the cart.

Then Shank settled down after putting two heavy logs in the fire. He used a blanket for a pillow and draped a heavy one over him. All three fell asleep in minutes.

Shank, flintlock under his pillow, despite his exhaustion, woke up from time to time throughout the night. A light sleeper by nature, he would check the prisoners.

William rolled over, his hands in front of him, eyes open.

Shank pulled his flintlock out, pointing it toward William, whom he could clearly see in the glow from the slats in the little woodstove. "One move, one false move, and I'll shoot you but I won't kill you. You aren't worth nothing dead. So you can live in pain or you can accept that you've got no way out."

William stared at him, then turned the other way.

Shank was half hoping he could shoot him. He, too, fell back asleep.

24

Saturday

"I love all this sunlight." Harry pushed the keeper on the back of her gold dome earrings.

"Won't be long before the solstice." Fair turned left on Turkey Sag Road as the long rays of late-afternoon sun slanted over deep green fields offset by shining white fences.

"God, look at the fences. A fortune in fencing, then painting them and repainting them. Well, we should all be grateful Castle Hill rises yet again."

"Given its long history, yes. I often think that losing the War"— Harry meant the war of 1861 to 1865, always referred to in Virginia as "the War"—"saved our architecture from the seventeenth and eighteenth centuries. No one had the money to tear things down and start over."

"What didn't get burned got saved anyway," Fair matter-of-factly replied.

"Do you ever get sick of it? Hearing about the War?"

He turned for a moment as he slowed the station wagon. "All the time. I'd much rather hear about new building materials, medical breakthroughs. Oh well, we get that on the big news channels. You know the old proverb, 'Until lions learn to write, the hunter will always be the hero of the story.' We don't know the truth about any war, not just that one."

Harry scanned the huge estate. "How beautiful. Honey, look at all the cars."

"The auction sold out. There must be hundreds here. Good for AHIP." He named the Albemarle Housing Improvement Program by its abbreviation.

The purpose of this organization, formed in 1976, was to repair and preserve homes, making sure families of limited means could live in safe, affordable homes. The success of dedicated people, most of them volunteers, proved once again that if people decide to do something and so-called authorities get out of the way, it gets done. And everyone learns to get along as they work together.

"What I like about AHIP is how they know what works and what doesn't. You want to talk about building materials, they know it all. If regular folks only knew how much they were being ripped off by some builders and suppliers, they'd burn them down."

"That's true in any business, honey. We are pretty lucky here. Aren't too many liars and cheats out there, at least in construction. We all know one another too well and even the new people eventually get told if they will listen."

"You're right. I guess I sometimes forget how deep we are in this county, our roots, I mean."

He parked a few rows away from the doors to the tasting room. The grass, though mowed, was thick. "Honey, can you walk through this?"

"Of course I can." Harry opened the door, swung her heeled feet out, and stood, immediately sinking into the earth.

Fair, now next to her, looked down, then roared with laughter.

"Shut up." She laughed, too.

"I can carry you."

"Don't you dare. I can walk. Get me out to the path where most of the cars drove in. It will take a little longer but I may yet retain my dignity."

So he put his hand under her elbow, keeping her upright as she pulled her heels out of the dirt, one step at a time. Took a minute or two but soon she was on firmer ground. She lifted up one foot, brushing off dirt and grass, then the other.

"Looks good," Fair said.

"Okay, not good."

"Well, honey, how many people are going to be looking at your shoes?"

"Fair, do you know nothing about women? Even my dearest friends will look at my shoes, at my earrings, at my off-the-shoulder peach-colored dress."

"Seems like a lot of trouble."

"It is. But if your girlfriend asks you the next day what did you really think of Janice Childs's diamond shell earrings, you'd better have something to say. Do I care? Not a bit. But I have to live here"—she paused—"as do you."

"Yes, honey, but all I have to say is how good a woman looks. I need not remember her shoes. All right, fire up your memory."

They stepped through the open doors into the tasting room. The band played on a raised floor, like a small auditorium in high school. Round tables for six, set with china and silverware, low center-pieces and candles, exhibited enough aesthetic charm without being overwhelming. In other words, when you sat down you could see your tablemates, mostly.

Jeannie Cordle, clipboard and cellphone in hand, approached Fair and Harry as they waited to sign in at the table.

"Dr. Haristeen."

"Jeannie, are you involved in every organization in the county?" He smiled at her.

"Fair, you're as civic-minded as I am but your work is for those on four feet. Hello, Harry."

"You clean up good, girl." Harry used the old horseman's expression for wearing "civilian" clothes.

"I didn't know you were involved with AHIP," Fair noted.

"Frank and I have worked on weekends for years. We love it. By the way, Harry, you look wonderful. When we see each other we're usually covered in dust or dirt."

Frank was her husband, a successful plumber.

"I'm so glad you could come." Jeannie meant it. "Now, do you have a cellphone?"

Fair reached into his inside coat pocket, producing the requested device.

"Good," Jeannie announced. "You see the long table there, our silent auction. We're doing something new this year. It's all high-tech. You bid on your phone. You can keep checking your phone to see if anyone has outbid you. Just punch in AHIPauction.com. Simple."

"Okay, thanks."

After shaking hands, moving on, Fair stopped looking at his phone. "Okay, baby doll, let's hit the table and see if this works. I'm used to a clipboard where you write your bid and either a number or a name. You ready?"

"Sure. Oh, there's Mags." Harry waved and Mags waved back.

She, too, was at the long silent-auction table, and once there Harry saw many of her friends from St. Luke's, her gardening buddies, too.

"Look at this bracelet." Mags pointed to an item.

"Lovely." Harry liked the turquoise.

"I'm making a sensible bid."

"You'd better. Your husband is right over there." Harry nudged her to look where Kevin was standing, drink in hand, talking to Olaf, Janice Childs's husband.

"Well, what do you think is sensible?"

"Mags, I'm the wrong person to ask. Susan." She called to her best friend, who had walked in the front door, waving her over.

Upon reaching her, Susan asked, "What? I left my husband at the door."

"Good place for him," Harry teased. "Ned can be too reasonable. Anyway, everyone will be at him."

"True. Okay, what's up?"

Mags pointed to the turquoise bracelet. "What do you think is a reasonable bid?"

Susan peered at the wide bracelet, unusual in that the turquoise was interspersed with same-size onyx squares that set off the turquoise. All was backed by heavy silver.

"Retail, I would guess over a thousand dollars. The design alone is so special. Given that this is for charity, it will go for more. Stunning. Your kind of piece, Mags."

Chewing her lip, Mags consulted her phone. Already three bids had been placed, the last being one thousand. "He'll have to get over it." She punched in her bid.

Laughing, the ladies walked down the long table as Fair grabbed Ned, knowing his buddy would be besieged with harebrained ideas plus some good ones. Also, anyone who had a complaint about government always felt compelled to dump it on him.

Reaching the corner of the now-packed table, the ladies nearly ran over Carlton Sweeny.

"How good to see you," Harry enthused.

"Who would miss this party?" He smiled back. "When I can, I like to visit the projects, bring a bush or two, something indestructible."

"That's good of you." Mags wanted that bracelet and kept checking her phone.

"Mrs. Nielsen, we need organizations like this in every county. In some of our counties, the old tobacco counties and the coal counties, the need is overwhelming," Carlton said.

"Governor Baliles sure pushed for those places." Susan mentioned an outstanding governor serving from 1986 to 1990.

"No easy answers because of the overwhelming need and the money. The state is the only way to funnel money there. Here in Albemarle County, a rich county, people can and do come through."

"Carlton."

All looked over to see a petite woman, maybe late twenties, her hair in a French twist, little jewelry, but then when you look that good you need no adornment.

"Be right there." He smiled at the ladies. "Good to see you."

After he left, Susan remarked, "If he doesn't marry that woman, someone else will grab her up in a hurry."

Harry laughed. "Susan, not everyone is meant to be married."

"Bull. Marriage is Nature's way of keeping us from fighting with strangers."

The party rolled along like that. Wisecracks, laughter. Clinking cubes in highball glasses, ladies usually sipping from taller glasses, some summer drink. The men, this being the South, stuck to the strong stuff. The din grew louder and louder. When they repaired to their tables, Susan, Harry, and Mags sat at one table with their spouses. Janice and Olaf sat at an adjoining table. Also at their table was Jane Andrews of AHIP and Amelia McCully, and Jeannie and Frank Cordle. Olaf, used to this, handled the stream of people coming to his table for financial advice. Like Ned, wherever he went he wound up working.

Dinner was served, followed by the requisite speeches, most of them mercifully short. People were told to check their phones, as the bidding was over.

"I got the bracelet!" Mags, thrilled, shouted. This was followed by a lowered-head discussion with her husband. He forced a tight smile.

Then the table cleared and out came the band. As usual, the ladies repaired to the ladies' room, the makeup mirror lined with women adjusting hair, bodices, making sure an earring wasn't loose. As the crowd moved along, the ladies eager to get to the dance floor, Harry, Susan, Mags, Janice, and Jeannie lined up at the well-lit mirror.

"I hate my hair," Susan complained.

"You've hated your hair since you were in first grade. Actually, you didn't get hair until then." Harry tormented her.

"God will get you for that," Susan intoned, her deepest voice.

Janice raised one eyebrow. "Sounded better when Bea Arthur said it."

"I don't think young people know who Bea Arthur was," Mags chimed in.

Jeannie, mother of three grown children, replied, "Reruns."

"Ah," the others chimed in.

Harry reached for her lipstick in a black case from her small silk bag, which she wore over the shoulder. She unscrewed the top, held the lipstick up to the light. "Magenta."

"Mine is better." Mags fetched her lipstick, also in a black case.

"Are you two still going on about those peonies?" Janice reached into her own small purse, pulling out a lipstick, unscrewing it. Janice's was black with a rose, in fake gold, on top of the cap.

"That's not magenta," Susan opined. "More of a dark ruby."

"I say it will pass as magenta with sparkles." Janice was defiant.

"Let me look," Jeannie offered, frowned, then pulled out her own lipstick, another black case. "Close."

"Well, what are you doing with magenta lipstick?" Harry asked.

"It's a great color. Jumps right out at you." Jeannie triumphantly held up her tube.

"Give me that." Mags playfully reached for it.

Within seconds five grown women, all college-educated, too, reverted to childhood, grabbing one another's lipstick.

Jeannie held Janice's. "It is magenta, Harry. But dark."

"It is not. Mine is," Harry argued.

"You're all full of it. Mine is the purest," Janice pronounced.

"Hold hard, girls. I've saved the best for last." With a flourish,

Susan reached down into her larger bag, hauling out a brand-new tube of lipstick.

It was damned close to the peonies. A silence followed this display. Then they started grabbing lipsticks again.

Mags wound up with Janice's as Janice snatched hers. Now everyone was reapplying lipstick while exchanging tubes. Some ladies managed two coatings of slightly different colors, some only one. Then the lipsticks were tossed back into bags, although not necessarily their own lipsticks. They marched out, still fussing and laughing.

Fair, leaving the men's room, asked, "What were you all doing in there? We could hear you."

"Obeying my mother's wisdom. There's no problem that a new lipstick can't cure," Harry told him.

He shook his head, which made the women laugh anew.

A good band fills up any dance floor. Big Ray and the Kool Kats had everyone shaking and baking. The floor became so jammed that mostly people stood together wiggling.

Harry never worried about being overrun thanks to a six-foot, five-inch husband.

Jeannie Cordle, face bright red, hollered to Frank, "I'm burning up. Let's go outside for a minute."

He nodded yes, stepped in front of her, and reached back for her hand as they threaded through the crowd.

Once outside, the stars against the black sky took their breath away, but Jeannie was having trouble breathing.

"Frank." She grabbed her throat.

"What, honey?"

"I hardly drank anything, but I feel so strange."

He touched her forehead. "You're burning up."

She grabbed his wrist. "Turn around." Her eyes were large.

He did. "What, sweetie?"

"It's Daddy. Daddy's come for me." She let out a piercing scream and then crumpled.

Frank knelt down, terrified and shocked, for Jeannie was not given to visions.

Cupping his hands to his lips, he bellowed for all he was worth. "Help! Help me, please!"

A young couple who had stepped outside for some cool air ran over.

The young man turned to his date. "Get Jordy. Fast."

Jordy was pulled off the dance floor and hurried to the fallen woman.

"I'm an ER doctor."

"Help her! Oh, please help her!"

Jordy took all the vital signs, looked up into Frank's face. "She's gone. I'm terribly sorry."

25

Friday

Clear deep robin's-egg blue skies arched overhead. The snows stopped. The road, rutted in the best of circumstances, proved more endurable as snow had packed into the ruts. The cold nights kept the road packed tight and the temperature in the day nicked above 32°F but not by much. Martin drove, observing the farms they passed, while Shank, scarf around his neck, tried to see mile-posts.

"Too many covered by snow but we should make Red Store in maybe an hour." He named a store at the crossroads of Alexandria Pike and Falmouth-Winchester Road.

"We'd better. Sun won't be up much longer. At least it's not snowing, but we're dragging along." Martin ached a bit.

"Yep. Might get better, though."

"We sure don't want it warmer. Roads will be slop. We'll be digging out of the muck. This cold is our friend." Martin sniffed. "Except my back hurts in the cold."

"Right." Shank shrugged.

"Might be no rooms at Red Store."

"Someone will know where we can stay, especially if we buy something," Shank laconically added, then looked back. "You know they haven't spoken for two days. Think they're struck dumb."

"No. What is there to say?"

"Got that right." Shank smiled. "Didn't Richard Henry Lee give land to the Red Store place? So now it's more than a crossroads."

"Imagine being that rich," Martin mused.

"Or as rich as Maureen Selisse Holloway. Three names. That way we have to talk about her longer." Shank laughed. "Not a bad-looking woman."

"Bet she was a beauty when she was young."

"You're right again. Bet she was a bitch young, too." Shank rubbed his hands together. The gloves could have been thicker.

"Aren't most women?" Martin posited.

"No. I expect there's about as many rotten men as women. Nature doesn't play favorites here."

Martin came back. "I was married once. I tell people I am still. Once was enough."

Shank grinned. "What's made you think of that?"

"Bitch." Martin laughed.

Riding in silence, they reached Red Store before sunset. The scarlet orb hovered above the horizon, turning the snowy fields equally scarlet.

Martin pulled up to the hitching post.

"I'll do it." Shank swung out. His feet touched the snowy ground, and he tied the mare to the post.

"If you want to make a run for it, go ahead." Martin taunted them.

Neither Sulli nor William said anything as they sat in the back wrapped in their blankets, surrounded by straw, which did help cut the cold a bit.

Walking inside, stove belching out heat, Martin and Shank sighed, for it felt so good.

Martin said, "If you give me a hammer, I'll break the ice on your water trough."

A man behind the counter sporting a thick, white, long beard grunted, bent down, and stood back up with a hammer. "Been doing that all day."

Martin took the hammer, went out, broke the water, untied the horse, and walked her and the cart over for a long drink.

Inside, Shank bought a thicker pair of gloves and asked about the closest inn. It wasn't far.

"Good food?" Shank asked a bit more.

"Rebecca, the woman there, good cook, makes a cobbler using her peach preserves. Pours brandy over it. Worth the trip, I can tell you."

Handing over money for the gloves, Shank turned when Martin walked back in.

"Think I'll buy a few bales of your hay. Stacked up outside."

The old man smiled. "Good hay, corn, oats. Wheat's off and on. Don't know why."

"How much?"

"Twenty-five cents a bale."

"Make it four bales, then." Martin reached in his pocket, pulled out some coins, counted them out. "One dollar."

"How far is Rebecca's Inn?" Shank slipped his hands into the heavier gloves.

As the two walked to the door, the old fellow followed. "If the road's good, ten minutes. If not, who knows?"

Running his right hand over his beard, he grunted. "New wagon?"

"Yes. Cost me one hundred and fifty dollars. My other one gave way. Pull on your coat. Come look at this," Martin suggested.

"Why?" the old fellow wondered.

"Because, you could sell wagons like this. Come and look. It's well built. Take a real beating." Martin enticed him. "Yes, it is expensive, but this wagon will last for years. In the long run it will prove a prudent buy."

The old fellow followed them out, paying no attention whatso-ever to the two young people in the bed of the wagon. He couldn't resist—he knelt down to look at the axle and the wheel wells.

"Sturdy." Shank echoed Martin's appeal. "Look again at that axle. It's heavier than what you'll find around here."

The old man knelt down again. "Take a hell of a thump to bust it. How much?"

This time Shank replied, "One hundred and fifty, what we paid."

"That's a lot of money." When the man stood up, his knees cracked.

"How much would it cost to keep repairing a cheaper one? Hours lost. Work lost. Repairs are what cost you."

"Well, that's the truth," the old fellow replied.

"Tell you what. You tell me what color you want. I'll bring you a wagon. Paint for free. Now, it will take maybe two months. If I can hurry it up, I will. You give me half when I deliver and half when you sell, and you will sell it. Before you know it, you will have good money coming in from something that doesn't spoil. You got food in that store. That spoils what isn't in jars."

Martin and Shank could almost see the wheels turning in the old man's mind.

"I'll bring it to you. If you don't want it, I'll sell it somewhere else." Shank shrugged.

"Bring one here. I may be old but I'm willing to take a chance. Like you said, it's repairs that fritter away time and money." He looked more closely into the bed of the wagon. "Runaways?"

"Yes," Shank replied.

"Young and healthy. Where are you headed?"

"Down to Albemarle County. Owner lives there. Lady from the Caribbean."

"Don't know where that is." The old fellow turned to go back into the store.

"No snow there." Martin grinned.

"Might like to see that." Then he shut the door.

The two climbed back in after untying the patient mare.

"One hundred and fifty dollars. Why didn't you add some?" Shank prodded.

Martin smiled. "Because if we can sell more along the way, I bet we can get the price down to one hundred and twenty dollars apiece. I'll start at one hundred but I know we can settle with Dipsy for one hundred and twenty."

"Dipsy don't run the farm." Shank pulled his cap down a bit.

"Mr. Finney is a shrewd man. He'll go for it. All Dipsy has to do is talk to him or allow me to talk to him." Martin was confident.

"We'll have to slip money to Dipsy." Shank knew the way the world worked.

"Yes. But maybe we can find someone to build carts here in Virginia. Someone who has a forge, ability. So we buy a few off Royal Oak, then we begin to make them here."

"Martin, you want to be a wagoneer." Shank laughed.

"It's better than fooling with runaway slaves."

A silence followed this as they drove south. Then Shank grinned. "We could own slaves ourselves."

"Damn right." Martin breathed a sigh as Rebecca's came into view, a two-story mustard-colored clapboard place, an addition to the side, and smoke curling out of the chimneys.

This time Martin went in, paid for a room, and paid for space in the barn where, as usual, there were groom's quarters.

They drove the mare inside the wide aisles and unhitched her. Shank wiped her down, grabbed her rug from the back of the wagon, tossed it over her, and put her in a stall. The water hadn't frozen. Then he put down three flakes of that good hay.

"Like to feed hay I picked out."

Martin nodded. "Lot of people charge you for stuff filled with broom sage. Only good for cattle. There's a thousand ways to cheat."

"My turn again in the barn." Shank found the groom's quarters.

"Yeah, but come on in. Let's eat together and try that peach cob-bler that old fella told you about. Been thinking about it since we left Red Store."

"Let's tie these two up." Shank helped Sulli down as Martin pulled out William. William refused to cooperate so Martin cuffed him, leapt onto the bed of the wagon, and kicked his ass out of the wagon. Shank looked out of the corner of his eye as once more he had to fire up the potbellied stove in the groom's quarters. "Sorry son of a bitch, ain't he?"

"He'll be sorrier when we get him back to Mrs. Holloway." Martin grinned. "Wouldn't want to be on the bad side of that woman."

The sparks caught in the kindling.

"You know once I saw a potbellied stove that sat in the corner of a house, rich people, Swedes. The damn thing wasn't iron, and it was huge, filled up half the wall, went to the ceiling. White with gold corners, kind of like a pattern. Huge and it heated most of the house. Don't know why we can't do that."

"Well, the Swedes do."

After tying up Sulli and William to a sturdy post, they went in-side, ate a good meal, then brought out potato salad and some sliced turkey for the two runaways. Shank untied their hands so they could eat.

The two talked for a while as their captives silently ate. Martin noticed that Sulli rarely looked William in the eye. As for William, he grew increasingly more sullen.

After they ate, Shank stood up and William grunted that he needed to go outside.

Martin handed Shank the flintlock as the slender man walked William outside where he relieved himself. Then he walked him back in, tying him with one leg, hands pulled behind his back.

The pallets, about the same everywhere, allowed some comfort. But William and Sulli's hands behind their backs, that hurt. Sulli, more tractable in the eyes of her captors, was allowed to have her hands tied in front of her.

"See you in the morning," Martin said, then checked on the mare as he left, closing the doors behind him.

Martin, awake before sunup, ate pancakes in the inn and then walked out to the barn to find Shank sound asleep but the other two awake.

"I'll bring you some food. Shank, up."

"Yep." Groggily the younger man sat up, looked around. "Good food?"

"Good as last night's. You go on in. I'll sit with these two. Bring something out when you're done."

Shank must have inhaled his food because he was back out shortly, carrying an old bucket, clean, full of pancakes and syrup. Untying their hands, they waited for the two to eat.

"I'll check on the mare. Maybe we can make fifteen miles today. Twenty miles would be better." Martin opened the wooden door to the center aisle.

Shank turned slightly to watch Martin shut the door. William saw his chance with his hands untied. He leaned over to untie his one foot, which Shank saw as he turned around.

Advancing on the much younger man, Shank underestimated William's dexterity. He'd untied his foot and that fast bolted by Shank, knocking him down in the process. Sulli stayed rooted to the post. Shank rolled, got up, ran outside the room.

Martin, in the stall with the mare, saw William run by. "I got the gun."

"Let's get him." The two flew out of the barn, oblivious to Sulli. William running through the four inches of snow, six in spots, was maybe one hundred yards away.

"Bugger is fast."

Martin said to Shank, "Not as fast as a bullet."

"You can't kill him. He won't be worth a penny."

"Don't worry. You run ahead of me, distract him if you can, turn him if you can." Martin checked his flintlock.

Shank tore after William, not gaining ground. The snow covered bad footing underneath. William went down, snow all over his face. He hurriedly rose as Shank closed on him and so did Martin, not far behind him.

Martin fired in the air, which made William drop facedown. He then got up again, ran to the left, but Martin had gained a bit more and so did Shank, who wasn't slow.

Stiff from sitting in the back of the wagon, William struggled. Youth was on his side but not much else.

Martin took careful aim and fired again, this time hitting William in the buttock. His hand flew to his backside; he stumbled. The pain burned but he got up again. Too late, for Shank reached him and kicked him, knocking him back over. Both men grabbed him now. William couldn't fight them off. He swung but missed and fell down again. This time Martin and Shank each grasped an arm as they dragged him back. William hopped from foot to foot.

Once back in the stable, Shank realized he'd left Sulli. Blasting into the grooms' room, there she was, foot still tied, resigned to her fate. Sulli had sense enough not to get beaten. She knew her captors carried a gun. She also believed they wouldn't use it, keeping her alive to deliver her to her fate.

Martin dragged William into the room, shoving him down face-first.

Sulli felt no pity for him. In her mind he was her enemy, as were Martin and Shank. At least Martin and Shank didn't beat her. Not yet anyway.

"Hold him down," Martin ordered.

Shank knelt in front of William as Martin pulled down his pants. "Butt?"

"Yeah. Keep holding him. I'm going to make sure he never runs again." Martin walked to his pack and pulled out a sharp hunting knife. "Keep holding him."

Martin then rolled up his pants leg, carefully placing the blade behind his kneecap, measuring. Then with one swift motion he sliced his hamstring in two as William screamed. Martin rolled the pants leg back down.

"He's not running anywhere."

Shank nodded.

"Let's get the wagon ready. Tie him up again."

"Sulli, do I need to tie you?" Shank asked.

"I am tied," she replied.

"Your hands? I expect you don't want anything painful to happen to you?" Shank warned.

"No, sir." She watched William sobbing, his hand reaching back to touch the sliced hamstring, but it hurt so bad he couldn't do it. She found she enjoyed watching him writhe and she also swore no one would ever touch her again. If Maureen beat her, nothing much she could do, but if anyone promised love and did her like William, never. She felt strangely calm and peaceful.

Mare hitched up, fed and watered, Martin doused the fire in the stove, grabbed his gear and Shank's as Shank, hand under William's armpit, dragged him to the wagon. He lifted him up as William whimpered, shoving him onto the wagon, making him crawl to the front.

Sulli, hands untied, walked out with Martin. She hoisted herself up into the wagon.

Martin, voice soft, reminded her, "If you don't try to escape or hurt either Shank or myself, I'll leave your hands untied. You've seen what we can and will do. It will be easier on both of us and your wrists won't be rubbed raw."

"Yes, sir."

"So you agree to be quiet?" Martin wanted a clear answer.

"Yes, sir, I agree to be quiet."

She moved up, leaning against the backrest, pulled the blanket around her as Martin pushed up straw. The day was going to be cold.

Martin threw William's blanket at him, which William pulled

around himself. Then Martin tied William's hands together in front of him. He pushed some straw up.

"I won't kill you," Martin promised. "But I'll cut your other hamstring or I'll geld you if you really bother me. If anyone kills you, it will be Mrs. Holloway, but I expect she'll work you until you die. Since you can't run away, you're probably worth more than before. You've been stupid, beyond stupid." He then climbed up into the front as Shank picked up the reins. It would be days before they reached Big Rawly. Days of suffering for William. Days of determination for Sulli.

It wasn't lost on Martin or Shank that she had not spoken to him since their capture. She evidenced no interest in his welfare. They each concluded that she hated him, which would make their job easier, but then he brought it on himself. He was hardheaded.

26

Friday

Solstices wriggle between three days. Same with the equinoxes. The span is usually between the twenty-first and twenty-third, but it's easiest to remember as the twenty-first, at least it was for Harry.

She considered these events moments of repose. A new season started. She liked to consider that, which is what she was doing early this morning as she walked through her house garden patch.

For income she had acres of sunflowers in the rear of the farm, along with hay, but she used the hay for herself. Now she scrutinized the shoots peeking up at her. Corn, potato, tomato, all in the grade school stage.

Pewter, flopped under the large walnut tree, thought vegetables a bore. Tuna, that's what mattered. Chicken and beef weren't so bad either, but fresh tuna was heaven. Mrs. Murphy tagged along with Harry, as did Tucker and Pirate.

"Pirate, honey, walk between the rows," Harry instructed him.

He gingerly stepped off the little line of peeping plants and stepped into formation. Mrs. Murphy went first, then Tucker, then himself, now on the narrow walk between the rows.

Kneeling down, Harry poked her fingers in the soil. "H-m-m. If we don't get rain in the next few days, I'd better water this."

The hose, coiled up at the house, wasn't that far away.

"Let's pray this doesn't turn into a drought year." Harry stood up.

"*Won't,*" Mrs. Murphy predicted.

"*How do you know?*" Tucker asked.

"*Same way you do. I can smell it and I can feel it. They can only feel it when it's a few miles away or the sky darkens. I wonder if once upon a time they could feel changes?*" Mrs. Murphy replied.

"*We'll get rain tomorrow.*" Tucker sniffed the air.

Pirate, taking baby steps since the two in front of him lacked his long legs, lowered his huge head, asking, "*What do you mean, humans can't feel what's coming?*"

Mrs. Murphy hopped onto the row next to the big fellow. "*If they could, we'd all know it. Harry wouldn't forget an umbrella or she'd throw snowshoes into the car. She listens to the Weather Channel, she goes outside and feels the air, but she's behind. I think in order to survive, they once could read these changes, maybe not as well as we do but they could.*"

"*It's terrible that they lost that ability.*" Pirate frowned.

"*They did it to themselves,*" Pewter called from under the walnut.

"*How can that happen?*" Pirate had learned to take anything Pewter uttered with a grain of salt.

"*Breeding,*" Pewter replied with relish. "*Instead of breeding stronger animals, they've bred weaker. The stronger ones died first in all their stupid wars. The cowards and weaklings lived. Bred more of the same.*"

"*Pewter, that's awful,*" Tucker barked.

"*No one wants to hear the truth.*" The gray cat flicked her tail in irritation. "*Plus they bred stupidity as well. Lots and lots of stupid people.*"

"*Pewter, there are courageous people on earth now. Look at what Mom reads in the papers about protesters jailed in Russia or China or God knows what Middle Eastern country. Those people are willing to stand up and take the consequences.*"

"*Where are they here?*" The gray fatty licked her lips.

"*In the military,*" Tucker fired back. "*And our mother is not a coward. She's faced danger.*"

"*O, la. The only reason she's alive is we saved her how many times? She's not the brightest bulb on the tree, you know.*"

"*You can't compare humans to us. They are limited, but if they stay within their limitations they do pretty well,*" Tucker thoughtfully said, then turned to Pirate. "*Maybe one way to look at how you lose sense or senses is to look at some purebred dogs. Bassets used to have beautiful voices. The hunting bassets still do, but most of the show dogs have lost it. They are dwarf dogs, which I am, too.*" He glared at Pewter. "*You shut your mouth.*"

Pewter replied with delightful maliciousness, "*If the shoe fits, wear it.*"

Mrs. Murphy warned Tucker. "*Ignore her.*"

"*It's hard to ignore someone that fat. Parts of her are in the next zip code.*"

Pewter shot upward, tearing after the corgi, not bothering to sidestep the tiny little corn shoots.

"Hey!" Harry yelled.

"*I will bloody that long silly nose of yours.*"

Tucker had a head start and she could move along. After all, she was bred to herd cattle. Pirate, dumbfounded, watched the drama as Mrs. Murphy rubbed on Harry's leg, hoping to calm the human.

"*Kill!*" Pewter sounded terrifying.

Tucker dodged to the left but the cat, fat or not, could easily change course.

Harry stopped to watch the drama. "She can run. Give her credit."

Pirate lifted a paw and patted Harry, as the wolfhound had stepped back into the same row as the human.

"You're a good dog, Pirate. God knows what any of us would do if you were a bad one."

"*I will always be a good dog to you. I will protect you and defend you for all my life,*" the youngster murmured.

Mrs. Murphy, now under the big dog, called upward, "*Good thing, Pirate, because you'll have to. Harry gets into the damnedest messes.*"

Tucker circled back to the little group as Harry left her garden, what she thought of as her best food garden, walking toward the barn. All the horses grazed in the verdant pastures. Every door and stall door had been flung open for the breeze. The upper doors where hay was stored were also open. The barn owl, asleep in the cupola, opened one eye, given Pewter and Tucker's screams. She shut it. This was old news to her.

The tack-room door, open, allowed the beguiling scent of cleaned and oiled leather to drift into the center aisle. Harry loved visiting stables and barns. When she'd gone to Kentucky, she marveled at the Thoroughbred barns, some of them so grand, the cost must have been punishing. Those places were built for people who were not horsemen but who wanted to enter the racing game. Show impressed them. They naturally believed the owners had made money. Some had. Others inherited it. Others were smart enough to make money from other people's money. No matter what, horse racing was tremendously impressive. Harry believed everyone should make a pilgrimage to Lexington, Kentucky, to take a stable tour. Maybe then they'd realize how important horses were to the economy. Of course, nothing was more important than dogs, who protected horses and humans, chased rats and other varmints, and even watched over children. Dogs truly were the center of the universe.

The center of Harry's universe, or so she believed, trotted into the tack room, but it wasn't a dog. It was Pewter, who had never lacked for self-regard even as a kitten.

"*Scared the poop out of her.*" She triumphantly jumped into Harry's lap, looking straight into her eyes. "*No one messes with Number One.*"

"Aren't you nesty." Harry stroked her sleek head.

Despite the weight, Pewter was a deep gray with electric green eyes. She was pretty.

Mrs. Murphy followed in, jumping on the old tack trunk.

"*Terrified. That dumb dog is terrified,*" Pewter crowed.

"*I'm sure,*" the tiger cat fibbed.

The old dial phone rang. Harry picked it up. "Haristeen."

"I know that." Susan's voice sounded over the line. "Why don't you say Farm Queen? Have you seen that show *FarmHer*?"

"No."

"I'll tell you when it comes on. Won't do me any good to tell you now. You'll forget."

"My memory's good."

"Okay." Susan took a breath. "But what I'm going to tell you will push other thoughts out of your head. Did you know Jeannie Cordle suffered from diabetes?"

"No. I wasn't that close to Jeannie. A warm acquaintance but I rarely saw her. Is that what killed her?"

"No. Frank asked for an autopsy because he was worried about the diabetes. Would the kids, adults now, be subject to it? It does run in families."

"Seems to." Harry was not very medical even though she was married to a vet. "How are Frank and the family?"

"About as good as can be expected. They waited for the funeral until the autopsy, of course. Also people are so far-flung now, it takes time to get everyone here."

"Did the diabetes contribute to her death?"

"No. Ned called me because he can reach people in Richmond and he wanted to know. He has some good contacts in the medical examiner's office. They wouldn't tell him anything until the family was notified. Fair enough. But something about the way whoever was on the phone said it set off an alarm bell in my husband's busy brain."

"And?"

"Ned called his contact back after the family was notified. I hope I can pronounce this right but she was poisoned—" Susan paused.

Harry interrupted. "What?"

"I'll try this. Atropine and scopolamine. Strong toxins."

"How in the world did she, what, eat that stuff or rub up against it? Wait a minute. If she ate poison at the auction, wouldn't we all have gotten sick or died?"

"Well, let me keep going here. Again, this is all new stuff to me. Those two substances I mentioned can act fairly quickly depending on how much is ingested. Again depending, it could take a few hours. The GI tract absorbs it and I think if you're active it might speed the process along. We need a real doctor here, but she was definitely poisoned. Ned, of course, has to be concerned with safety in his district. But what they told him was, 'Think of belladonna, deadly nightshade.'"

"What the hell?" Harry was incredulous.

"The Solanaceae family is large. These damn words are hard to pronounce. But she had ingested poison, a natural poison. The question is how?"

"Don't they have tissue samples?"

"They do, but they don't tell anyone how she came by it."

"Could it have been an accident?"

"Highly doubtful."

"So the toxin wouldn't be hard to get?" Harry's mind whirred.

"Not if you know what you're doing. Fields are full of weeds containing this stuff. Plants like angel's trumpet. This is the *Datura* genus."

"If it's so common, why aren't more of us getting poisoned?"

"People don't usually go around eating flowers and weeds."

"So much for organic farming," Harry quipped. "If you don't know what you're digging up, you can die."

"Yeah, but we've always known that. Think of mushrooms."

"True. So her killer must have known what they were doing? You think?"

"I don't know. But why Jeannie? They are pretty sure it was angel's trumpet, jimsonweed."

"You know, Susan, it's been a strange time. There's two stills above my farm on either side of the ridge. Old bones, and hey, what about Bottoms Up's beer truck getting emptied? Weird stuff."

"Jeannie being poisoned is beyond weird. It's incomprehensible," Susan said.

"Something is wrong here." Harry spoke with conviction. "Jeannie Cordle wouldn't harm anyone. She was well loved."

Susan, pondering this, replied, "There has to be a reason. There's always a reason."

"I don't know," Harry thoughtfully said. "Maybe Jeannie was in the wrong place at the wrong time."

Pewter, great ears, heard every word. She leapt off Harry's lap, ran over to Mrs. Murphy, telling her all she had heard.

"That really is the worst," the tiger cat said.

"No. The worst is we'll be dragged into it. You know Harry will never let this go. She'll have to figure it out. I guess we'll have to inspect her food."

"Pewter, why would anyone want to kill Mom?"

"Because she sticks her nose where it doesn't belong."

"Why can't people be more like cats?" Mrs. Murphy bemoaned.

"We can be curious but at least we have nine lives," Pewter replied with some satisfaction.

"You hope."

27

Monday

Wrapped around the midsection, Ralston, slow but up-right, worked in the mare barn. He could fill water buckets and troughs, throw hay, mix up a bran mash. Picking out hooves proved harder, for he had to bend over to do it, and rare was the mare who didn't take this opportunity to lean on him. He combed out a few manes.

Each chore took twice as long as it had before his injury. Miss Frances wrapped him up, telling him a few ribs were cracked, and not to lift heavy objects. Time would heal the ribs as well as the puncture wounds.

The bitter cold added to his stiffness, but Ralston felt he needed to work. He didn't want Mr. Finney to think he was a layabout.

A flea-bitten gray mare, young, nickered. He walked over to her, running his fingers down her neck under the mane. Most horses liked this, and she certainly did. She turned her head to nuzzle him.

By early afternoon all the mares, turned out, were brought back in. That, too, proved difficult, for the footing was slippery, icy where the snow had melted a bit then refroze. Given that the sun set so early, he wanted to bring them back, groom them a bit, feed and bed everyone down for the night.

The mares, happy to be inside the barn now, seemed happy to see Ralston. Ard had checked the mares for him, as did Leo, when he could hardly move. But they particularly liked Ralston, who might slip them a sweet now and then. As Christmas had passed, sweets were plentiful. Horses and humans both craved sweet things.

Rechecking the blankets, he patted everyone in turn, then swept out the aisle. That hurt. Bending hurt, too, but he persevered. Mr. Finney, should he walk into this stable, would see everything clean, tidy, in its place. Ralston had learned from Barker O, "A place for everything and everything in its place."

Sometimes he thought about Cloverfields. Barker O taught him a lot. He watched Catherine and learned from her. He was glad not to have to see Jeddie, nor did he much care about any of the young women at Cloverfields, who all thought they were better than he was.

But Sulli still inhabited his thoughts. He wondered where she was. He figured William could no longer beat her since he had been captured. He prayed God would give him the chance to kill William. All he could think about was: How could he get to Sulli? How could he free her? He pushed open the door to the tack room, his sleeping quarters when he wished it. The men in the bunkhouse treated him kindly, especially Leo, but he wanted to be alone. Here, he could bed down on a double pallet, near the stove, a blanket rolled up for a pillow, two blankets covering him. He could even remove his clothes. He didn't like sleeping in his clothes but he always kept some on in the bunkhouse. Others did not but he had a streak of modesty, except with Sulli.

Feeding the fire, he walked back to the wall containing the saddle racks. Holding on to one, he tried to do knee bends. He could very slowly. They hurt, not his knees or thighs but his back. Every tine hole, weeping a bit, stung. He'd been hit so hard that muscles were bruised and a deep breath let him know two of his ribs ached. He kept at the knee bends, then sweating—which surprised him— gingerly walked back. Hanging his pants up over a saddle, he wiggled out of the heavy Irish sweater, old and torn, that Miss Frances found for him. Ralston was gaining appreciation for Irish ways and attire. The sweater kept him warm and the old cotton shirt underneath kept the heavy sweater, with a cable front, from scratching him. He felt the bandage around his midsection. Miss Frances told him not to take it off. He needed to leave it on for two days; then she'd remove it, wash his wounds, and wrap him up again.

It was strange but he wasn't shy with Miss Frances, gruff though she was.

Finally down, he pulled the blankets over him as he watched the fire inside the slats of the stove. The stove, set on a large, heavy piece of stone, maybe slate—he wasn't sure because it was a pale color— kept everything safe. The only way a fire could spread is if he or someone else left the door open and a spark flew out.

The main doors opened. He heard them slide, so he sat up.

A soft voice called at the tack-room door for there were no lit lanterns.

"Ralston?"

"Come on in."

Leo stepped in. Maybe mid-twenties, Leo—also African American but he had been born free—pulled up a clean bucket, turned it over, and sat down.

"How is it?"

"Better. By spring I won't even know I was hurt. Be riding all the horses Mr. Finney will allow."

"Good. Tomorrow is a New Year." Leo smiled. "I always wondered why is the New Year in the dead of winter? Shouldn't it be in spring when everything is new?"

"Never thought about it." Ralston said, pulling the blanket around him.

His chest, smooth, embarrassed him. He would have liked a little chest hair. His voice, deep enough, was manly, but he wished he could grow a heavy beard for show plus have some hair on his chest. At least his chest was broad, even though he was skinny. Sulli had never complained.

"Sometimes my mind wanders. I think of things like why I can't hear an owl fly but I can hear the rustle of a blackbird's feathers. Know what I mean?"

"Well, if you or I can find feathers, maybe we'll find out."

"Good idea." Leo smiled. "Thought you might want a bit of company. You didn't eat today. Miss Frances fretted."

Ralston smiled slowly. "Miss Frances lives to fret. Tell you what— she knows what she's doing. She cleaned me up, cleaned out those damned holes, wrapped me up. She knows a lot."

"She does."

"Was she ever married? I kind of wonder what he would be like. Miss Frances could pass for a boxer, know that?"

Leo laughed. "Could. They say when she was young and her hair fire red, she married. Wasn't here then. He died at Valley Forge. That's what I heard, anyway."

"Ever notice how hard it is to imagine someone old, young?"

"I do. My momma has gray hair. I kind of remember when she didn't when I was little. Guess it happens to all of us. I don't think about tomorrow. I just poke along, you know?"

Ralston leaned back against the tack trunk he used as a backstop so he wouldn't roll over the floor. He could be restless in his sleep.

"I think about the future. I think about William. I want to kill him, but more than anything I want to find Sulli and bring her back."

"You know where she's going?"

"Yeah. Place called Big Rawly. Big house, full of silver and paintings and stuff you can't imagine. Mr. Finney is rich. He's done well but this is money like Midas. Gold everywhere. Silver everywhere.

The Mistress wears jewels so big and heavy, I can't imagine having something like that around my neck or in my ears. Must be two hundred slaves working at Big Rawly. I don't know. I'm from another plantation. Big, too, thousands of acres, but the Garths—their name is Garth—don't show off."

"Were they cruel to you?"

"No. If I asked Barker O, the man who ran the stables, best driving man I ever saw, he told me what to do when I was little. Mostly told me to keep my mouth shut. The rich people called him a Whip. Well, he'd give me a brass chit with a number on it. I could come and go if I was running an errand. My trouble was with another fellow in the stables, Jeddie Rice. He got all the good rides and he treated me like dirt. I hated him."

"Mean?"

"No. Snotty." He changed course. "I don't know how I can get Sulli, but when it's spring and there's no more snow and you can sleep out without too much trouble, I've got to go back and try."

Leo's face changed. "Don't do it. You go back to Virginia, you'll be picked up. And you might not wind up at wherever you came from. You might get sold downriver. Stay here. It's safe here."

"Well, Leo, if it's so damn safe, how did William and Sulli get caught?"

"Oh, bounty hunters come through. No one has ever been taken from Royal Oak. Those two men who bought the cart. It had to be them and they must have been paid a whole lot of money."

"Was Mr. Finney mad when he heard?"

"I don't know. You'd have to ask Ard, but he knew William jammed the pitchfork in you. Maybe he thought good riddance. William said Sulli was his wife, so they grabbed them both."

"She's not his wife. He lied."

"She stuck with him," Leo evenly said.

"He filled her full of dreams when they lived at Big Rawly. He wanted to sleep with her and he wanted her to steal from the big house. She knew where some stuff was but it turned out not enough. She only grabbed small stuff. And he got a cabin, saying she was his wife. He beat her. I will kill him, I swear."

"He's not worth it. He'll get beat plenty when he gets back to Big Rawly. You don't need to trouble yourself." Leo folded his hands. "Don't go. There will be other Sullis."

"No." Ralston raised his voice. "I love her. Only her."

Leo remained silent for a bit, then spoke. "And what good do you do her if you get enslaved again? Even if you're sent back to the people who owned you, what good does it do? If you're caught, I wouldn't bet on being sent to Virginia. You're young. They'll ship your ass to the rice growers or the cane cutters and you'll be old and broken by the time you're thirty. This is a good place to work. You've kept your nose clean. You have a place here."

"Haven't you ever been in love?" Ralston was exasperated.

"No. Looks like trouble to me." He covered his mouth for he yawned.

Dark outside made Leo sleepy, plus he was up and working mornings in the dark. Farm chores took time. Let one go and it's harder the next day. Got to keep at it.

"Nothing feels like that. Nothing feels like holding a woman and hearing her say she loves you."

"Ralston, I'll take your word for it but it's not worth being a slave. Look, heal up. There might be another way."

"What?"

"You stay here. Work. Save your money. Then you send a white man down to Big whatever. Give him your money and see if he can buy Sulli."

Ralston considered this. "Leo, I could buy her."

"They know who you are down there. Don't be a fool. You'll never be free again. Work hard. Save your money. Send a white man."

They sat in the warmth, both staring at the slits in the stove, the reflection of the flames on the one tack-room wall.

"You've given me a lot to think about."

Leo smiled. "I hope so. Well, time for the bunkhouse. I'm tired. Ard says this winter will be hard; all the signs are it will be hard. We're chopping wood, splitting wood, filling up about every empty building we can find. Fill up Mr. Finney's woodbox outside the kitchen door every day. I'm glad you're coming along."

"Yeah." Ralston smacked at his blanket for pillow, lying back down. He winced as he reached for another blanket to pull over him.

"I'll do it." Leo knelt down, pulling up the blanket. "Take it slow. Maybe spring will be early this year."

"You never know."

"Night."

"Night, Leo. I really will think about what you said." He heard the doors open, then slide closed.

28

Tuesday

Brilliant blue skies and a few thin white stratus clouds announced a clear, cold day. January in Virginia fools you. Occasionally, snow on the ground, the mercury would rise up in the high forties, only to plunge the next day, snow flying everywhere.

Martin and Shank relished the good weather. The night before they cleaned up Sulli and William at the Ordinary in Orange County. Today would be the day they reached Big Rawly unless a wheel rolled off the cart, and this wagon was too well built for that, rough roads or not.

Cold though it was in the stable, the two men stripped down William, washed him, fished out a pair of pants not cut behind the knee. The two carried odds and ends like clothing to hide the booze for selling. This proved useful on many levels. They carried a few sweaters, bonnets, and canvas pants. Not much but items that could cover their travels. They'd have to post a guard to protect the liquor every night if people had any idea how much liquor they carried.

They allowed Sulli to clean herself using a stall. She had a bucket of water, soap, old towels.

One man held William's arms behind him; the other washed. They took turns. William, erratic, could easily take a swing at them. Cold though the water was, it felt good being cleaned up. William cooperated enough to put the pants on. When his hamstring was cut, the wound bled very little. The slice was healing. The hamstring would never mend. William was crippled for life. Still they tied his hands together.

On the drive into the next county, the two captives sat in the back, a blanket over them.

The day, cold, was offset by the sun, a welcome bit of warmth.

The steep decline onto the old east-west road to Big Rawly proved no trouble at all. The wagon brakes, well made, could handle a slow-down without a stop. The steep rise up on the western side of Ivy Creek proved no problem either. The mare was strong, the cart about perfect in balance.

Not even two miles down the road, wide enough for two wagons to pass in opposite directions, the Big Rawly sign announced the estate.

Martin, reins in hand, clucked to the mare, who picked up a trot as they turned left. Shank checked on the captives. Sulli, no expression, looked around at surroundings she had known since childhood. Tears streamed down William's face.

Pulling up to the stables, Shank jumped down and walked inside to find DoRe, whom he had met when he took the capturing job from Maureen. DoRe described William as well as Sulli, with Maureen standing there. If the big man had left out a distinguishing feature, the mistress would think him a liar. He described them vividly.

"Delivery," Shank called out.

DoRe, harness bridle hanging over his shoulder, stepped into the aisle and recognized Shank, following him as Shank motioned.

Outside, immobile, sat Sulli and William in the wagon.

"Wanted you to see them before we took them to the house."
Shank held his hand out as though presenting the captured young
people.

"I'll be." He studied the two, neither of whom looked him in the
eye. "You might want to leave the wagon and mare here, I'll take
care of it, and walk those two up to the back door. Elizabetta will
answer. She's paid dearly for these two." He didn't elaborate but Sulli
lifted her jaw as DoRe relayed that message to the two bounty hunters.

Sulli and William didn't budge.

Martin stepped over the backrest, took a knife, and cut free William's hands. He pushed William forward.

Sulli stood up. Martin had to haul up William, who did nothing
to help.

As the two moved to the end of the wagon bed, DoRe lifted his
hand to Sulli but she stepped back as William, dragging his leg, was
pushed forward by Martin.

William stood looking down. DoRe did not offer his hand. Sulli
moved behind William, put her foot on his ass, and shoved hard. He
flew off the wagon, sprawled facedown in the snow, and was left on
the ground. Then she took DoRe's hand and hopped down.

DoRe allowed a small smile as he looked at Sulli, bent down, and
put his hand under William's armpit to haul him up.

As the four started walking to the big house, DoRe studied William's gait.

Martin simply told him, "I cut his hamstring. He was too stupid
to learn. If he'd cooperated, things would have gone better. No riding for him. But he won't run away."

DoRe nodded.

Reaching the back door, imposing for a back door, Martin
knocked. Within a few minutes Elizabetta opened the door, beholding the two whose escape had brought down a savage beating on
her. The scars would never go away, inside or out. Shocked to see
them, she stepped back.

When Maureen and Jeffrey visited England, Elizabetta over-stepped her boundaries by assigning other people her own jobs while she laid around. Doubtful though it was that any slave on Big Rawly enjoyed watching her back get shredded, no one especially liked her or trusted her, although Kintzie nursed her and DoRe originally had carried her to the healer's cabin.

The others managed to get along with Elizabetta but no one drew close. She had learned, brutal though it was. She knew she could never ask for help. She was alone.

Once the shock and disgust registered, she opened the door wider, allowing the four inside so they stood in the small back room, a coatroom for chore coats for Maureen and Jeffrey plus the usual odds and ends of daily life on a farm.

"Please wait here. I'll announce you to the Master and Missus."

Two benches, wrought-iron legs—Maureen favored wrought iron—faced each other as they stood against the wall. Martin and Shank sat down. Sulli and William stood, although William stood on one leg.

The rustle of a voluminous skirt could be heard, followed by a man's heavier tread. Maureen appeared, followed by Jeffrey.

The Missus walked right up to William and hit him across the face with the back of her hand. She repeated the procedure with Sulli.

Jeffrey took her by the elbow, pulling her slightly aside as he moved in front. He had seen enough of his wife's vicious temper when crossed. No point giving her room to vent.

"Where were they?" Jeffrey asked.

"Working in Maryland."

"Did anyone want money to turn them over?" Maureen focused on the cash, of course.

"Surprisingly, no," Shank smoothly replied, not offering the information that they had been abducted.

"I see." Maureen appraised Sulli, a bit worse for the wear, but that would pass. "Elizabetta!"

The Mistress's dresser returned, hands folded together. "Yes, ma'am."

"Elizabetta, where do you think Sulli should lodge?" Maureen used a generous term, "lodge," but she asked Elizabetta for the reason that the message is: You cause trouble, I will hand you over to the people you troubled once I am satisfied.

Without betraying her pleasure, Elizabetta nodded her head, replying smoothly, "Perhaps, Mistress, the Hill."

"Very good."

The Hill was where the simpleminded lived. Every large estate, slave or free, produced some people a bit slow or hampered in other ways through no fault of their own. Often they could be taught simple chores: The physically strong could sow and harvest, plow and cut, but many could not even do that. So Sulli would be surrounded by people needing constant supervision. The other able-bodied person at the Hill was becoming elderly. Sulli's would be a severely circumscribed life.

"And William"—Maureen sounded almost sweet—"you will return to the stable, of course. You will be chained at night, by manacles attached to a center pole. You will be here until you die, William."

"What about the stealing?" Elizabetta inquired, with barely concealed malice.

Light voice, Maureen waved her hand. "He's not going to steal. Not unless he wants his hands cut off. His leg looks bad enough."

"Hamstring, Mrs. Holloway," Martin simply reported.

"He got violent. Kept trying to run away," Shank declared in an even voice.

"That was prudent of you," she replied. "Jeffrey, dear, allow me to leave you with these gentlemen." She didn't think they were gentlemen for one minute, but why not flatter them. "I'll retrieve the funds." Turning to them, she smiled. "With a bonus for your speed."

Both bowed slightly.

Jeffrey, relieved that Maureen didn't explode, looked at the two slaves and in a low voice said, "If only you hadn't taken some of her jewelry. Bad enough you ran, but it was the theft, especially after the pearl and diamond necklace Sheba stole when she left."

Both hung their heads as Maureen returned with two heavy leather pouches filled with coins. She handed each man a pouch. "Thank you. I do hope I will never need your services again, but I will highly recommend you to others."

"Yes, ma'am."

Jeffrey, eager to be out of this, smiled. "Allow me to walk you down to the stable."

Grabbing a heavy coat, Jeffrey ushered out Martin, Shank, and William, whom Shank pushed to keep up. William hopped down to the barn.

Elizabetta, also wrapped up, riding crop in hand, took Sulli down to the Hill.

"You take one wrong step, you filthy slut, and I will beat you as badly as they beat me."

Sulli remained silent.

Elizabetta walked in front of her, slamming the riding crop across her face with all her might. "Answer me, bitch."

"Yes."

Another crack. "Yes, what?"

"I will not take a wrong step."

Satisfied, Elizabetta moved beside her, walking Sulli to a dismal fate.

Back at the stable, DoRe greeted Jeffrey.

"Master, come look at this." DoRe led Jeffrey to Dipsy's wagon. "Nothing like your work, but people need more carts and wagons than coaches. Look underneath."

Down on one knee, Jeffrey checked the axle and the alignment of the wheels as best he could. "I see."

"Mare's good, too," Martin remarked in an offhand manner.

"She looks strong enough. Age?" DoRe asked.

"Well, you can look at her teeth. I say she's five." Shank had sense not to make her out to be younger. You couldn't fool DoRe.

DoRe checked, holding open her lips for Jeffrey.

Quick to put the pieces together, plus a big workshop, allowed Jeffrey to make decisions without dragging it out. "How much do you want for the cart and the mare?"

"Well," Martin drawled, "we weren't planning to sell her."

"Two hundred," Jeffrey said.

"Three hundred. You're getting a good mare. The wagon is worth two hundred alone," Martin countered.

DoRe patted the mare's neck, then stroked her muzzle. Jeffrey got the signal.

"That's pricey for these parts. I don't think I can sell a wagon for two hundred dollars, but I'll give you three hundred for the wagon and the mare. I'd like to study this wagon."

Martin held out his hand. "Done."

Shank did also. "A good choice."

"Gentlemen, I'll be right back." Jeffrey left the stable and trotted to the house to get the money. He'd tell Maureen later, although she rarely interfered in his business decisions. He never inquired about hers, especially since his coach building proved quite successful. The sales were finally paying for the expense of that large, impressive shop. Jeffrey had every tool known to man.

Martin, directing his gaze to William, sitting on a trunk against a stall, said, "You can't trust him. Not for a skinny minute."

DoRe nodded. "I know. He stole another man's horse. Broke the other jockey's collarbone in a race. Pushed him hard. Snuck back months later. The horse actually showed up down along the James, down near the falls. Anyway, he showed up, stole Sulli and some things from the Mistress."

"Maybe you should put an iron collar on him," Shank suggested.

"Up to the Missus," DoRe replied.

Jeffrey returned with more money and said to DoRe, "How about if you take them down to Hare Field. Good place to stay for the night. Give you a chance to test the wagon."

"Yes, sir, I will, but let me turn this mare out and harness a fresh horse. Won't take long." DoRe called for one of the stable boys, who stopped cold when he stepped inside and saw William.

As the mare was unhitched and a Percheron put in her place, Jeffrey mentioned to DoRe, "Mrs. Holloway wants you to chain William at night. Granted he can't get too far, but she is deeply angry as well as mistrustful. I think she'll come down here to tell you exactly what she desires."

"Yes, sir. In the meantime, I'll"—he looked around—"chain him to one of the stall rings. Can't leave him here while I take these two to Hare Field."

The stall rings were round iron rings used to tie those horses in an open stall. Some had regular boxes; others stood with lots of water and food in a closed stall. Over time DoRe was switching from open stalls to those with doors. He was finding he liked them better and he felt the horses could move around more.

The young man hitching up the Percheron heard every word, which were also meant for him. William as well as Sulli would be ever-present examples of what happens when you cross Maureen Selisse Holloway.

If they proved more considerate of those harmed because of them, maybe over time a few people would sneak them helpful things, better clothing, food, perhaps. But it was doubtful anyone, slave or free, at Big Rawly would ever help William or Sulli, because they had never been kind to others. Those two especially must pay for their selfishness.

The biblical lesson, "As you sow, so you shall reap," was vividly apparent.

29

Thursday

Blistering heat had not yet descended upon central Virginia. The daytime temperatures might reach the high seventies, even the low eighties, but a pleasant breeze kept summer lovely. Enough rain guaranteed leaves darkening in their green; those early summer flowers exploded; the grass felt like a thick carpet, springy.

Harry, Susan, Mags, Janice, Pamela, and Carlton Sweeny walked along the middle quad at St. Luke's. Fortunately for Carlton, he enjoyed flexibility in his job. This doubled as a research trip for him as well as a helpful visit for the ladies of the Dorcas Guild focused on the grounds.

"Charles West had grown up among fabulous gardens in England. He was the younger son of a baron." Harry noticed a chipmunk scurrying away, as did Mrs. Murphy and Pewter, who followed.

The dogs paid little attention to the chipmunk, a bit of a surprise, but perhaps they waited for larger game.

"How did your peonies do?" Carlton asked.

"Divine." Harry beamed. "Such an old plant, shrub."

"You know, really, there aren't that many new plants. Humans have bred them for color and for size over the centuries but the fundamental properties of, say, a rose remain."

"'A rose is a rose is a rose.'" Pamela Bartlett quoted Gertrude Stein, which made the little group smile.

"Could you understand what she was writing?" Janice wondered. "I read one book in junior English at Sophie Newcomb. Didn't understand one word."

Sophie Newcomb was a college in New Orleans when Janice was young.

"All I can say about Gertrude Stein is I was force-fed the present participle." Harry smiled, as she had read a lot of the unique writer while at Smith.

"I can't stand fiction," Mags grumbled.

"Oh, Mags." Susan grimaced.

"Well, I can't. None of it is true."

Carlton stopped as they approached the large red oak, the dead tree nearby. "But it is the truth, Mrs. Nielsen. Nonfiction is the factual truth. Fiction is the emotional truth."

"There you have it." Janice couldn't help but tease. "Mags is emotionally stunted."

"What's this?" Carlton stopped in front of Sheba's grave. Mags gave him the story to the extent that they knew it and somewhat redeemed herself, if in fact she needed redeeming.

"I remember reading about the exhumation, the necklace and earrings. Who knows how many people we are standing on?"

"Carlton, that's a scary thought," Susan quietly remarked. "I, well all of us, were taught not to disturb the dead."

"Standing on someone isn't disturbing them." Janice popped up. "Digging them up, yes. And didn't you all dig up bones at Big Rawly? Bones related to these bones. It was in the news."

Susan shook her head slightly. "We did. It was a surprise. We had no idea what was under that shed. If we are allowed to keep the bones, if no family members claim them, we will do as was done for this woman: provide a Christian burial."

"I doubt anyone will claim them." Mags stared down at the tidy area. "Too far back, and if anyone does share that DNA, there would have to be plenty of others." She looked at Carlton. "Ever have the ancestry test?"

"No, but my great-grandmother, still here, and my grandmom are genealogy nuts. There are Sweenys littering all of central Virginia."

They laughed.

Carlton walked past the grave to a brush area behind the red oak. He stared down, then knelt down.

"What?" Harry hoped he wouldn't suggest more yard work.

"You know Solanaceae is one of the largest families in the plant kingdom. Potatoes, tomatoes, ornamental plants that you have mixed in here, Nicotiana, and some of the Datura genus. All over Virginia."

"How big a family is it?" Mags inquired.

"Three thousand members. Big. Stuff you see every day. Mostly the members are good actors, either edible or decorative, but there's the motorcycle gang element. Belladonna is probably the most famous, one called Purple Hindu, angel's trumpet, large and showy, pretty, and then our own jimsonweed. Effects range from hallucinations to death."

"Jamestown had a lot of jimsonweed." Susan had done a bit of research. "In time, a short time, the settlers realized not to eat the stuff, although you can use it for medicinal purposes."

"And something like that substance or deadly nightshade was what killed Jeannie Cordle," Pamela recalled.

"The difficulty is, where did she ingest it? The first thought was some kind of potato, or something injected in a potato, God knows why," Susan told them. "You can imagine the law enforcement people going through every bit of food from the AHIP fundraiser. They found nothing. Not one thing."

Mags trudged along with the rest of them as they headed back up to the church. "She might have eaten something by mistake."

"Well, if she did, it would have hit her either before or shortly after she reached Castle Hill. Whatever she touched or ate, she did it at Castle Hill." Harry had been keeping up with Susan on research.

"Good. Maybe we can go to Reverend Jones's office." Pewter picked up her step. *"Be good to see the cats."*

"I had no idea you were becoming so social." Tucker caught up with her.

"We've eaten communion wafers together." Pewter let out a puff of laughter in which Mrs. Murphy joined.

Some years ago the cats pried open a not tightly shut closet door in which were stored communion wafers. They ate every one, with a little help from Cazenovia, Elocution, Lucy Fur, and Tucker.

"We all ate the same food. Couldn't have been that," Carlton posited. "And if something had been altered just for Mrs. Cordle, wouldn't the chef have known or someone working with the food? You'd have to grab her plate to make sure only she ate it."

"That's true." Pamela agreed. "I wasn't there, but I can imagine it was deeply upsetting."

"It was," both Mags and Janice said in unison, while Harry and Susan nodded their heads.

"Rev." Harry tiptoed to Reverend Jones's door, lightly knocked.

"Come on in. Saw you all out on the quads." He rose as Harry opened the door, his three cats bounding up to meet the other animals.

"Drinks, cookies?" Reverend Jones offered.

"Catnip!" Pewter hollered.

Pamela took charge. "Reverend Jones, you sit down and entertain. I'll take care of the libations."

Susan and Harry joined her in the small kitchen as the others picked a drink.

"What do you think of our grounds?" Reverend Jones asked Carlton.

"Beautiful. And much of it is the original, or at least the original layout. I was here once in my early teens, when I thought I might like horticulture. Visited every old garden I could. The proportions of St. Luke's are lovely and the quads in the back reflect that, too."

Herb smiled. "We all benefit from those who have gone before."

"I heard the story about the grave. It's peaceful under that red oak." Carlton stood up to take his drink, as the seat swallowed you up if you were on the sofa.

The chairs offered more support.

"Given that there are so many Sweenys, as you said"—Mags sipped a sweet tea—"maybe you're related."

"You know, Mrs. Nielsen, I bet if we all did the ancestry DNA thing, we'd all be related, especially those of us who have lived here for generations. It's inevitable." He, too, took a sip. "Just like finding members of the Solanaceae family in our gardens is inevitable."

"Have them in mine. Well under the yews," Mags confessed.

Harry, eyeing Pewter, who was about to jump on the large coffee table, stood up. "Don't you even think about it."

She walked to the kitchen, opened a cabinet drawer where the treats were kept, and tossed out tiny colored fish goodies to all the cats, fetched two bones for the dogs. "I'm stealing your cat and dog treats, Reverend Jones, but it's the only way."

Pewter, having gobbled her fish, purred to Pirate, *"You know there might be poison in your dog biscuit. Think about what the gardener guy said about belladonna. You never know."*

The innocent youngster opened his mouth and dropped the medium-sized biscuit. That fast, Pewter dove toward it, picked it up, and ran out the opened door.

"Pewter," Mrs. Murphy called. *"You can't steal in a church."*

Calling from the hall while she tried to eat the hard dog biscuit, refusing to admit defeat, she hollered back, *"They'll forgive me. They're Christians, remember?"*

Harry gave Pirate another bone. "Pay her no mind."

30

Tuesday

Apart from less pain, Ralston had more energy. He still needed to take breaks, to sit and breathe deeply, before returning to his chores, but all was in order.

Miss Frances cleaned his wounds and complained he wasn't eating enough.

"Keep your strength up."

He nodded. "Yes, ma'am."

Ralston knew she was taking as good care of him as she could, so he let her boss him about. Miss Frances lived to boss.

Snow packed down. At least when the horses walked, those who were not shod didn't carry half-moons of snow in their hooves. That would make a horse lurch a bit; then the snow would pop out. This repeated process slowed them down. Not having to put up with it was a relief.

It still hurt to bend over to pick out a hoof, but Ralston did it with the sturdy hoof picks Dipsy forged.

Night arrived early. It was time to bring the horses in.

Spring seemed a lifetime away.

Tidbit, a small mare, nickered, running up to him when he entered the paddock. She followed him into the stable, zipped into her stall. As he liked her so much, he lavished special attention on her before heading out to bring in the others. For those girls he'd slip halters on his shoulder, lead ropes attached. No one pulled on him as he carefully walked into the barn. Once everyone stood in their assigned stall, he closed the doors. This ritual always involved each horse, save Tidbit, seeing if she could duck into another stall. The food might be better there. He'd call their names, admonish them, halter still on so he had some control. They'd go to their stall, crabby as they did so. Then he would head for the doors, smiling.

Equine antics never failed to raise his spirits.

Ferocious cold numbed his hands. He closed the door behind him to the tack room, removed worn gloves, held his hands toward the potbellied stove, which he religiously kept going all day. Dog tired at the end of the day, having to fire up the stove seemed like the last straw—hence his devotion to that potbellied stove.

Hands working again, he walked out, finishing his chores. The last was sweeping the center aisle, straightening out anything hanging on hooks that may have become a bit crooked.

Finally back in the tack room, he pulled his pallet nearer the stove. Removing his clothing, he sat with his back to the stove. His healing puncture wounds itched. The heat also helped his back muscles loosen. The cold tightened him up. Ralston was determined to regain his suppleness and strength.

A small window, glass handblown so a bit wavy, bits of old towels stuffed around it, showed brilliant stars.

Seemed to the young man that the winter's sky made the stars bigger and brighter. He watched them glitter, wondering if Sulli was watching the night sky.

———

Sulli, worn out, wouldn't be able to drop into bed for at least another hour. The people living at the Hill often cried or put up a fuss. Wes, a slave so old his eyes were milky, would hold her hand at night. His mind was that of a child's. Finally he would fall asleep. Then she could leave him. He cried frequently. Difficult and painful as Sulli's situation was and appeared would forever be, she recognized that at least she was able-bodied and of sound mind.

Those most able at the house often assisted those who were not. Sulli, before her escape, rarely ventured down to the two-story cabin. The cooperation between the residents surprised her. This was the only life they knew. They couldn't truly participate in the affairs at Big Rawly.

When Maureen was out of sight, with no snitches around, less afflicted people were free to follow their passions and curiosities. Small though that time might be, it was their own and they made the most of it. That was also the only life they knew.

Annie, same age as Sulli, would rock and sing the songs she heard others sing. She remembered every word, although she couldn't carry on a conversation.

Olivia, frail now, had been in charge of the Hill since she turned twenty, a good fifty years ago. She thought of the residents as her children. Loving, patient, intelligent, Olivia never missed Sunday services at Big Rawly. She absorbed every reading, every lesson, memorizing parts of the Bible when she heard the Good Book read. Olivia couldn't read, nor could most of the workers, including the white ones.

Wes now asleep, Sulli dropped on a stool in front of the stone fireplace. The logs' aroma smelled wonderful.

Olivia, pulling her shawl tighter around her narrow shoulders, sat next to her in an old wooden chair.

"Cold gets me. Didn't mind it so much when I was young." She stared into the leaping flames. "Missus call for you?"

"No."

"H-m-m, you've learned a lot in a short time. These children, even if they have snow-white hair, need gentleness, patience. If you gain their trust, they will try harder for you."

"How did you wind up here? It's a job nobody wants."

"Meaning you don't want it," Olivia shrewdly said.

"I didn't. But now—" She shrugged.

"They have no guile. It's a gift God gave them. Their honesty is a rebuke to us." Her quiet voice vied with the fire's crackle.

"I've seen enough guile to last me until I'm as old as Wes."

Olivia replied, "I expect you have. Don't need to leave Big Rawly to see that."

Shifting on the stool, Sulli bitterly remarked, "I believed William. I was a fool."

Olivia tapped her foot, then slowly replied. "Every woman does that once. Fool me once, shame on you. Fool me twice, shame on me."

Wrapped up in bed later, Sulli reviewed Olivia's words. She vowed never to repeat her mistake. She thought of Ralston, sweet enough, but in time he would have pushed her around, given orders like William. Seemed to Sulli men were all like that.

She realized Olivia didn't answer her question about how she wound up at the Hill. Was it because of a man? Would she ever know?

But she did know she would spend the rest of her life at Big Rawly unless Maureen sold her for spite. She'd tasted freedom. Sweet though it was, William soured it. Olivia's words on being fooled came back to her again.

She didn't think Maureen would sell her. She'd use her for an example, for show. Sulli took comfort in the thought that she'd out-live that bitch and she would make certain to outlive William. Anything she could do to bring pain upon him she would do. Slave she might be, but she wasn't helpless. She would never be a helpless woman.

31

Friday

Susan allowed the motor to run. While not sticky hot, it was hot enough for air-conditioning as she was parked at Mags's.

Harry fished in her purse. "Why is it, no matter what you want, it's always at the bottom of your purse?"

Harry's finger found what she was looking for. "Aha."

She pulled down the visor, mirror on the reverse, and pulled off the cap.

"You and your magenta lipstick."

"You bought a tube." Harry lifted one eyebrow.

"To show you up." Susan dug out her tube, top off, twisting the lipstick up. "Better than yours."

Patting her now-vibrant lips with a Kleenex from the glove compartment, Harry rolled her lips inward. "Dream on."

Susan grabbed the Kleenex, patting her own lips.

"Mine is better."

Harry snatched the tube, holding it next to her own. "Close but no cigar."

"Cigar, hell." Susan grabbed her lipstick back. "Out of the car. We can see better in the natural light. Next year when the peonies bloom, we can compare for real."

"How do you know we won't have used up all our lipstick?" Harry challenged her.

"Well, Harry, you could bite it in half. Then you'd have a magenta tongue and teeth."

"You're nuts."

"Remember that line from our senior class play, *Charley's Aunt*? Oh, you remember. 'I'm . . . from Brazil. Where the nuts come from!' "

At this they both laughed.

Susan grinned. "What fun. Even funnier, my future husband played Charley's aunt." A deep sigh followed this memory. "I miss those days."

"Because we were young?"

Susan thought. "Kind of, but more because we were innocent. We believed what we were told. At least, I did." She paused. "You did, too."

"Yeah." Harry put the lipstick back in her small purse. "Isn't it odd that we were all so silly at the AHIP fundraiser? A bunch of middle-aged women grabbing one another's lipsticks. We aren't silly enough, Susan."

"That's the truth." Susan opened the door, tossing her lipstick on the driver's seat of the station wagon.

"That will melt."

"I'll pour it on you." Susan closed the door, not bothering to lock.

"Do you lock your car when you go into Charlottesville?" Harry asked.

"You know I do. I don't know who those people are anymore."

"You only have to worry about the city council." Harry took a jaunty step. "They need money. They'd open your car. Might have pennies on the floor."

Susan laughed. "How did we get into this mess?"

"We didn't. We're part of the county." Harry squared her shoulders. "Everyone's in a mess."

"You know, Harry, I think about that AHIP fundraiser. To think that about an hour after our hijinks in the ladies' room, Jeannie Cordle would be dead."

"You never know." Harry stated the obvious.

"At least she died happy. Almost on the dance floor."

Mags, stepping out from her impressive home's side door, waved. "You two are prompt. Come on."

They walked back behind the house, through the graceful door to the garden.

Stopping at the end of the arbor, the entrance to the horseshoe garden, Harry asked, "Where's the bench? Sort of Chippendale?"

"Moved it. Blocks the view and I have those table and chairs on either side of the door."

Noticing the comfortable cushions on the chairs, Susan inquired, "Shouldn't those cushions be waterproof?"

"Doesn't matter. If it rains, I still have to wipe them off so I untie them, bring them into the outside shed over there. Granted, it's one more thing to do, but I am not buying more cushions."

"One good thing about daily chores, they keep you fit." Harry's eyes swept over the garden, even more lush than at their first visit.

"Your chores." Mags laughed. "Come with me. Let's stand in the middle of the horseshoe."

As they did so Susan remarked, "I really love the way you laid this out. No juniper."

"I thought you liked juniper," Harry came back at her.

"I do, but this garden is so soft. Maybe I'm not using the right descriptive word. Juniper is kind of edgy. Spreads, though. It can be a godsend."

Mags nodded in agreement. "I used juniper on the edges of the walk down to the creek. Trickle, actually." She smiled. "I was going for the effect here of black locusts and hemlock on the curve of the horseshoe, a bit away, but then once in the horseshoe, I wanted color."

"All your rhododendrons, azaleas give you that. The iris and coreopsis. Mags, you've done such an interesting job." Harry meant that. "By the way, where is Janice?"

"Brewery. We each take two days apiece, one day together. The other two days go to the managers. You'd be surprised how exhausting running that brewery is."

"Any time you deal with the public it's exhausting." Susan knew she was not born for any kind of service or retail.

"Your hops look good." Harry then added, "Drove over with my boyfriend for a look."

"Now, that was a fight. Janice said, 'Why go to the trouble of growing our own hops when farmers around us are doing it?' I swore just like wine, the earth leaves a distinctive taste. The soil is good at Bottoms Up. We have thirty acres. I prevailed and our beer is better than ever."

"Fair thinks so, too." Harry smiled. "I stick to Coca-Cola."

"Bet I can change that," Mags teased. "You two garden, have done so for all your lives. Susan, your mother and grandmother garden."

"Keeps Gran young." Susan adored her grandmother.

"You are both good to look this over with me. I have another reason." Mags put her hands together. "Poisonous plants. The cause of Jeannie's death disturbs me. I have jimsonweed here."

"We all do, Mags," Harry reassured her.

"What else do I have? You all will know. I go for size, texture, color. I'm not thinking about anyone eating my garden, including the rabbits."

Harry and Susan looked at each other. Then Susan spoke first.

"So many trees and plants have parts that are poisonous or times of year when they are dangerous. See your impressive English yews?"

"Yes."

"There's poison in the berries."

"Why didn't anyone tell me?" Mags complained.

"Who is going to go to the trouble to climb up, get berries, and eat them? The berries are short-lived."

"I see. So they aren't dangerous?"

"Not unless someone makes a point of harvesting berries." Susan then pointed to the rhododendrons. "Now, those can get you. They produce a honey-like substance and it's poisonous. You don't want horses to eat rhododendrons. As for us, we'd have to eat a large amount to kill us, but a small amount can make you sick."

"Such a beautiful shrub." Mags's brows wrinkled. "But okay?"

"Sure. So are azaleas, which have a little goo, enough to make you queasy." Harry shrugged. "Given all the pesticides people spray on their plants, that's more dangerous than some of the plants. You breathe in the pesticides."

"True enough," Mags agreed.

"Foxglove, seeds, stems, flowers. Those happy flowers contain poisons." Harry walked into the garden. "But then again, you'd have to go to a lot of work to collect the flowers, press them, find a way to make them edible." She walked out and over to the yews. "Now, this stuff, jimsonweed. First, if you ingest a small dose, hallucinations. More, boom, you're dead."

"Should I pull it out?" Mags asked.

Harry smiled. "It's all over Virginia. Unless you are planning to serve it to someone at Bottoms Up, no."

"That's just it, Harry. Someone did serve it to Jeannie." Mags's voice rose.

"No one knows how she got jimsonweed. All they know is, given the time frame of her death, the severity of the symptoms, she had to have eaten it at AHIP." Susan stated the known facts.

"Someone knew what they were doing." Mags crossed her arms over her chest.

"Yes, but maybe they did it to the wrong person." Harry truly believed Jeannie could not have been the intended victim. "Look at the still way up behind my house, up in Susan's walnut acres. Bones. A natural death? A murder? Then another still. Now we know the profits involved with selling black-market booze are enormous. Someone stole your beer."

"I hope I get my hands on them," Mags vowed.

"Not that Jeannie was involved in any such thing, but here's another thought. What if timber is being harvested illegally on government lands and sold? Susan fusses at me, but I think we're in the middle of either some kind of rivalry or a threat to illegal profit."

"Mags, don't get her going." Susan then looked at the large plants under the English yew. "You're safe."

32

Friday

The January thaw, a bit late this year, ushered in temperatures in the mid-forties during the day. Given the bitter cold and snow, this felt like freedom. People could wear lighter clothing, perhaps even dispense with a scarf.

Maureen looked over the mare her husband had bought as he stood next to her.

"She is uncommonly sweet, my dear. I thought if you wished to drive alone, she would be most reliable. I don't want to take any chances with my bride." Jeffrey called her his "bride" because she liked that.

"Not much to look at," Maureen commented.

"No matter. All eyes will be on you."

DoRe, hearing this as he was kneeling down to feel one of the elegant coach-driving horse's legs, shook his head. Jeffrey knew exactly how to handle the Missus.

"And what coach do you suggest I drive?" She paused. "What's her name?"

"Penny."

"Ah."

"In summer, you have many choices. I always like seeing you drive the dog cart."

The dog cart was a short two-seater, two large wheels, a popular choice on many farms in warm weather.

"We'll see. What about cold weather?"

"I prefer you be in a closed cart, my dear. No need to expose you to numbing temperatures. DoRe can drive you as he always does in rain, snow, cold."

"Yes."

At that point DoRe emerged from the far stall. He nodded, wiping his hands on an old towel hanging outside the stall.

"What do you think?" Jeffrey asked DoRe.

"About what, Master?"

"Barney's leg."

Maureen turned to her husband. "What's the matter with Barney's leg? Why wasn't I told?"

DoRe stepped in to help Jeffrey, whom he thought a good man. "Missus, he's stocked up. Now that the weather's better, he can be turned out all day. He just stocked up."

Horses' legs, like humans', will swell if they stand for hours. Horses and humans are built to move.

"DoRe, what do you think of the work cart Jeffrey purchased?"

"A wise buy. We won't need to be constantly fixing it."

"My darling, I can sell more carts and wagons than I can coach and fours. This adds, um, faster income. The coaches take longer to fashion, which means longer to receive as due."

Shrewd about money, Maureen probed. "Who will you take off the coach building?"

"Only Mason to work with and train two younger men. The underpinnings will take the most skill."

"How quickly can you produce such a vehicle once the men are trained?"

"Three weeks." He held up his hands. "Given the equipment we have, maybe two weeks. The painting will add a bit of time but it's the axles and wheels that matter. Of course that is critical, important for the coach and fours, but think of how intricate and elegant those coaches are. The windows alone add a big bump to the cost. And people want a coach in their colors. Even down to pinstripes on the wheels."

She nodded in agreement. "You get what you pay for and you, husband, really are an artist. Sublime work." She kissed him on the cheek, satisfied with the explanation.

"As long as you are pleased."

DoRe had many chores to finish but he couldn't just walk away. He caught Jeffrey's eye, raising his eyebrows. Before he could be dismissed, Maureen spoke.

"Who might you train?"

"Young Louis." He stopped.

"Who else?"

"William. He can't ride anymore. He can't really work in the fields. This way he can be useful."

"If I have to feed him, he'd better be useful."

"My sentiments, entirely," Jeffrey soothingly agreed.

"DoRe, is he useful to you?"

"No, Missus."

"Where is he?"

"In the lower barn mixing bran mash."

"Fetch him," she commanded, then turned to her husband. "Let's wait in the sunshine. I want to feel the warmth on my face."

"Of course." Jeffrey lifted a small bench from the large tack room, carrying it outside.

"Jeffrey, we have men who can do that. I do wish you would more often employ them."

"Yes, but I don't want you to wait until I find one. You should sit right here, face turned to the sun. Would you like me to find a foot-stool?"

"No, dear."

The sight of William, dragging his one leg, next to DoRe, who also limped, from old horse injuries, made Maureen laugh.

Finally, standing before her, she looked William up and down. "Did you learn anything?"

William bowed his head, silent.

She barked, "Did you learn anything?"

"Yes, Missus."

"My husband is willing to have you taught how to build carts. Mason will be in charge. You will live at the workshop and be chained each night."

"Yes, Missus."

"Perhaps in a year or two, with good behavior, you can sleep un-chained. I'll be decent. In the carriage shop you need only be chained by the ankle. One false move and your hands will be chained to a beam. Do you understand?"

"Yes, Missus."

"What else?" Her voice rose threateningly.

Head down, he replied, "Thank you, Missus."

She tapped her small foot, encased in a lovely shoe, thinking. "William, do you know where my pearl and diamond necklace and earrings might be? Did you steal them?"

William's head shot up, eyes wide with fear, for he had heard from DoRe what happened to Elizabetta. No one else would talk to him. William was utterly distrusted and despised.

"No, Missus. No."

Jeffrey quietly affirmed, "Dearest, if he had that exquisite neck-lace and earrings, he would have gotten a lot farther, although I grant you his disappearance so close to Sheba's raises questions."

Maureen now tapped her other foot.

"William, my husband, who is far too kind, will supervise you at the shop." She turned to Jeffrey, sitting next to her. "When do you want him there?"

"Now would do nicely." Jeffrey stood up.

Maureen did not stop him as this exchange further provoked her. "On your way, send Sulli to me at the house."

He stopped for a moment, then smiled. "Of course. You know, I long to find that necklace and those earrings. You looked so radiant wearing them"—he paused one short beat—"although no jewelry can ever do you justice."

Then he left as DoRe returned to the driving horses. Jeffrey, along with William dragging his leg, headed toward the shop.

DoRe, halter over Barney, walked the big boy out to his paddock. He thought Jeffrey Holloway sang for his supper daily. He thanked God for a good woman who loved him. Slave he was and always would be, but he had more than his master. He had the love of Bettina.

"Barney, life is confusing." He patted the fine animal, slipped off the halter, and watched him run and kick, happy to be out of that confining stall.

Back in the big house, Maureen told Elizabetta to expect Sulli.

Within five minutes Sulli was let in the back door. Elizabetta said not a word but led her to Maureen, sitting on the porch, flooded with sunlight.

"Elizabetta, stay here. You should hear this." Maureen turned her luminous eyes, one of her best features, to Sulli. "Have you learned your lesson?"

"Yes, Missus," Sulli quickly responded, bowing her head like William.

"Do you know where my necklace and earrings are?" She had no need to explain.

By this time most of Virginia knew the story.

"No, Missus."

"But you knew Sheba?"

"Yes, Missus, but she was far above me, working in the house."

"Yet you, Sheba, and William ran off not far apart in time."

It was far apart in time, for Sheba disappeared in 1786, October. However, no one, including her husband, would point that out to her. Maureen did not take well to correction in any form.

"Missus, Sheba would have nothing to do with me. She never spoke to me."

"H-m-m. Never?"

"No, Missus. I was far beneath her."

"But you knew when she ran off."

"Yes, Missus."

"And you knew she stole a necklace and earrings of great value."

"Yes, Missus."

"Do you think William knows where Sheba is or where the necklace might be? After all, you two stole from me."

"Yes, Missus. I was wrong to do that. I was wrong to listen to William."

Maureen was enjoying this, as was Elizabetta.

"Tell me, Sulli, what did William promise that could turn you into a thief and a fool?"

Sulli took a deep breath, lifted her head. "He told me he loved me. He told me we would be free and make lots of money."

"And you believed that?"

"Yes, Missus. I most particularly believed he loved me."

"You aren't the first woman to be misled by a sweet talker, but you knew right from wrong. 'Thou shalt not steal,'" Maureen said. Then she called out. "Kintzie, come in here."

Kintzie, the herbalist and healer, walked in.

The woman exuded a natural dignity and kindness.

"Yes, Missus."

"Help Elizabetta show her back."

Kintzie did as asked, sliding the sleeves down. Elizabetta turned her back to Sulli, whose reaction was a slight narrowing of her eyes.

Maureen waved her hand. Kintzie helped Elizabetta with her top.

"Sulli, Elizabetta's negligence allowed you and William to steal the pin money out of the kitchen plus a small necklace. She has paid for it. How should I punish you?"

Sulli kept her mouth shut.

Maureen stood up, slapped her hard across the face. "If you ever do anything like that again, if you ever steal from me, if you know where Sheba is and I find out you know, I will do worse. Far worse. Do you understand?"

Sulli nodded.

Maureen slapped her again. "Do you understand?"

"Yes, Missus."

"Get out of my sight."

As they left, the last rays of the sun shone on the meadows. Maureen would kill to find her necklace, but who to kill?

33

Saturday

"How much longer do you think this will last?" Barker O asked DoRe.

"Day or two. I never let my defenses down." DoRe watched Penny turned out with a few old mares in a field at Cloverfields.

"U-m-m. That mare has good cannon bone. Why doesn't Mrs. Selisse want her?"

"She's not elegant enough. Her comment was she's not riding a horse that should pull a plow."

Barker O shook his head. "Jeddie!"

"Yes, sir." Jeddie, who was in the field, trotted to the fence.

"Go find Miss Catherine. Ask her if she has time to look at a horse."

"Yes, sir." Jeddie, one hand on the top board, vaulted over the fence in one smooth motion.

Barker O looked at DoRe. "Remember doing that?"

"I do." DoRe shook his head.

The two friends, driving competitors, leaned on the fence, caught up, talked of their favorite subject, horses.

Shortly, Catherine, a light shawl over her shoulders, joined them, as did Tulli, the little fellow, closing in on his twelfth birthday but looking younger. He kept his mouth shut, as all youngsters should around the adults.

"DoRe, feels like spring," Catherine said.

He grinned. "Does."

"What have you?"

DoRe pointed to Penny, contentedly grazing. "Mr. Holloway bought a cart. Penny came with it. Mrs. Selisse Holloway"—he cleared his throat, couldn't get used to calling her Holloway— "thinks she looks too common."

Catherine, half-smiling, studied the gentle girl. "Tulli, hop on. Jeddie, help him up."

"I can do it." The little fellow rushed out, guided the mare to the fence, climbed up, and slid on while Penny remained still.

"I can see that." Catherine smiled.

Jeddie, just in case, had moved to the other side of the mare.

"I can make her canter." Tulli smiled.

"That won't be necessary, plus you don't have a bridle."

"I can do anything." He puffed out his scrawny chest while Jeddie shook his head.

"All I want you to do is walk the fence line, come back, walk away from me, turn, walk toward me. Walk, Tulli."

"Yes, Miss Catherine."

Observing the mare's stride, Catherine said, "DoRe, she's good off the shoulder. I don't see any major flaw. Do you?"

"No. She'll cover ground. She's kind."

"Yes." Catherine agreed. "DoRe, what does your esteemed mistress want for her?" She drug in "esteemed."

"She didn't say. She just said she doesn't want to feed a horse who doesn't meet the Rawly standards."

"Ah—yes. Jeddie, go up to the house. Tell Father I want forty dollars plus ten."

"Yes, Miss Catherine."

Tulli ran along with Jeddie, who told him to hurry up. Tulli never wanted to miss anything, so while he tried to keep up with the long-legged nineteen-year-old, he blabbed the entire time.

"If you shut up, you'll run faster." Jeddie picked up the pace to torment Tulli.

As the three adults waited, DoRe told them about Sulli and William.

"No sign of Ralston?" Barker O inquired.

"No one said anything. William's had his hamstring cut. The girl is put with the simpleminded. The men who caught them drove a cart that the Master wanted to study. That's how we came by this mare."

A deep breath, then Catherine, voice low, remarked, "I expect William and Sulli's lives will be unremitting agony."

DoRe nodded. "The Missus, well, you know."

"I think I do. Ah, that was quick."

Jeddie, breathing more heavily than Tulli, handed her the money.

"For the mare." She then gave DoRe ten dollars. "For coming to me first. Penny will be good for John." She named her son, who was coming onto three.

"He's growing, growing, growing. He'll soon outgrow his pony." She reached over to pat the mare standing by the fence, seemingly interested in the conversation. "Penny will solve that problem. Thank you, DoRe. By the way, I'll go write Maureen a letter thanking her, of course, which will give you time to visit Bettina."

A broad grin revealed his feeling. "Yes, Miss Catherine."

"She's in the kitchen. Go in."

For a man with a limp, he moved fast up toward the house.

Turning to Barker O, a tall man, Catherine remarked, "Sooner or later, I, too, will limp. All horsemen do."

Barker O smiled. "Not you."

Jeddie and Tulli listened. Then Tulli piped up. "What about Sweet Potato?"

Barker O gave him a stern look. "What's the matter with you, boy? You don't go asking the Missus or any of us questions."

He hung his head.

"You will ride Sweet Potato and keep John company."

"Oh, yes, Miss Catherine." He was thrilled.

"Jeddie, you'll wind up watching both of them."

"I'll do my best."

As they watched Penny, two old retired "girls" came over. Everyone visited.

DoRe no sooner stuck his head in the kitchen than Bettina hugged and kissed him, putting a moist slice of pound cake in front of him.

"Fresh."

"Great day." He took a bite. "Where's Serena?"

He named her assistant.

"Back pantry."

He then told her everything about William, Sulli, the slave catchers, and Maureen's chaining William.

"William was a fool. He'll probably always be a fool, but I hate to see a man chained by the wrists. He's been moved to the carriage workshop. Heard now it's only one leg."

"Given that he stole a horse, beat Jeddie with his crop after pushing him off, and ran off, then came back to steal more, he's lucky to be alive."

"If you call what he'll be facing for the rest of his days life." He polished off that pound cake. "Missus Selisse has never been a merciful woman."

"That's a nice way to put it."

DoRe shrugged. "Bettina, if she were a horse, I'd say she broke bad. This all goes back to Sheba and the jewelry."

Satisfied with the fire level, Bettina sat opposite the man she loved. "You would know better than any of us."

A flash of fear, quickly conquered, coursed through him. "Why do you say that?"

"You've lived at Big Rawly all your life. You've known Sheba's mother, her two crazy brothers, and Sheba. And you all knew Sheba when the Mistress wasn't around."

"She was worse than the Missus." He exhaled loudly.

"She fooled everyone. She escaped with a fortune."

"Maybe," he said noncommittedly.

Bettina, eyes narrowed slightly, said not a word, but she realized for the first time that DoRe knew a lot more than he was telling.

34

July 1, 2019

Monday

Sitting at a lunch table at Keswick Golf Club, Harry and Carlton talked about everything. They knew so many of the same people.

Finally, Harry focused on what was bothering her.

"Jeannie Cordle's death at the AHIP fundraiser. You kindly explained to us, as did the medical people, about the Solanaceae family. How easy would it have been to make, distill, crush, whatever, a lethal dose?"

"Pretty easy. There are three thousand members of this particular family. Potatoes, eggplants, tomatoes, and the killer ones, like deadly nightshade. Lots of choices."

"Is there any other way she could have been poisoned? The sheriff's department focused on the obvious method, ingestion, but no one else's food had been contaminated. And there would have been no way to guarantee that only her plate was touched. Sheriff Shaw said they thoroughly questioned the waitstaff."

"To be poisoned by one of these plants, it has to enter your system. Your digestive system. For instance, Hindu Datura, the common name, was used as knockout drops to snag virgins into prostitution, especially in the eighteenth and nineteenth centuries. And in answer to your question about formulating a lethal dose, if you know what you're doing, it's time-consuming but fairly simple."

"Could Jeannie have drunk it?"

"It would have shown up on the glass. Since she died at the fundraiser, I am sure everything was closely scrutinized. Or at least everything from her table."

"What about putting the dose on someone as a cream?" Harry wondered.

"The skin would react quickly. And to administer a lethal dose, I'd think you'd need a trowel to apply it. That I don't know. Perhaps a toxicologist would or even a general practitioner."

Harry, leaning back in her chair, watched the line at the driving range for a moment. "And this poison would have to have entered her system at the party?"

"Given the speed with which she presented her symptoms, yes. For instance, in murder the spouse is always the prime suspect. Frank, if he had wanted to kill her and had given her, say, drops or some food laced with the stuff, he would never have gotten her to Castle Hill. Not that I for an instant think he did it. If he tampered with her food or drink at Castle Hill, someone would have seen him."

Harry shook her head. "She was the easiest person to get along with, helpful, fun. Just makes no sense. Of course, Frank didn't kill her. No sense at all."

"Murder sometimes only makes sense to the killer."

"I agree. But what if this was a mistake? You know, they got the wrong person."

"It's possible. Let me go back a minute. You can die from topically absorbing the alkaloid, but it's not that common and no one having stuff rubbed on them would ignore the rash, the discomfort."

"Is exposure always fatal?" Harry leaned forward, a sliver of chicken on her fork.

"No. For thousands of years humans have understood the properties of various plants, herbs. In controlled doses hallucinations can occur, so let's say someone is passing her- or himself off as a prophet or a witch. Slip a tiny bit of the stuff in tea or have your client smoke it."

"So our killer went out, found or had planted angel's trumpet, jimsonweed, what have you, and chopped it up or pureed it?"

Carlton shook his head. "These herbs can be dried and stored. When you go into an herbalist's place, think of the plants hanging upside down. Again, Harry, humans have known about this stuff for thousands of years. Rarely is it fatal unless it is intended to be fatal."

"All the symptoms, flushed skin, trouble breathing, dilated pupils—I checked, read everything I could—well, seizure and then cardiac arrest. Right?"

He nodded. "Harry, whoever wanted Jeannie Cordle dead knew what they were doing."

She sat silently for a moment, eyes drawn back to a fellow at the driving range with a most peculiar swing. "I still can't believe anyone wanted that woman dead."

"Well, someone, somewhere, was supposed to die."

Smiling sheepishly, Harry said, "Apart from the fact that I wanted to see you, I really asked you here for my book. I kind of wandered off into stuff. Do it all the time. Drives Susan crazy. My husband tunes me out, I suspect, but at any rate he is used to it."

"I'm not tuning you out." Carlton smiled.

"Okay. The Dorcas Guild—you met some of us at St. Luke's—we are going to research everything we can for a written history of the church, the people, everything we can think of. I think I backed into being the editor in chief."

"I see."

"St. Luke's has preserved its records and many of the old families, early congregants, still live in the area. So we'll be asking to read family documents, Bibles, lots of stuff. I was wondering if you might be willing to look over what we pull together for the plantings, the garden designs. We could pay you." She hastily added, "We intend to do so."

He held up his hand. "Harry, I am not taking money from St. Luke's for doing what I love to do. Of course, I will read whatever you put in front of me. In fact, if any of the early design papers remain, I would love to see them. Having spent time in England, as you know, I am fascinated by the horticultural knowledge our ancestors brought with them as well as the adjustments they had to make."

Harry soaked that up, then connected.

"Imagining the adjustment coming from a vastly different latitude? I think of that when I think of those early slaves. Losing a war or being captured by your enemy tribe and sold to some Portuguese who then sells you to the English slavers. Nothing would be familiar. Maybe not even a rose."

He nodded in agreement. "I am continually humbled by how people survived." Taking a deep breath, he added, "But I think some of those early slaves had a gift for growing things, a curiosity about plants. As animals we differ more than, say, giraffes. We are so weak, we need groups, and in those groups we all need different abilities for all to survive. Someone who can grow things, identify species, use herbs to heal, that's a really valuable person. I truly think some people arrived here with those abilities, just like some people are natural healers."

Harry thought long and hard about this. "Yes. It's odd how we don't want to think of ourselves as animals who must adapt like any animal must to survive. We think we are above other species. I don't. I think we had to work together, create tools and stuff because we are weak and slow compared to other species. Your idea about inborn abilities makes so much sense." She paused. "I'm not certain I have any, really. I bump along."

"You don't give yourself credit," he generously replied.

"Ah." She shrugged.

"You got me to open up. You have curiosity and you can get people to work together. I'd say those are inborn talents."

"Well," she thought, "good for me." Then she laughed and he laughed with her.

Driving back to Crozet, Harry sang to herself the whole way. Her singing lowered to a hum as she reviewed what Carlton had told her about those dangerous plants and herbs. She just couldn't believe anyone would want to kill Jeannie Cordle.

Reaching home, she bounded out of her Volvo station wagon, miles starting to show, and skipped into the house.

"*Must have had a good time,*" Tucker remarked.

"*She didn't bring us any treats,*" Pewter grumbled.

Pirate stood up, putting his head under Harry's hand, his tail wagging.

"*Suck up,*" Pewter complained.

"*Go eat crunchies,*" Mrs. Murphy advised.

"*I have a delicate system. I need steak tartar, not something manufactured by a large company. Who knows what's in that stuff?*"

"Susan." Harry reached her friend on the phone. "Carlton said he would do it. He doesn't want a penny. I had the best time with him."

"Good for you. He will be a big help." Susan liked hearing good news.

"We talked about a lot of stuff. He's so thoughtful. Kind of intellectual. I'm not." She paused.

That pause gave Susan her chance. "Have you only just figured that out?"

"You can sit on a tack," Harry fired back, then laughed, and Susan laughed with her.

"I have news." Susan baited her.

"Tell."

"Maybe."

"Susan, I hate it when you do this."

"Okay. The bones we uncovered, well, dug up, really, at Old Rawly appear to be related to the bones buried under the red oak. Ned pushed the medical examiner's office and they were interested, so they hurried things along."

"What can that mean?" Harry paused. "Our unknown woman was a slave?"

"Maybe. Maybe not. She could have been exceedingly beautiful and had freedoms not shared by women not so blessed by nature. Think of the gorgeous women in New Orleans, all living in houses kept by white men, men married to white women. A beautiful woman is a trophy in any century."

"New Orleans wasn't ours until 1803."

"Harry, that doesn't mean women weren't kept no matter whose flag they were flying."

"True." Harry inhaled. "Instead of making things clear, this is more confusing."

"Gran is going through all the Bibles, all the records, grain purchases, you name it. Given this information, she is even more driven to read everything. I guess some of this will show up in our St. Luke's history."

"The Selisses were Catholics."

"I know that, but Jeffrey Holloway was not. After Maureen died and he married Marcia West, he attended St. Luke's. They are buried there."

Harry paused. "They are. Seems we have a lot of interesting dead people. Susan, the head of UVA's theater department won't have answers about bones, but rather clothing and fashion from other centuries."

"Yes."

"Let's get them to look at the necklace. That might help us with one set of bones."

35

Tuesday

"It's cooler down here," Harry noted as they walked along Ivy Creek.

"Before paved roads, the people at Big Rawly and those at Cloverfields could simply walk across the dirt road if they wished. Well, anyone could, really."

"Do you think of your ancestors? You know, that 23andMe stuff or Ancestry.com?"

Susan shrugged as she ducked under a low-hanging cedar limb. "Cedars breed chiggers, I swear it."

"True." Harry ducked as well.

"Ancestors. Well, the paternal half we know because Big Rawly is still in their—I should say *our*—name. But it's funny, much as I love history, I have never cared that much about my own. You know, Gran has started on the first family Bible. She's excited about the St. Luke's history. I kind of am, too."

"Me, too. Maybe if Mom and Dad had lived longer, I would have asked questions about our own ancestors. Sometimes Dad would talk about the potato famine in Ireland when his people first came over. Mom swore her line was descended from a Frenchman who jumped ship during the Revolutionary War. One way or another, we're here."

"And our people chose it," Susan added.

"I don't know. I think thousands were driven to it, but that's better than being carried against your will. But when you lose a war, I expect you get brutalized one way or the other." Harry's voice fell.

"Going on, as we speak, somewhere in the world." Susan pointed out the obvious.

"Think wars will end?"

"Never." Susan said this with finality. "Look, there are the caves."

They walked a bit faster, the running water of the creek soothing.

Harry stepped into a large opening. "You could hide in here. Goes back a ways."

"This one, too." Susan walked into a smaller one, the dampness immediately apparent despite the July heat. "Used to be an old still down here somewhere, back in the mid-nineteenth century. Grandpa said the still was used to divert people from their cover, being a hiding place for runaways."

"When we really start digging into St. Luke's history, these caves will be important. Better take good photographs."

Susan agreed. "When we get to it. I wish I had known the Wests. In middle age they helped start the Underground Railroad. By that time William Wilberforce had made a big impact in Parliament in England. Charles always had good information from his brother, I expect. I can't quite imagine it."

"You'd think Rachel's sister would have picked up on it. But we don't know so much about the Schuylers, as they were Anglicans. I guess those Bibles are around somewhere."

Susan replied, "The University of Virginia has them in their Virginiana collection. Ned's already on it. I think he's more excited about the history than we are."

Walking on, they found the narrow path up to the easternmost pastures of Ingleside, once part of the former Cloverfields into the mid-nineteenth century. Stopping, they surveyed the land.

Susan looked over the higher pastures. "What a beautiful spot. Our ancestors sure had an eye, didn't they?"

"It's a perfect place until the wind blows hard from the northwest in winter." Harry stood up, the soil falling to the ground. "We at least have central heating."

"A triumph." Susan grinned. "You know, when Mom and Dad would go up to the Adirondacks for the summers, it was so gorgeous. I can't imagine the winters. Really, all those states bordering Canada, the winters are too extreme for me."

"Shorter growing season, too." Harry felt the sun on her head.

Susan looked up when Harry did. "High noon."

"Yep."

"Let's go back. We need to be at the schoolhouses by one-thirty. We'll just about make it."

The two dear friends arrived at the schools right on time. Half of the Dorcas Guild was there, along with people from St. Mary's, the Catholic church; Mount Olivet, the Presbyterian church; the Methodist church; and a goodly smattering of Baptists. For whatever reason, the church groups, once they became aware of the potential destruction of the three buildings, had all banded together. Tazio took charge. The bringing of electricity up to grade meant the walls all needed to be repainted and repaired first.

So every wall had its crew.

Janice called out as she was carefully doing the bare-bones trim, "Is the potbellied stove staying?"

Tazio, opposite wall, replied, "Yes. The question is: Can we actually use it?"

Mags quickly added, "I thought the point was we cycle the kids through here in each of the different buildings from all the schools in the county for two weeks apiece. You know, living history."

Harry called back, "Some kid might burn himself on the stove."

"Oh, come on," Janice answered. "Do we really think kids are that stupid?"

A long silence followed this and then Susan said, "Best not to examine this too closely."

"It's not the kids. It's the county board of supervisors." Tazio dipped her brush in a bucket. "If anyone gets burned, they fear they will be sued."

"Hell, Tazio, if the kids are in a brand-new school and trip down the stairs, they'll be sued. And it can go all the way to the state board of education. Everyone is scanning the horizon to find someone upon which to blame their troubles." Harry shrugged.

"Don't you think it's always been this way?" Pamela Bartlett asked as she measured windows.

"Probably, but now we have the media to tell us twenty-four hours a day how grim and dangerous every single day can be." Mags laughed.

"Rats." Tazio stepped down the ladder. "Need a hex screwdriver."

"For painting?" Harry asked.

"No. I noticed a . . . well, no matter." She went to her large bag, started rummaging.

Harry laughed at her. "What do you have in there?"

Tazio pulled out a small kit filled with screwdrivers, one adjustable wrench, followed by a tube of something, a toothbrush and toothpaste, powder.

Harry couldn't stand it. She had to climb down her own ladder and peer into the cavernous canvas purse/bag/carryall. "That's one hell of a ditty bag."

"Here." Tazio, laughing at the description, handed her a tube, Bougie Bee emblazoned on it. "Rub some on your arm. Try it."

Harry unscrewed the top, screwed up the bottom to make the hardened creme stand up, and did as she was told.

"Rub it in."

Again Harry did as she was told. "What is this stuff? Makes my skin feel soft and I'm out in the sun all the time."

"I use it on my face but it's for your skin wherever you want," Tazio replied.

"Where did you get this? I've never seen it."

"A friend of mine gave it to me. She's from Kentucky. I expect if I look for it on the Internet I'll find it, but I'll probably wait until I run out. Then again, I could just call her."

Harry looked into the bag. "Tazio, you could start a beauty parlor with all the stuff you have in here."

"I need to sit down and divide this up into a tool kit and a real handbag. I forget. I go home, take a shower, and go to bed."

Harry lifted out a compact as Tazio pointed for her to do so. "This is lovely." Opening it, she sniffed the packed powder, the usual take-the-shine-off-your-nose stuff.

"Susan!" Harry looked at the compact and then again picked up the Bougie Bee cylinder.

"What?" Susan looked down at Harry.

"Jeannie's purse. What if whatever killed her was in her purse?"

Now they all stopped.

Janice placed the paintbrush across the can.

"What do you mean?" Mags carefully stepped down.

"We know the poison, we know the family. What if it was in her purse. A candy that had been altered or something like Bougie Bee, very absorbent." Harry quickly fished her phone out of her back pocket and dialed the county sheriff's department. "Is Sheriff Shaw there?"

"No, Harry." They all knew her, thanks to her getting into scrapes. "Call him on his cell."

"Harry, you can't do that. You don't know anything," Janice counseled.

"He's used to me," she replied, and he was.

Punching in the numbers, she waited.

"Hello." Sheriff Shaw answered as he was driving down to White Hall.

She told him of her idea and wondered if he might see if Frank still had her purse.

The sheriff actually listened, agreed, and hung up.

"There," Harry triumphantly declared. "He did not cuss me out. He thought it was worth trying." As they climbed back up on their ladders, Janice shaking her head, Susan saying nothing, Harry loudly said, "I know you all think I'm crazy, but you never know."

4:00 p.m.

Harry, Susan, Pamela, Janice, Mags, and Reverend Jones met Professor Cynthia Lindstrom at St. Luke's. They went down to the large basement where Reverend Jones unlocked the safe, twirling the large wheels like a pilot's wheel. With the door open, the reverend placed a large block against the door kept for this purpose. One never wanted that huge door to close.

Switching on the lights, Reverend Jones said to Professor Lindstrom, "This is climate controlled. You can see the filled shelves. Those boxes contain records starting with construction. University of Virginia, William and Mary, would like these records. To us they are invaluable. There is not a year that passes that I don't consult them for something."

Professor Lindstrom, mid-fifties, stared at this historical treasure. "What about the Lutheran Church, the national council?"

"Yes. Everyone wants our records, but they belong here." He smiled, a warm smile.

Walking to a shelf, Reverend Jones carefully lifted down a wooden box, one and a half by one and a half feet.

"The jewelry?" Professor Lindstrom was anxious to see it.

"Let's go upstairs. You need to see it in natural light." Reverend Jones smiled.

They tromped back upstairs as Pamela explained to the curious professor, "We are all from the Dorcas Guild, the women's organization. We have reburied the skeleton, bones, of course, and one of our number, Harry Haristeen, was the person who called our attention to the tipped tombstone of the Taylors. Also, there were cutting marks, like a big stiletto had been driven into the soil."

Harry nodded to the professor. "I'm in charge of Buildings and Grounds."

Once in Reverend Jones's office, he opened the box where the necklace and earrings glittered in the rich blue velvet.

"How beautiful!" Professor Lindstrom exclaimed.

The ladies stepped back, throttling their urge to crowd.

"May I?" She reached for the earrings.

"Of course," Reverend Jones said.

She turned the earrings over, then turned them to their front side again. She replaced them, drawing her face closer to the necklace. "Extraordinary."

Mags, thrilled, offered, "Put it on me. Seeing it on a person might help. Reverend Jones, may I?"

"If it will help," he agreed with some hesitation.

Janice lifted the pearls interspersed with diamonds from the velvet. "This is heavy." She then placed it around Mags's neck, fastening the old golden clasp, itself fine workmanship.

"How could anyone walk?" Mags asked, as she in fact walked to the mirror on the back of the door. "I have never seen anything so gorgeous in my life."

Professor Lindstrom stared intensely at the heavy treasure. "It falls perfectly on you. Would you say you are, m-m-m, five foot three?"

"Close," Mags rejoined.

"That would be about average. There were tall women, of course. These were made for a woman who could carry them. The style is high Spanish, most likely, given the design, from the early seventeenth century."

"So by the eighteenth century they were already heirlooms?" Susan was quick to figure things out.

"These were made for a high noblewoman at the Spanish court.

Remember, Spain was the richest country in Europe for centuries. There was a reason Queen Elizabeth encouraged Sir Francis Drake and others to fight and rob ships from the New World bound for Spain. Anything to weaken Spain and enrich England."

"Think that's what happened here?" Harry was fascinated.

"No way to tell unless we find records or portraits of an English duchess or powerful woman like Bess of Hardwick wearing them. Bess was rich, probably the richest woman in England. Convention meant little to her." Professor Lindstrom couldn't take her eyes off the necklace. "One of the reasons the necklace is so heavy is it encouraged the wearer to move slowly with a stately tread."

"Is it possible this necklace was bought from a Spanish family by new money here? In South America or the Caribbean?" Harry asked. "Families do lose money."

"It is. However, it is highly doubtful that anyone from our colonies bought it. This was not our fashion, plus the kind of public display did not come into fashion until much later, really with industrialization."

Reverend Jones folded his hands. "Fashion reveals much, I assure."

"Who would wear this here in Virginia in 1786?" Janice asked.

"A woman, possibly titled, married to an ambassador from Spain, possibly a businessman from what we call South America, then called New Spain."

"Professor, why wear it, given our aversion at the time to such display?" The reverend wondered.

"Well, it would display quiet arrogance, speaking of display. It would show us, former colonists, how drab we were, how insignificant in the Old World. This, whoever wore it, was a display of raw power. One could read it as a warning."

This created silence. No one had considered that.

Finally Susan spoke. "So, whoever owned this, she, her husband, or possibly her keeper, might be in politics but not in tune with the New Republic."

"Exactly," came the quiet reply from the professor.

"Could it have been bought by a foreign businessman living here or visiting here but doing business outside our country?"

"Yes. This would make a statement to whomever he did business with in Europe, even Russia. There was trade with Russia. It was picking up."

"Professor, any idea why the woman who wore it died of a broken neck?" Janice asked.

A long pause followed this until Professor Lindstrom, forefinger touching her lips for an instant, proclaimed, "Obviously, she was hated, perhaps feared. Then again, maybe she should not have been wearing the necklace. She might have aroused a lethal jealousy."

Susan stepped around Mags. "We don't want that to happen to you."

As she unclasped the fabulous piece, a dark cloud scudded overhead with a gust of wind.

Harry shivered. *No good will come of this,* she thought to herself.

36

Like a thief in the night, the January thaw came and went. Ralston, Tidbit next to him, walked out to the large paddock, a few flakes smacking his face. Determined not to move like a man in pain, Ralston held his back straight, his head high. Opening the gate to the paddock, he turned Tidbit around, slipped off her halter, told her to go. She turned around, beheld her equine sewing circle, and off she galloped. Tidbit made him smile.

Walking back to the mares' barn, Ralston felt he would never be happy again. Without the horses he would feel even more lonely, miserable, angry. Believing he would find a way to free Sulli and kill William drove him on. Unrealistic as this was, the hope kept him moving.

Ard waved to him. Ralston stooped.

"Yes, sir."

"Mares look good. Be sure to tell me if anyone comes into season. Mr. Finney wants to breed a few of his mares."

"Yes, sir. He has some good ones."

"It's a good thing they exercise themselves out there."

"Yes, sir. I'll ride anyone, anytime, but it's so hard to keep your fingers and toes warm. Can't feel my feet."

Ard chuckled. "Winter's hell. Why the priest tells us hell is fire and brimstone, I don't know. I say it's frozen." He pulled his scarf tighter. "Next stop, Dipsy."

"He can talk," Ralston observed.

Ard laughed. "Sure can, but I've never found he says anything."

Ralston watched as the farm manager walked off, then returned to cleaning the stable. Scrubbing the water buckets irritated him. Everyone has a least favorite chore. That was his. He picked up a stiff brush, chopped out last night's frozen water, got to it. He wished he had asked Barker O more questions. Ralston was beginning to realize good people lived, worked, were enslaved at Cloverfields, and he was too foolish to learn from them. He swore he would learn from everyone around him here. He'd make money on the side. No matter how many years it took, he would one day make enough to free Sulli.

Sulli, resigned to never being free, held a baby born blind. Olivia told her that blind people could do any number of things but you had to teach them. So Sulli held the baby, putting a rattle in its tiny fingers.

Olivia came back into the building, unwound her scarf, and draped her heavy shawl over the old chair close to the fire. "Winter's back."

"It is."

Olivia bent over, tickled the baby. "She'll learn quickly. You'll be surprised."

"Her mother takes her at night. Better she be with her mother," Sulli responded.

"People underestimate the blind, the deaf. But we have her in the day now and I'll show you what to do." She smiled broadly. "And we have years. But oh how fast they grow. Do you want children?"

"No," Sulli firmly replied. "I don't want a man. I don't want children. Why bring a child into slavery?"

Olivia listened, thought. "I don't have much of an answer, Sulli, but I truly believe if a child is brought into this world and loved, it is a good thing, no matter what the circumstances. And I also believe our Moses will come. I probably won't live to see it, but I hope you do."

"Olivia"—Sulli's voice registered sorrow—"no one is going to free us now or ever. We're like this blind baby. We have to grope our way through life."

"Chile, you've suffered a harsh lesson. Don't let it spoil what joys you may have."

Sulli looked at Olivia, whom she respected. "I hope you're right, but I'm not holding my breath." She used the old phrase.

Olivia sat next to her, took the baby, kissed her soft cheek. "In Christ we are all free. Give yourself to the Lord, Sulli. Look around you, look at the unhappiness. Doesn't matter if they are rich, poor, white, or black. A lot of unhappy people. Jesus died for our sins. Believe in Christ. Have faith. The kingdom of heaven will be yours."

Sulli didn't believe a word of it but she said nothing. It's one thing to disagree, another to be blasphemous. She held out her finger and the baby wrapped her fingers around Sulli's. A flicker shivered through Sulli. Maybe she wasn't dead inside after all.

While the flakes lazed down, Barker O and DoRe high up in their separate carriages, each wrapped in a heavy coat with an extra layer across the back, looked down at Jeffrey.

"DoRe, you go right. Barker, left. Figure eights. I need to see the turning radius."

The two drivers did as asked. They arrived back in front of Jeffrey.

"Drive almost down to the house. Turn back to me. Come straight at me."

Jeffrey knelt down, the earth cold and his knees now wet as he watched the carriage move off. His eyes never left the wheels. A badly set wheel is a disaster waiting to happen. He wanted to build carriages that could take punishment but have a bit of give. Both of the big beautiful carriages came toward him. They looked good.

He stood up, oblivious to the cold, and gave more instructions. When all was done, Barker O and DoRe's shoulders were white, as were their beaver top hats. The two men then unhitched the horses, leaving the carriages outside the big workshop. Men pulled those elegant conveyances inside, which Jeffrey also watched.

"Balance. Balance. Balance," he said to himself.

Barker O and DoRe, all that leather in their hands, walked behind the unhitched horses, back to the barn. Pete and Norton ran out when they saw them, both young men deeply impressed by the skill the two drivers displayed. Barker O and DoRe, the best at what they did, possessed powerful upper bodies, sensitive hands. Joking, teasing each other, they walked into the carriage barn, DoRe first.

Norton walked up to DoRe. "How about if I start with Doubloon?"

"Fine. I'll hold the reins until you're done."

Pete ran up to the four that Barker O had driven and duplicated Norton's method, which was to take the inside front horse first.

Unhitching took twenty careful minutes. Once each horse was in his stall, the fellows took the heavy harness, then the reins from the drivers.

Barker O walked to a far stall. "You know that sweet mare, Penny? Doing great. Miss Garth hopped up on her. Loved her. Said Penny would take care of her father. You know, this horse . . ." He turned, stopped talking, because Maureen walked into the stable.

"How were my husband's carriages? You know he wants everything perfect."

"Drove light as a feather," DoRe answered.

She nodded to Barker O, then stopped a moment.

"I was surprised that you wanted the mare. She's common look-ing."

"Yes, ma'am, but she will take care of Mr. Ewing and in time young John." Barker O agreed with her, or at least said what she wanted to hear.

"I suppose that's wise, but your master looks good for his age. He should be on an elegant, powerful horse. Well, let me check with my husband to see if he is pleased." She left them.

No one said anything, continuing with their chores.

Finally Barker O whispered, "She has eyes and ears everywhere."

"H-m-m." DoRe nodded.

"Where's William?"

"Working in a smaller workplace. Mr. Jeffrey wants to build work carts, wagons. He's chained at night."

Whispering again, Barker O said, "Surprised she didn't break his other leg."

"There's still time," DoRe whispered back.

The two worked silently as the young men cleaned up the horses and then all would clean that heavy leather.

While Jeffrey acted thrilled to see his wife and answered her questions about the drive, he mentioned that Barker O and DoRe had done a wonderful job, and might she send DoRe back to Clover-fields with Barker O so the two could work out a driving path and a field so he could run the same tests on all his carriages and the wagons he hoped to build?

"Give the good man a night with his lady. I know I would be be-reft if I could only be next to you once a month or so. A man needs the woman he loves." This was followed by a warm kiss. She said yes.

Later

Bettina and DoRe sat by her fire. DoRe, in a close chair, held her hand.

"Today I tried to wrap lamb chops in bacon. Have to try new things."

DoRe smiled at her. "You're always coming up with something. Barker O and I are trying to figure out a course where Mr. Jeffrey can test his carriages and wagons. Can't say as I have your flair, but I like new things, too."

"How's William?"

"He's chained at night. She's making an example out of both of them. Not that anyone at Big Rawly needed examples." He sighed. "Elizabetta gave everyone that."

"She was never well liked. Not hated like Sheba but not well liked," Bettina remarked.

"Whoever gets close to the Missus thinks they can give orders. Goes to their head. No one can trust Miss Selisse."

"Not even Mr. Jeffrey?"

He shrugged. "Maybe. He dotes on her, tells her she's beautiful. The man is no fool."

"You'd think that Sulli and William would have learned from Moses and Allie." Bettina named the two accused of killing Francisco Selisse, who then ran off.

"Young. Thought they were smarter." He shook his head. "Every now and then Mr. Charles tells me about my boy. He's doing good. Even when he was a boy, Moses watched and listened. William always shot off his mouth. People are just different."

"Moses still with that Irish captain?"

"No. He lived there and worked for them. Still does things for them but he mostly works with carriage makers."

"Quakers?"

DoRe shook his head. "No. The Captain is a Catholic. His wife, a Lutheran, and I don't know what the carriage makers are, but the Quakers have people thinking their way. Never happen here."

"Surely William and Sulli knew that Moses and Allie ran away?"

"Everyone did. My boy didn't kill the Master and neither did Allie. I tell you, Bettina, I think it was the Missus herself or Sheba or both. Thick as thieves and they both hated Francisco."

She rocked, then slowed. "DoRe, you know that Moses and Allie hid in the caves. Rachel and Charles helped. Mr. Ewing doesn't know and he never will. What I never told you was that Allie had a baby, white as snow."

DoRe nodded. "Francisco's."

"That man deserved killing even if Sheba and the Missus did it. Both, well, all three, cruel."

"I know Allie hanged herself. I thought it was because she couldn't follow Moses."

"No. If the baby had been his, she would have lived for it. I expect Mr. Charles and Mr. John would have gotten her up to Pennsylvania somehow. The sorrows of the world, DoRe. Such sorrow."

DoRe was quick to put it together. "Marcia. The baby Rachel passes off as her cousin's, an unwed cousin, so it's a family scandal?"

"Rachel is clever. This way people can talk about the child but they have no idea."

"Miss Catherine and Mr. John?"

"They know, of course. As does Father Gabe. I think Ralston figured it out because he was always lurking around the weaving cabin where Allie was hidden and delivered the baby. Another no-good one. Somehow he didn't get caught."

"Miss Selisse didn't pay for him."

"Still, they could have caught him."

DoRe grunted assent. "Sold him if they did. William says nothing. Sulli is with the simpleminded. I don't guess they care."

"Seems to be so."

"So people here know?"

"Our people know. No one will ever tell. Ever."

"She can pass that child."

"She can. I say good luck to her. If I could pass I would, wouldn't you?"

"Yes," he said, and cleared his throat. "Bettina, you and I will spend the rest of our lives together. You've told me a secret. I never suspected that little girl being Allie's. Well, here's my secret. I killed

Sheba and buried her in the Taylors' grave at St. Luke's. They'd just died. Easy to do and no one would suspect. What she did to my boy, lying that he had killed Francisco, and that beautiful girl he loved, it was all unforgivable. My only regret is I killed her quickly. I wish I could have made her suffer."

"I understand," Bettina calmly replied, for she did. "Did she steal the Missus's jewels?"

"Wore them. Wore them."

"Are they with her?"

"They are. If even one of those diamonds or pearls showed up, well, I don't know. Miss Selisse is still in a rage about those things."

"Anyone suspect you?"

"No. I threw her in a cart, covered her with a horse blanket. Buried her in the night. No one will ever know."

"I truly hope not." She rocked more again, then said, "You did the right thing."

"Bettina, some people are on this earth to hurt others. To lie, cheat, and steal. No one was ever safe at Big Rawly as long as Sheba was alive. The Missus has her spies, always will, but Sheba knew us, knew how our people think. She knew how to tell a lie with just enough truth to fire up the Missus. No one is really safe there now, but it's not as bad as it once was."

"You did the right thing," Bettina repeated. "And soon I pray to the Good Lord you will be here."

He squeezed her hand.

37

Wednesday

"Did you find a pair of shoes you can walk in without crippling yourself?" Susan asked Harry as they ate lunch at Bottoms Up.

If you can support the businesses of people you know, you should. Both friends did this on a regular basis, whether it was the feed store, the grocery store, or any other store. If you knew the owner, that's where you shopped. No big-box stores for them if they could help it.

"Bought a pair of Stan Smith sneakers. Bright white. Fit like a glove." Harry picked up a french fry, dipping it in mayonnaise. "I won't shame St. Luke's for the Fourth of July parade."

"You and mayo."

"We all have our little ticks." Harry popped the dripping slender french fry into her mouth. "So what are you walking in?"

"Like you. Tennis shoes. Had to wash them."

"At least you didn't have to spend money."

"Harry, you can afford new sneakers. Anyway, you can't walk through the town for the Fourth of July parade in your work boots."

"Yes, Mother." Harry's lip turned up slightly.

"Well, someone has to dress you. God knows you can't do it yourself. Speaking of Stan Smith sneakers, it's interesting what's coming back into fashion. Sneakers more or less got so technical. You looked as if you were ready for a moonwalk."

"What's old is new again," Harry mentioned as two young women walked in wearing tie-dye T-shirts. "Glad we were born after tie-dye."

"Not anymore." Susan laughed. "The colors are pretty. Pamela says the sash is ready for us, by the way. So we all wear our blue T-shirts and white skirts. Another purchase—I'm surprised you didn't have the vapors."

A wry grin started on Harry's pleasing face. "You know why?"

"I'm all ears."

"Because we'll be cooler marching in a skirt than pants. And think of our people on the float, eighteenth-century clothes. They'll be sweating bullets."

"Bet they will. This has been a big time for us. Herb's birthday, our homecoming, and now the float. I still can't believe St. Peter's Guild built a small replica of St. Luke's. To the T."

"What I like is how on both sides of the float, the text of the First Amendment is written. Freedom of religion and here we are, still freedom of religion."

Susan nodded, then looked up as Janice strode over, trailed by Mags.

"How is everything?"

"Wonderful, as always," Susan replied as Harry agreed.

Mags smiled. "Always good to see friends in here."

"We're being served by one of your boys. You have good people."

Janice smiled. "I do. Mags and I pride ourselves on our hiring. We've got four of the young men in the back now loading up trucks.

Our beer will be well represented throughout this county and Virginia tomorrow. The Fourth of July is heaven for a brewer."

"Never thought of that." Harry hadn't either.

"Most businesses have a season. I mean if you're selling to the public. I don't know as lawyers have a season." Janice sat next to Harry on the bench while Mags slid in next to Susan. "Actually beer does well in the summer, as you might suppose, falls off a bit in the winter, but what is making a comeback is hard liquor and cocktails."

"The perfect martini." Susan watched as the tie-dyed girls were seated. "Think it will take that generation a little time to discover a whiskey sour?"

Janice looked around. "You know it does. Being in the business, my analysis is that once people enter the workforce and climb a bit—say, get into their early thirties—their business socials are more sophisticated. Mixed drinks are sophisticated. A lady isn't going to drink out of a bottle of beer; the smart men aren't either. They may stop for a beer after work, but when it's business you need a halo of worldliness, a veneer of sophistication. At least, I think so."

"Never forget country waters," Harry added. "I hear people are paying a bundle for the stuff across the Mason-Dixon Line."

"Always have," Mags remarked. "And the truth is, some of that stuff is remarkable. A great distiller is a great distiller no matter what he, well mostly he, is making. It's both a science and an art."

"People ever ask for it here, under the table?" Harry blurted.

"Sometimes. We can't sell it, of course. Would I like to sell it here? You bet I would," Mags stated.

"Janice, do you think alcohol will always be so strictly controlled?" Susan knew Ned's take on this.

"The amount of money we all pour into Virginia's coffers, without a doubt. My prayer is it won't get worse. Well, I believe we are about to legalize marijuana. First it will start as medical mumbo-jumbo, but then no holds barred. Those tax dollars will roll in like the tide."

"The real question is where does the money go after it rolls in?" Harry then paused. "I sound cynical. I didn't used to be but, except for Ned, I don't trust anyone in public office. Just don't."

Mags smiled. "What about paying them off?"

"Maybe that's the real question. Well, hey, what do I know? I grow hay, sunflowers, and a terrific vegetable garden. I don't make enough to pay off anyone, plus apart from people in the Department of Agriculture, who comes after farmers?"

Janice observed a hand motion from her manager. "I do. Back to work. See you all tomorrow."

As Mags also moved out from the booth, Harry said, "Speaking of illegal hooch, I am going back up to that still one more time. This will be my second time."

"You've already been up there," Mags noted. "Let the sheriff's department go back."

"I know the mountain, they don't."

Harry paid up, her turn, and she and Susan walked out into the brilliant sunshine. Harry's old Ford, a vehicle Susan had ridden in for much of her life, as it had belonged to Harry's father, was parked way in the back, for Bottoms Up was packed.

Passing the rear of the building, a large steel container of hops was attached to the side like oats containers often were at the side of barns. In the shape of large cones, they could hold any grain, horse pellets, too. This allowed a stable to save money by buying in bulk. It also dispensed with all of those fifty-pound bags. You can carry one or perhaps two over a shoulder, but oh, how easy to just turn the stop, out ran the goods, turn it off. While Bottoms Up grew their own hops, they still had to dry them and store them. In the case of a light harvest, hops had to be purchased. The large container illustrated their growing needs.

"Four trucks lined up. I expect they will be coming and going all day."

Susan noted, "That's why the girls put in a big circular road back here that comes out above the car road. Otherwise the traffic jam would have residents in an uproar, justly so."

"Looks like they thought of everything." Harry motioned for Susan to follow her, so they walked to the loading dock. "Given the different kinds of beers they brew, they have stripes on the cartons to read them—easier to load and unload. See, the white stripe for Weiss beer, wheat beer?"

A loaded truck drove off, two young men dropped down the back of another truck, and two more readied to do the same for a third.

"Lots of room." Susan studied the clean interior as boxes were walked in from the loading dock. The door flipped onto the loading dock, which saved time lifting and carrying. A person could pick up a carton and walk it right into the truck.

"Don't most of these trucks have a bit of room so the driver can hang his stuff?" Harry wondered.

"Yeah. Those big trucks, the long-haulers, have all kinds of room. I don't think I could drive one of those with the gears at different levels."

"Be fun to try." Harry grinned. "Well, girl, let's check back at St. Luke's before finishing up our chores. I'm sure yours involves ironing."

Susan shrugged. "You know what? Ten minutes outside on a July day and that skirt will hang perfectly. I'm not ironing anything."

Driving to Susan's brick house, after a quick stop at St. Luke's, the two talked about tomorrow, summer projects, the heat.

"Those trucks aren't huge. If they were carrying contraband, they wouldn't attract as much attention as some of my bigger trucks. I mean like cigarettes or our famous country waters. Never thought much about that stuff before, I mean, before finding the still."

Susan answered. "Think of the fortunes being made from illegal activities. Not just millions but by the drug kingpins, billions."

"You think there's billions in moonshine?"

"I don't know. Look at all the money that was made during Prohibition. Kennedy's father is reputed to be one of those people bringing in liquor across the Canadian line. Guess Al Capone did all right." Susan lifted her purse on her lap as Harry stopped in the driveway.

"Films, TV shows have all these people getting caught. The newspapers print it up but what I wonder is who and how many get away with it? Like those trucks. If they stopped at weigh stations, they would have to hide the stuff and somehow disguise the weight. Right?"

"You'd think so. I don't know how you could disguise the weight of filled bottles."

"What if"—Harry's mind was turning—"what if before you arrived at a weigh station, and they all know where those places are, you pulled over, unloaded the stuff. Someone in on the game could put that in a small truck or a couple of car trunks and would meet you down the road. Takes some care but it could be done. You know, if a truck had a compartment or something—"

"Or people could take cartons up north in their cars. No stopping. Course, you couldn't carry a lot, but still, free money, sort of." Susan considered this.

"The other way"—Harry leaned back on the old bench seat—"would be to get to the coast, either the Chesapeake Bay or the Atlantic, load the stuff on a boat. The boat sails to Philadelphia, New York, Boston. When you think of all the rivers we have in Virginia and the bay, that incredible bay, it'd be easy. You know in colonial times New Jersey was a hotbed of smugglers. Maybe it still is."

"I had no idea." Susan's hand rested on the door handle. "Oh, I almost forgot, Ned said the medical examiner couldn't tell much from the rib cage and the partial skull found by the still. If they'd had the teeth, they would have had a better chance. He was young. They are treating this as a suspicious death. While they have no pelvis, they are pretty sure this was a male. Women rarely are near stills."

"You'd think somebody would miss him?"

"What if that somebody is in Alabama?" Susan opened the door. "Okay, tomorrow. Put Band-Aids on your heels just in case."

"Okay." Harry waited until Susan opened the door to her house, then backed out, headed for home.

The animals, using their animal door, except for Pirate, too big, were flopped in the front yard. Pewter sprawled on the bench with the cushions.

"*You're home!*" Tucker joyfully rose up.

Mrs. Murphy also trotted up to greet Harry.

"*Let me out,*" Pirate pleaded from inside the house.

"*Quiet, please.*" Pewter lifted her head.

Harry pushed open the screen door, which squeaked, opening the door to the kitchen.

"*I missed you. I want to go where you go.*" The long tail smashed against the screened-in porch where Pirate now stood.

Petting the big beautiful head, Harry informed the fellow, "You're still a bit of a puppy. No staying outside until I'm one hundred percent sure."

"*I'll take care of him,*" Tucker promised.

Walking inside the kitchen, Harry tossed her bag on the square, small table. She checked her messages. No reminders about tomorrow's time to rendezvous at St. Luke's since she had talked to everyone in the morning. Fair was still at St. Luke's, putting the finishing touches on the scaled-down model of the church, which would be the centerpiece on the float.

"I need to burn off that lunch. Why do I let her talk me into eating so much?" Harry grumbled. "Come on."

Outside, Harry walked to her trusty truck, opening the door. Pewter and Mrs. Murphy jumped in. She dropped down the tailgate. Pirate leapt up easily. Harry bent over to lift up Tucker.

"Umph." She groaned.

"*Fatty!*" Pewter triumphantly yelled from the truck cab.

Tucker flattened her ears, bared her teeth, as Harry shut the tailgate.

Once in the truck, key turned, that wonderful old V-8 engine rumbled and grumbled.

Harry sat for a moment to listen to what she regarded as a true internal combustion engine. Then she popped it in gear, shift on the floor, backed out, and headed for the road.

Pirate sensibly sat down. *"She's never put me in the back like this."*

"Means we aren't going far. Mom doesn't like us in the back."

"Then why are we here?" the gray-coated big dog asked.

"Not enough room in the old truck. Fair's truck has extra seats but he uses it every day for work," Tucker answered.

"Couldn't Mom buy a new one?"

"Pirate, she'd faint. We'd have to lick her face to revive her. The price of a new truck with extra seats is through the roof."

"Oh. I don't understand money." He dropped his handsome head.

"Nobody does. Humans make it up as they go along. Really."

Turning left on a tertiary road, Dog Leg Road, Harry headed up the mountain. The road became gravel, but Harry kept her foot steady on the gas and the truck made it to the top of the ridge. Harry turned left again, stopping near the switchback path that would lead down the mountain, land she owned on the south side. Susan's land was on the north. A quarter of a mile down the path was a clearing where one could park a vehicle. There was no way to drive down from up here.

Some hunters knew of this location, as did the sheriff's department. GPS proved less useful than old county maps, which were detailed. The department kept decades of such maps.

Cutting off the motor, Harry stepped out and let the dogs down. The cats had already disembarked.

Eyes down, Harry walked slowly to the top of the footpath, pushing the grasses aside with her feet.

A coin, brass, the size of a half dollar, revealed itself in the grasses right at the edge of the big timber.

Harry knelt down. The animals surrounded her.

"Keep your noses out, kids."

"*Who wants a coin?*" Pewter sassed.

Pulling on thin summer work gloves, Harry picked it up, turned it over. Nelson Mandela's face was on one side. The reverse was a representation of the South African flag. Mr. Mandela's birth date and date of death encircled his face, as Harry had turned it back over again. She slipped it into her pocket.

Then they all walked down to the still, untouched since Harry's last visit. Harry stood in the open doorway, stepped inside for a moment, wondering what the glass containers, the tubes, cost. Seemed like the equipment wasn't pricey. Anyone with knowledge could start and run a still.

The others also sat down outside, except Mrs. Murphy who, inside, pushed something around in the dirt.

"What do you have there, Murphy?" Harry knelt down, running her hand over the dirt. "Huh?"

Mrs. Murphy patted the small piece of onyx.

It had chipped off something.

Harry walked outside, the piece in her palm, so she could better examine it in what sun filtered through the trees.

Holding the piece, she dropped it into her jeans pocket.

Once back on the farm she called the sheriff. A squad car, having been parked close by in Crozet, by the library, drove out and took the brass memento coin.

Harry did not offer the cut chipped onyx square. She should have, but she wasn't ready to believe what it could mean.

38

Thursday

What a day to celebrate. Sunshine flooded the tops of the Blue Ridge Mountains, turning them scarlet, then gold. Below, a slight breeze beckoned, combined with decent humidity; maybe this wouldn't be a Fourth of July that turned into a steam bath. One could always hope.

As the numerous marchers for Crozet's myriad organizations drove toward their rendezvous destinations, people remembered former Fourth of July days. Those World War II veterans, long years, long memories, wore their uniforms. Each year that number dwindled but a few determined to walk, at least part of the way. Others rolled along pushed by Boy Scouts, which confused a few people. Many men and women who had served wore their old uniforms, whether from Desert Storm or the endless conflict in Afghanistan. Those still serving and home dazzled in their Army black, Navy whites, full-dress Marines, Air Force blue, and Coast Guard blue. Flags fluttered everywhere. The world for one day was red, white, and blue. All three Albemarle high schools sent their bands. A fife and drum corps in Revolutionary blue and buff, snare drums, fife, and tricorn hats would lead the parade. Naturally civic worthies rode in open cars. Other groups built floats. The grade schoolers built a Snoopy; they all knew Snoopy.

Mrs. Murphy and Pewter, languishing in the kitchen, discussed their fate.

"I belong on the float. Cats hunted mice at St. Luke's. Thanks to us, their grain supply stayed safe, and think of the diseases we spared them. Mice are terrible disease carriers." Pewter vilified mice although she had yet to catch one.

"Then the mice in the barn must be germ-free and flea-free." Mrs. Murphy sat on the windowsill behind the double sink.

Pewter ignored this, warming up for a rant against Tucker and Pirate. "Can you believe those suck-up dogs are going to be on the float. On the float. It's an outrage. Just because Colonel Henry Shelton, USA retired, gave Mom the history of Irish wolfhounds here as well as in war. So maybe there was an Irish wolfhound in the early years at St. Luke's. I don't believe it. No."

"We know there was a corgi because Charles West made many drawings of him. Called Piglet." Mrs. Murphy resisted the obvious jab at the fat cat.

"Big deal." Pewter turned up her black nose, whiskers back.

"I wonder if any regiments have a cat insignia. The Twenty-Seventh, Irish wolf-hound insignia. Got the nickname in 1918 for pursuing the Bolsheviks. Least that's what Mom read."

"Who cares? If we were in the parade, it would be better. Cats made this country great. Wherever the humans settled, we did our jobs. And you know what else is dis-gusting? She shut the animal door. We're stuck in the house. I am getting even. I'm going to go into the library and push books off those shelves. That will teach her."

"Pewter, that's not a good idea."

Too late. Pewter dashed into the library, crawled behind the books on a midlevel shelf, then kicked that whole line of books onto the floor. Mrs. Murphy heard the slap, slap, slap of hardbound books hit-ting the wood. Some of Harry's books had been printed in the mid-nineteenth century and two in the eighteenth, prized possessions of early ancestors.

"You know what else I'm going to do? Bite the Roman candles."

"Pewter, calm yourself."

"This will be a July Fourth no one will forget."

Perhaps Pewter possessed the gift of prophecy, but at ten in the morning no one was in danger of forgetting. The parade would start at the post office, head east, and end at Starr Hill Brewery, a happy outcome for Starr Hill. The idea, to beat the heat, was a good one.

The residents of a six-story home for older people stood or sat on their balconies, waving small flags. The post office parking lot, jammed with the front of the parade, was about ready to start.

Sheriff Rick Shaw, in the third car, a squad car, watched the veterans in front, the very first marchers being the fife and drum corps.

Pamela Bartlett, at the head of the Dorcas Guild, intended to march the length of the parade, about a mile. A gold sash with DOR-CAS GUILD in blue letters captured the eye. It ran from the woman's left shoulder to her right hip where a large bow secured it. Behind the impressive St. Luke's float the men of St. Peter's Guild marched, sashes without the bow.

Fair, thanks to his height, stood on the float as Charles West, both men blond. Charles had been shorter than Fair but tall for his time. A young parishioner, black cascading hair, doubled for Rachel West. They wore clothing of the period. Tucker sat at Fair's feet. The Very Reverend Herbert Jones, at the front of the float, waved. He was dressed in his Trinity robes. Other men represented some of the more famous pastors, wives at their side. A church bell, small but perfect in tone, rang from the steeple. The church on the float had been built to one-fifth the size of the original church.

On the sides of the float was painted the First Amendment guaranteeing the freedom of religion.

The Dorcas Guild had printed up the Twenty-third Psalm. Janice on one side of the marchers, Mags on the other, handed out copies of the psalm to people.

"All right, one, two, hup," Pamela called out as the group in front of them, the Western Albemarle Band, moved out playing John Philip Sousa.

Children waved as the men and women on the float waved. They hollered for Tucker as Pirate, resting next to the Very Reverend Jones, wondered what this was all about. Not that he minded, but it was loud, people happy.

As St. Luke's blessed animals on St. Francis Day, people loved that the dogs graced the float. Anyone in the crowd who attended St. Luke's told those around them about Piglet, the corgi.

St. Mary's also blessed animals on St. Francis Day, as did the Episcopal church.

The African Methodist Episcopalian church also presented its history. The people on the float sang hymns from the ages.

The Dorcas Guild walked in unison, Harry and Susan shoulder to shoulder. They had loved this parade since childhood.

Behind St. Luke's slowly cruised the fire truck from the Crozet Volunteer Fire Department, a dedicated group of people, as firemen and -women are.

What moved the crowd, clearly everyone in Crozet whether a newcomer or an old family person, was the sight of the remaining World War II veterans. People cried. The men waved. But everyone that day knew that fewer and fewer of this generation remained. And the service people behind them understood the sacrifice.

All across America people marched, flags flew. A birthday is a birthday.

Harry and Susan couldn't talk for the music. They kept in step and from time to time Harry would sneak a glance at her husband, Tucker, and Pirate. One husband, two dogs, representing those who had gone before.

Crozet was bigger than a minute, five minutes maybe. Wasn't much to the town hard by the Blue Ridge Mountains. A little place

known as Wayland's Corners back when St. Luke's was built. Over time it became known as Crozet when Claudius Crozet, once a young engineering officer in Napoleon's army, fled to the New World after Waterloo. He hung on, and his abilities finally brought him to Wayland's where, without dynamite, not yet invented, he and his men burrowed four great tunnels through those Blue Ridge Mountains for the railroad.

Harry's new sneakers held up as she thought about this place. It wasn't quaint, it wasn't really even pretty. The land was, the mountains inspirational, but Crozet—well, you could blow through it and not really notice it.

But it was home. The people she loved lived here. Listening to John Philip Sousa, Harry wondered how many people loved where they lived and the people who lived with them or next to them. She hoped most Americans felt that deep taproot.

Pamela's memories, longer than Harry's, included ghosts, those people who once marched along, who now were in another sphere. Pamela had no doubt about an afterlife. Didn't mean she wanted to find out anytime soon. A day like today was too sweet to want to leave the earth.

Finally St. Luke's reached Starr Hill Brewery. Those finishing the parade moved toward the vet clinic. The floats lined up there. When the last group, the Charlottesville High School band, finished up, the parade was over. Most people repaired to the brewery, including the band kids who dutifully drank sodas.

Tucker and Pirate, sitting in the shade, were beset by children. A few adults asked would Pirate hurt their cherub? Most of the kids were already hanging on the giant dog.

Fair, joining Harry, patted the big boy's head while Tucker laughed with everyone.

"You look impressive in those clothes. The hat does the trick."

He doffed his tricorn to her, putting it back on his head. "Keeps the sun out of my face. Actually feels good. I expect the cowboy hat came from the tricorn."

"Could be. Well, sweetheart, you go have a beer with Ned and the boys. I'll stay here with the dogs. Then we can catch a ride back to the truck."

"Sure?"

"I'm sure. I'll stay out here and pass and repass." She used the old Southern expression for talking to everyone, which she did.

Mags came by. "Handed out every leaflet."

"Really started to get hot at the end." Janice walked up. "Well, partner, we should patronize another brewery. It's only right."

Harry looked down at Mag's turquoise and onyx bracelet. She reached for Mag's wrist.

"This is so beautiful." Then she noticed the little bit missing from one of the onyx squares.

Mags, seeing this, said, "Kevin was ready to shoot me. Well, I did bid a lot for it and yes, I've already damaged it, but it can be fixed. Come on, Janice. I'm dry. Harry, come on."

Harry couldn't speak. Swallowing, she rasped out, "Need to stay with the dogs. Fair's in there. I'm fine."

As the two women walked inside, a flood of conflicting emotions filled her. For once in Harry's life, she kept her mouth shut.

In full sheriff's uniform, Sheriff Shaw came up. "Some parade."

"Yes," Harry replied.

"I've got all you girls together. Bring me your lipstick, the . . . I don't know the color. I know you don't have it with you. Your purse is somewhere else, but get it to me no later than tomorrow. If you're coming to the fireworks tonight, bring it then. When you told me to check Jeannie's purse, we checked everything. Susan told me about the lipstick exchange at AHIP. I need your lipsticks."

"Is there something about you I don't know?" Harry smiled. "Is this the new you?"

"No. We checked Jeannie's lipstick, and found it was loaded with deadly nightshade. Best I check everyone's. Is Susan's in there?"

She nodded.

"Have you used it?"

"I have. So has Susan."

"Probably nothing to worry about, but I have to check."

"Of course."

Harry dropped on the half barrel filled with bright pansies, that most serviceable flower.

"Mom, what's wrong?" Tucker stood on his hind legs to lick Harry's hand.

Pirate, standing now, reached over to lick Harry's face. *"I can help."*

"You two are the best dogs. I feel kind of faint." She dropped her head a minute, then lifted it up, taking a deep breath. "I don't want to know what I think I know about two of my dearest friends. I'm not sure what to do. I think I know what to do and yet, and yet, I can't believe it."

39

February 6, 1788

Wednesday

"Extraordinary." Ewing removed his glasses to stare into the fire on this bitterly cold day.

Catherine, glancing up from papers filled with columns of numbers, returned to the columns of potential seed orders and costs.

"My dear, we are living in extraordinary times. The Baron writes that on November 19 the King banished his brother, the Duc d'Orleans, to his estate north of Paris."

"What happened?" She noted her father's perplexed look.

"No Princes of the blood have ever questioned the King in any type of government meeting, for lack of a better term. They have so many qualifications in France, it's confusing. But the technicality addressed by the Duc was: Was this gathering a bed of justice or a royal sitting? The King replied a royal sitting. The Baron couldn't believe what had transpired and he writes that Princes have often crossed their brother throughout France's turbulent history, but when they did so, they had a sword in hand. The King walked out after holding to his views, moved by the solutions of those gathered to speak. The royal family doesn't speak. He and he alone speaks for France. Not a hint of flexibility. Catherine, this can't continue. Seventeen eighty-eight is not the France of Francis I or even Louis XIII."

"There goes trade." Catherine, practical, cared little for what she considered high-flown promises about the future and people's places therein.

"Yes, but the Baron remarks that most people, educated people, considered the King's older brother, Monsieur, to be the source of unrest, a future rival. No, it's Philippe, younger. He's playing to the people, of course. He can do that as easily from his estate as he can in Paris. This will affect us and it won't be just trade."

"Why? What's it to us if a rich nation clings to absolute monarchy?"

"Because that time had passed. Even King George recognized that and he didn't need our war to see it. You know, it's a funny thing, the further away I get from our break with Britain, the easier it is for me to understand why King George and Lord North feared our separation. We were one of many colonies, outposts."

"The others seem quiet enough," Catherine noted.

"For now. Once people believe they should control their own political destiny, anything is possible. Even here. What if we fall afoul of one another? Look at the enmity between Jefferson and Hamilton."

"But surely, Father, they won't resort to arms."

He leaned back in his chair, the letter on exquisite parchment, thin, in his left hand. "No, but that doesn't mean we are incapable of it. The Baron makes me think not just about France but about us."

"We should be grateful there's an ocean between us as well as the English Channel."

He sighed. "Indeed. Well, this confirms what we've kept in the corners of our mind. We'll not see any money from France. No more tobacco shipments. And I could guess no shipments of other things we grow here." He shifted in his seat. "Of course, the French can produce some of these things, but not tobacco."

"Before I forget, Bettina told me that the two slaves who ran off, in love, supposedly, have been captured and returned. Maureen appears to enjoy punishing them. The girl must tend to the simpleminded and the fellow, William, you remember the jockey who broke Jeddie's collarbone?"

"I do."

"Had his hamstring slit by his captor."

"Well, that is rough justice." Ewing shook his head. "I'm surprised Maureen hasn't formulated worse punishments."

"Give her time."

He grunted.

"Speaking of Maureen, she has contacts in France. I expect she's made arrangements to protect herself."

"Oh, when I first approached her concerning DoRe's proposal to Bettina, we did discuss the situation. She's moved her funds out of Paris, to London and, of course, the Italian bankers. The Italians have been handling money, the loans, investments, longer than the rest of us. Not that I trust them," he quietly said.

"I do hope she'll finally come to terms concerning DoRe."

Ewing sighed again, placing the papers on the corner of his polished desk. "Never, never have I dealt with anyone so difficult and truthfully, my dear, so greedy. Francisco was a hard man but essentially fair. Not so, Maureen."

"I sometimes wonder was she born like that, with that streak of cruelty that runs through her?"

"I don't know, but I do know she will torture those two recaptured slaves in ingenious ways."

Catherine folded her hands on the desk. She sat across from him, for the desk was wide. Through her father, Catherine, a quick study, learned the ways of the world. She understood a man's world and was prudent enough to keep it to herself. Given her mental abilities, her father taught her well and enjoyed the partnership.

As those two discussed what may or may not come to pass, Ralston, better, settled into hard work. He wanted to prove himself to Mr. Finney in the hopes of advancement but also in the hopes that people would bring horses to him as they did to Catherine Garth Schuyler. If he served Mr. Finney well, it might be possible for him to work horses at Royal Oak with the owner's permission.

Ralston foresaw but one future, work, saving money, buying Sulli's freedom.

Sulli believed she had no future. The need these poor souls had for her began to give her a purpose. While this was not a life the young woman would ever have selected, it was one with meaning. Olivia provided an example. The older woman would quote those Bible passages she memorized and she would tell Sulli she was part of God's plan.

While Sulli could not foresee God's plan, she felt small gratitude for being far away from the big house, away from Maureen's gaze, as well as the gaze of most of the other people on Big Rawly, especially Elizabetta. Nor did she want to see William.

William felt exhaustion and pain. He was too tired for rage, plus rage cost him the use of one leg. He wanted to live, but he didn't know why.

Whether at Cloverfields or Big Rawly, no one could imagine what the future would give or take from them. The one thing that was certain is that no one could imagine that future.

40

Evening

Seeing the books scattered on the floor was a relief for Harry. They took her mind off the onyx chip and the lipstick bombshell. As Fair drove them back from downtown Crozet, she told him everything, including finding the brass Mandela coin.

She ran through every possibility she could imagine until finally at home, sitting at the kitchen table, she asked, "What do you think?"

"I think you should talk to Sheriff Shaw."

"But if I do, then doesn't Mags, if she is guilty, have time to hide more evidence?"

"Here's the issue: guilty of what? murder? murder by lipstick?"

"Well, crazy as it sounds, yes. And don't forget where I found the onyx chip, at the still, and don't forget the body parts discovered not far from the still."

"I found them," Pewter interjected.

"Cat, if I were you, I'd shut up." Harry closed one eye, looking mean.

"*She understood.*" Pewter's jaw dropped, revealing white fangs.

"*Maybe.*" Mrs. Murphy leaned on the kitchen chair leg. "*Then again, you were loud.*"

"Pfft," the gray cat responded, a flick of her impressive tail.

"You think the motivation is money?" Fair pressed. "It's possible that Jeannie crossed her in some fashion."

"Fair, can you think for one minute what that sweet woman could have done to get herself killed?"

He threw up his hands. "No, but often the most ordinary people, or ones you like a great deal, are hiding something dark or are stealing. I never think of stealing as dark, do you?"

"Depends on what is being stolen." She rose and opened the refrigerator door, pulling out a tonic water. "Drink?"

"*While you're up I could use some bite-size fishies, the ones in different colors.*" Pewter blinked her eyes, followed by a purr.

Harry opened the cabinet door, tossing the cats tiny fishes and the dogs small Milk-Bones. Then she sat back down, a wedge of lime in her hand. She kept precut lemons and limes in the fridge.

"Call Sheriff Shaw. Or find him at tonight's fireworks. He'll be there. For my edification, let me work this out. You believe this is connected to the still, to the trade in moonshine."

"Yes. It's taken me time to figure it out but Mags could easily send shipments weekly up to New Jersey, New York, wherever the taxes shoot through the roof. And what is more appealing than contraband? It's why I think drugs are prevalent. It isn't just that they make people high or that they're addictive. They're illegal, so they're cool. You're a rebel. Same I think for country waters."

He half-smiled. "I can see it now. Two men at a bar in New York, drinks in hand, arguing about the merits of moonshine from Virginia versus North Carolina. Each has to one-up the other guy."

"I suppose. But here's how all this could be done. Is being done even if Bottoms Up Brewery isn't in on the game. First, you create a network of distillers, suppliers. They receive a steady income. Either the distiller or a third party picks up the bottles, all will be bottles, and stacks the cartons in a beer truck. But it has a false floor or siding."

"But that would change the weight at the weight station."

"I thought of that. Unload the contraband at a rendezvous on a back road, go to the weigh station, all is well, then meet the people down the road."

"Honey, that's way too complicated. Too much work and packing and repacking. All someone has to do is have a row of moonshine in beer bottles on the bottom row of the carton. Even if an official picks out a bottom bottle, it would look like a beer bottle. Or it could be a carton full of moonshine marked in some way so it could easily be unloaded by whoever knew the code."

"Fair, that's brilliant. You could be a crook."

He smiled. "No, I'm trying to be practical. And I think you're on to something. If the booze is the trigger for one murder and possibly two, given the profits, no tax, I guess that would be a powerful motivation."

"Fair, a small, steady operation would net half a million." She snapped her fingers. "If you had a network of suppliers, high-grade stuff, and you shipped out, say, even two trucks per day, you could make millions. Of course, you'd need to pay people off, but the profit would be enormous."

He nodded. "Would. It's a twofold problem."

"What do you mean?"

"Raising taxes destroys initiative and encourages smuggling, cheating. We have thousands of years of history to demonstrate a direct relationship. However, any nation needs large-scale projects that need to be funded by government."

"Why, Fair, look how the Romans tied service into the super wealthy building roads and public works. The Via Flaminia was built by one man, Gaius Flaminius, in 220 B.C." She cited a road from Rome to the Adriatic Sea, almost two hundred miles, which is still in use today.

"Maybe once upon a time we, too, as an early republic, put honor and acclaim for public works above private profit, but those days are long gone." He rose, got himself a tonic water, too, sat back down. "It would be like Jeff Bezos repairing bridges in Colorado or Verizon installing optic fiber in poor neighborhoods for families at no charge. Never happen. So we tax."

"How'd we get on this?"

"Illegal profit. Is Bottoms Up raking in an avalanche of money?"

"Next question: Are Mags and Janice in on it together?" Harry slapped her hands on the table so the salt and pepper shakers jumped. "I like them. Well, sometimes they can get on my nerves in the Dorcas Guild, but I like them."

"Well, maybe it could be done. Look how bookkeepers embezzle and aren't discovered by their co-workers for years. Crooks rely on people's trusting nature and their own winning personalities. Baby Face Nelson, in the thirties—people adored him."

"Their husbands? Would they know?"

"That's a good question. In the old days, wives would plead they didn't know of their husband's criminal activities. And maybe they didn't since men and women lived in such different worlds. It's possible to keep information from your spouse. Who knows?"

Pewter reached up to pat Harry's leg. The human's hand reached down to pet the gray head.

"More."

"Well, I'll call the sheriff."

"More." Pewter followed Harry as she walked to the landline.

"Pewter, forget the food for a minute. Mom's about to put herself in a mess. She has an idea but no, what do they call it?" Tucker stopped a moment.

"Evidence." Mrs. Murphy supplied the word. "She has an onyx chip and a coin memento. Something but not enough."

After the call, Sheriff Shaw having listened to Harry without comment, saying he would be at the fireworks tonight, Fair stood up.

"I'm going to take a shower before we drive back to the firehouse."

"Okay."

A shower restored Harry as well. As the sun moved toward the Blue Ridge, the heat shimmered. Sunset would help a little, but chances were that this would be a warm evening.

The horses, turned out to enjoy the slightly cooler night temperatures, looked up as Harry walked out to their pastures to double-check.

Tucker and Pirate tagged along. The cats stayed in the house. Leaning over the fence, Harry smiled. Her hooved friends nibbled the grass, now filled with nutrition.

"Okay, guys. Let's check the barn."

"*She checked it when she turned them out.*" Pirate wondered why she needed to go back.

"*She wants to make certain she's turned off the fans. A summer electric bill can be higher than a winter bill. Mom hates bills,*" Tucker advised.

The youngster, puzzled, asked, "*Why doesn't she keep them outside all day?*"

"*Heat is harder on horses than the cold. Their ideal outside temperature is a good twenty-five degrees less than a human's. Ours is less than a human's, too, but higher than a horse's. Mom studies all this stuff.*" Tucker tagged behind Harry, who checked each stall. "*She's dedicated about horses, crops, us, of course. The stuff she doesn't care about she ignores.*"

"All in order." She stepped into the kitchen. "You ready?"

"I am."

"*I'm going.*" Pewter jumped on the kitchen table.

"We'd better shut the animal door." Harry ran ahead to do that exact thing. Otherwise Pewter and Mrs. Murphy would have shot right by her.

"*No fair!*" Pewter yowled.

"You don't need to see fireworks," Harry advised her.

"*Right. You'll pee on yourself,*" Tucker maliciously called up to the cat. "*You can take Pirate and me. We'll sit with you,*" she told Harry.

"Fair, what do you think about the dogs?"

"They'll be all right. Tucker isn't afraid of booms and bangs. She'll calm Pirate if he doesn't like it. We can put them in the car with air-conditioning on if needs be." Fair opened the door a crack so the dogs could squeeze through.

Pewter yelled, "*You'll poop in the car.*"

"*Pewter, fireworks are awful. And don't forget the screaming kids. Let's stay home. We won't miss a thing.*" Mrs. Murphy leapt onto the kitchen counter and walked to the window over the sink to watch everyone drive off.

"*I hope they come down with heatstroke,*" Pewter complained.

"*They'll be in the car.*"

"*Murphy, they'll have to step out. Maybe it will hit them all at once.*"

Fair drove to the post office. They'd come in early enough to find a space. The actual display would be down the road, Route 240, at the firehouse. But one could see the colors, hear the booms, just as well from the post office lot. Parking otherwise would be along the street. Many others felt the same way. Susan and Ned preceded Harry and Fair, nabbing a wonderful spot right in front of the Crozet Post Office. Janice and Olaf were up near the road, as were Mags and Kevin. By now, the place was packed, so people drove onto the field to the west of the post office and behind the Whistle Stop Grill, a large grass lot.

The road to the firehouse was already packed with vehicles nose to tail on the railroad track side and cars also parked on the other side of the railroad tracks if they could. Wherever one looked in Crozet, cars filled the spaces and trucks, jammed with people in the bed, hosted parties.

Susan walked over, seeing the Haristeens park. "Good timing. It's hot but we've been through worse Fourth of Julys than this. Come on out. If it gets to you, you can always sit back in the air-conditioning. Save gas. Remember your carbon footprint."

Harry opened the door. "I'll remember my carbon footprint when Congress remembers theirs."

"Come on, kids." Fair opened the door for the dogs.

"Ned drove the truck. Come on. We've got chairs in the back, libations. Janice and Mags have their trucks. The Dorcas Guild has shown up in force. I would have thought the march would poop out some of us." Susan laughed as they walked back to her spot.

"We're tough. Lutherans have been tough since 1517." Harry named the year when Martin Luther nailed the Ninety-Five Theses onto the door of the cathedral in Germany.

"Drop the tailgate down, honey," Susan called to Ned. "We need to climb up."

"Gotta lift up Tucker first." Then Harry turned to Pirate. "Kennel up."

With one graceful bound, the Irish wolfhound vaulted onto the truck bed, immediately sitting down as Harry sat down.

Folks called to one another in the various trucks, glasses were raised, and then, into the twilight sky, red, white, and blue fireworks announced the beginning of the party.

Everyone cheered, rapt attention to the sky.

Next came a rat-a-tat-tat as smaller fireworks lofted up, the crackle adding to the excitement.

The distinctive whoosh of a canister pushing through the tube could be heard, then a boom as a gigantic white star appeared, its arms filling the sky, white turning to gold thence to gold bits as a marvelous sound, a kind of whoosh itself, caused loud cheers.

The cheering ran the length of the streets and the parking lot. That made it all the more exciting to hear the human sound traveling.

Tucker explained to Pirate what it was all about. The big fellow showed no fear. He enjoyed hearing the humans roar with delight.

Mags, Janice behind her, climbed up into the truck bed to hunker down in front of Susan. "Sheriff Shaw took our lipsticks. Heard he took yours, too."

Harry, highly alert, replied, "Did. He must have told you the lipstick in Jeannie's purse was loaded with deadly nightshade."

Mags waited for another boom to pass. "Since the rest of us are fine, don't you think this is something crazy like when Tylenol was poisoned? I don't remember but I looked it up on the Internet. Then there was a rash of products tampered with bad stuff. Died down for decades. Maybe we've got another nutcase out there."

Surprised, Susan responded, "I hadn't thought of that."

"Me neither," Harry echoed.

"I'd say we're lucky. What if one of us had used the wrong tube of lipstick?" Janice hastened to add, "Not that I want to see Jeannie dead."

Harry thought to herself, *Maybe Mags is right. Maybe this is the work of a nut.* Then she felt the little triangular piece of onyx in her pocket. The questions returned.

Harry, unwisely, baited the two women. "I went back up to the still and I found a brass medallion with Nelson Mandela's representation on it."

Janice's brow wrinkled. "A little coin thing?"

"Yes."

"Mags, remember Pieter, the South African who would come by for driving jobs? Haven't seen him in months, half a year maybe."

"No. Can't say that I do."

"Sure you do. Medium height. Black hair. Spoke with a South African accent. Once he showed me the coin. He was proud of it. Oh, I hope those bones aren't his."

Mags thought. "I kind of remember. I should keep better track of who shows up at the dock. Well, let's get back to party central."

Mags climbed back over the tailgate, foot on the back bumper, dropping down.

Janice, a bit disturbed, followed.

Harry, who had told Susan everything before coming tonight, moved over to her best friend. "I never had thought of the Tylenol case."

"Let's get through the Fourth of July. Then you or both of us can go see Sheriff Shaw. Bring him the broken piece of onyx. I tried to see her bracelet. Couldn't really."

"It's one little piece of evidence but it's peculiar."

Susan put her hand on Harry's shoulder. "Yes it is, but it's a damning piece of evidence."

Looking up, Harry said, "There's one with screamer streamers. I love those." Harry looked at her dogs. "Come on, guys. Let me take you to the grass over there. Just in case."

Once on the ground, the three walked to the grass at the side of the post office. Mags climbed back out of Kevin's truck as Janice watched her go. She had a small cloth purse stuck in her deep skirt pocket.

"Mags, where are you going?" Janice called out.

"For a walk." She headed toward Harry, Tucker, and Pirate. "Harry, walk with me. Let's go toward the library," Mags said upon reaching Harry.

"Why?"

"I have something of interest for you." Mags smiled.

"Don't take your eyes off her," Tucker commanded Pirate, for the corgi smelled danger.

Pirate did as he was told because he could smell it, too.

Overhead, fireworks glistened, boomed, shook the ground, it seemed. The colors filled the sky. Sometimes the fireworks managers sent up four or five simultaneously, a magnificent sight.

"Tell me here." Harry, on alert, stood her ground.

Mags, gun in the small fabric purse, held the gun barrel, gun still in the purse, against Harry's back. "Walk."

"So you did it." Harry calmly accused Mags.

"Did what?"

"You poisoned Jeannie and killed whoever was left at the still."

"If I did, why would I ever tell you? I'm warning you to butt out."

Janice, watching, climbed out of the truck bed in a hurry, to run after them. Harry and Mags were three hundred yards ahead and Mags pushed Harry. Janice didn't know what was going on, but she knew something was wrong.

Susan, beholding Janice's face and her now running toward the two way ahead, also climbed out. Fair stood up, all six feet five inches of him. He, too, climbed out.

As he did so, he told Ned, "Get Shaw down here. Tell him to head toward the library."

Ned didn't waste time asking questions. He heard the urgency in his friend's voice.

"Why did you do it, Mags? You have everything."

"You're nosy, Harry. If you had minded your own business, none of this would be necessary."

They climbed the sidewalk uphill toward the main entrance of the library.

"What made you think I knew something?"

Mags, breathing harder for the grade was stiff, rasped. "I overlooked things because you are known for your curiosity, but I knew when you turned the bracelet on my wrist. I figured you must have found the missing piece that I lost in the walnut grove. Then you found the damned Mandela coin."

"In the still—you killed him."

"Maybe, maybe not, but I have always liked the view up there." Mags coolly denied the charge.

"Mags, what you like is nontaxable profit."

Mags laughed. "Who doesn't?" Reaching the top of the hill, she said, "Move along."

"No."

Meanwhile fireworks burst overhead with all the noises that could cover other noises.

"Move."

"No." Harry took a step toward Mags and swept her hand toward her purse, knocking it onto the ground. Then she turned left, running as fast as she could past Over the Moon Bookstore. She was heading toward the railroad tracks. If she made it, she had buildings to cover her. If she headed back to the post office parking lot, she would be exposed. Foolish as it would be for Mags to shoot her in the parking lot, Harry felt no obligation to present an easy target. Then again, that lot was full of people. Mags, out of control, might shoot anyone or miss and hit someone else.

Picking up her gun, Mags began running toward Harry. Given Harry's head start, she figured she'd need to fire if given a clear shot.

Now one hundred yards behind, catching up, Janice, fast, shouted, "Mags, no."

Mags ignored her partner.

Fair, with his long legs, was closing on Janice, soon passing her. He saw the gun, did not see his wife, but knew if he was going to see her he had to run as fast as he ever had in his life.

Susan ran, too, closing the gap.

A shot rang out, but to anyone except the five humans, all running, it sounded like part of the fireworks.

Harry reached the corner of the small shopping center by the railroad track. As she turned left to run by the buildings down to the road toward the railroad underpass, a huge boom, a fabulous scarlet firework, exploded overhead. Mags used the opportunity to fire again. She hit the side of a painted brick building. A spray of paprika, like a tiny firework, fanned out as the bullet tore through the side of the corner.

"*Stop and turn,*" Tucker, voice firm, barked.

Pirate obeyed.

Mags approached the dogs, barely noticing them, for they stood like statues.

"*Now!*" Tucker speeded toward Mags's ankles.

Pirate ran alongside the little dog. Mags paid no attention to either dog. Tucker closed in but Pirate passed Tucker, seeming to pass Mags. Then the giant shot into the air, turned midair, and grabbed the back of her neck, throwing her on the ground. He could have snapped her neck but he did not. He sat on her as Tucker grabbed her right hand, ferociously biting while blood spurted. Mags dropped the gun.

Harry, hearing Fair call to her, stopped, looked back. Susan called also.

Janice now reached Mags, gasping for breath.

"Get this dog off of me. Get Tucker off. She's tearing me to pieces."

Fair leaned over, took the gun. Mags's fingers were gnawed, bloodied.

Susan now reached the prostrate woman.

Harry carefully walked back up as she was below them. "Pirate, enough."

The big boy dutifully moved off Mags. He went over to lick Harry's hand as Tucker also returned to stand by his human.

Fair leveled the gun at Mags. Nothing to say.

Janice stood still, shocked. "Are you out of your mind?"

Mags shook her head. "I had to do something. I'd be ruined."

"You *are* ruined," Janice curtly replied. "What were you doing? Were you stealing from all of us?"

Mags didn't answer.

The fireworks crashed overhead, each series more impressive than the last. Blue light swept the buildings as Sheriff Shaw and a deputy slowly drove to what they now observed.

"Are you all right?" the sheriff, hurrying out of the squad car, asked Harry.

"Thanks to my dogs, yes, I am."

Fair handed Rick Shaw the gun, handle first.

"She's under stress. She needs psychological help," Janice pleaded, trying to help a woman she had trusted.

"Old habits are hard to break. Mrs. Nielsen, get in the back of the squad car, please."

"No." Mags resisted, at which point the deputy came behind her, lifted her one arm behind her, way up, which hurt, and pushed her into the car.

Janice began to cry. Susan took her hand.

"Do you want me to send someone to drive you back?" the sheriff asked.

"No, thanks. I'll walk back with Fair, Susan, Janice, and my dogs. Will settle me down."

"I'll get a statement later."

41

Friday

Harry, Fair, Susan, Ned, Mrs. Murphy, Pewter, Tucker, and Pirate sat in Reverend Jones's office with Cazenovia, Elocution, and Lucy Fur.

Harry and the others felt Reverend Jones should be consulted as soon as Sheriff Shaw informed them they could do so.

The chase made the morning news on TV and in the papers. All wanted to talk to their pastor.

"Mags hasn't confessed. She was part of a smuggling network to carry illegal liquor across the Mason-Dixon Line." Ned, who as an elected official could question the sheriff, informed them, "She testified that neither Janice nor their husbands knew anything."

"This network is well organized, stretching from the mountains of Georgia to Virginia," Fair added, as he and Ned had spoken. "Millions, Reverend Jones, millions. And millions to Mags for God knows what purpose."

"How did she think they would get away with it?" Reverend Jones was aghast.

"Mags has gotten caught, but that doesn't mean the network will be brought to justice," Ned reminded them. "The kingpins are highly intelligent, can hide behind all manner of buffers, plus they can hire the best lawyers in the country."

"Will they abandon Mags?" Susan asked.

"Of course," Fair answered. "The question is, did Mags kill the South African, Pieter, as she knew of the still, or did someone in the syndicate kill him. Chances are he wanted a bigger cut."

"I don't know if I would be here if it weren't for Tucker and Pirate." Harry praised her dogs.

"If I'd been there, Mags would never have gotten as far as the library. I can smell evil. Oh, yes I can," Pewter bragged. *"And I found the skull at the old still."*

"Dead humans are disgusting." Elocution grimaced.

"A rib cage and half a skull with a ball cap. Not enough left to be disgusting." Tucker wearied of Pewter's blabbing.

Ned predicted, "If Mags will tell everything she knows about the syndicate, maybe she can plea-bargain."

Reverend Jones, wise in the ways of the world, replied, "If she tells everything she knows, she'll be killed."

"It's odd, isn't it?" Harry added. "Here we've all been focused on the necklace. Our attention was only on that."

"But who would think about contraband?" Fair asked.

"When the truck was robbed at Bottoms Up, that was a clue. As it turns out, the sheriff's department and other agencies knew of the network, but they didn't know how extensive it was or exactly who was in on it. Then they found the still and later Harry produced the piece of the bracelet." Ned spoke again. "Little things, but they add up. All supplied by Harry." He praised her again. "There's a good chance Mags had the beer stolen from her truck, a diversion, if you will. Then again, she could have done it to pocket the money herself. Any way you look at it, Mags is in deep trouble."

"Given how much we've all worked together, including Mags and

Janice, we thought we should come to you." Susan looked to her pastor.

He exhaled deeply. "Thank you. I must say something tomorrow. I can't pretend this hasn't happened. I don't know what my sermon should be, but I won't hide from it."

"Greed," Susan simply stated.

"Never goes out of fashion." Her husband smiled at her.

"What I can't believe is that Mags is a Lutheran," Harry exclaimed.

No one said a word.

Then Pewter purred. *"Death by lipstick."*

ACKNOWLEDGMENTS

Without Cindy Chandler many things in my life would be deadly dull. She and her son, Jeffrey Howe, own Windridge Landscaping. Together with Jennifer Huges, certified arborist/estimator, they knocked themselves out researching common plants which can be lethal. Cindy drew up the horseshoe garden, identifying each plant and listing its properties, including germination, flowering, harvest time, berries, even the stems, should they prove dangerous. Not only does Cindy refuse payment, each Christmas she gives me something I can plant in the spring. Often, Jeffrey checks on my site choices, etc. If you live in central Virginia you may have seen their work but not known that landscaping was theirs.

Michael Gellatly, the artist for this series, surprises me. His point of view can make what might be a mundane picture exciting. The illustrations are in black and white but I have seen how he handles color. Michael can do anything.

The late John Holland, ever a ready source of country waters, was always helpful in explaining how this liquid magic is made. It is not hard to do but it is hard to do well. The water off the Blue Ridge mountains is perfect. Over more than a century Virginia men have created incredible liquors, managing to avoid being caught by the feds and therefore being some of the few Americans who actually reap the fruits of their labors. Of course, I am just horrified that they do not pay taxes, just horrified.

Joy Cummings typed the manuscript and did not go blind in the process. My drafts leave a great deal to be desired. I fear I do, too, but I soldier on.

Whoever I have forgotten to thank, cuss me like a dog when you next see me. My notes for some were shredded during feline drama.

Dear Reader,
I did not do it.

Pewter

the Saint

Dear Reader,

She did, too. She had a snit because our human would not give her dried treats in the shape of little fish. I saw this with my own eyes.

Mrs. Murphy

Dear Reader,
I don't have a dog in this fight.

Tucker

Dear Reader,
It's a wonder I don't lose my mind.

ABOUT THE AUTHORS

Rita Mae Brown has written many bestsellers and received two Emmy nominations. In addition to the Mrs. Murphy series, she has authored a dog series comprised of *A Nose for Justice* and *Murder Unleashed*, and the Sister Jane foxhunting series, among many other acclaimed books. She and Sneaky Pie live with several other rescued animals.

ritamaebrownbooks.com

To inquire about booking Rita Mae Brown for a speaking engagement, please contact the Penguin Random House Speakers Bureau at speakers@penguinrandomhouse.com.

Sneaky Pie Brown, a tiger cat rescue, has written many mysteries—witness the list at the front of the novel. Having to share credit with the above-named human is a small irritant, but she manages it. Anything is better than typing, which is what "Big Brown" does for the series. Sneaky calls her human that name behind her back after the wonderful Thoroughbred racehorse. As her human is rather small, it brings giggles among the other animals. Sneaky's main character—Mrs. Murphy, a tiger cat—is a bit sweeter than Miss Pie, who can be caustic.

ABOUT THE TYPE

This book was set in Joanna, a typeface designed in 1930 by Eric Gill (1882–1940). Named for his daughter, this face is based on designs originally cut by the sixteenth-century typefounder Robert Granjon (1513–89). With small, straight serifs and its simple elegance, this face is notably distinguished and versatile.